WITHOUT RIGOR MORTIS

WITHOUT RIGOR MORTIS

B.J. LUCKNOW

Copyright © 2013 by B.J. Lucknow.

Library of Congress Control Number:		2013914197
ISBN:	Hardcover	978-1-4836-8135-1
	Softcover	978-1-4836-8134-4
	Ebook	978-1-4836-8136-8

All rights reserved. No part of this book may be reproduced or transmitted in any form or by any means, electronic or mechanical, including photocopying, recording, or by any information storage and retrieval system, without permission in writing from the copyright owner.

This is a work of fiction. Names, characters, places and incidents either are the product of the author's imagination or are used fictitiously, and any resemblance to any actual persons, living or dead, events, or locales is entirely coincidental.

This book was printed in the United States of America.

Rev. date: 11/26/2013

To order additional copies of this book, contact:
Xlibris LLC
1-888-795-4274
www.Xlibris.com
Orders@Xlibris.com
140233

CONTENTS

Prologue 9

Chapter 1	Full Moon	11
Chapter 2	The Locker	18
Chapter 3	Shock	22
Chapter 4	Answer the Damn Phone	24
Chapter 5	Facing the Dean	28
Chapter 6	Guess Who's Surprised	32
Chapter 7	Unidentified Intern	36
Chapter 8	Tunnels	42
Chapter 9	Eavesdropping	45
Chapter 10	Promotions	49
Chapter 11	Dead Man Walking?	52
Chapter 12	Haunted Halls	54
Chapter 13	Endless Emergencies	58
Chapter 14	Isolated	60
Chapter 15	Consoling Samantha	63
Chapter 16	Accidental Casualty	66
Chapter 17	Lost and Found	69
Chapter 18	Encounter	73
Chapter 19	Friends and Acquaintances	76
Chapter 20	Gossip	80
Chapter 21	In a Snit	82
Chapter 22	Why Didn't I Stay Home?	84
Chapter 23	Connecting the Dots	86
Chapter 24	Unexpected Company	87
Chapter 25	Who Drugged the Coffee?	89
Chapter 26	Who's Who of the Auxiliary	93
Chapter 27	Reunion	96
Chapter 28	Warning	98
Chapter 29	Tracking the Special Blend	102
Chapter 30	Investigation	104

Chapter 31	Fingerprints	107
Chapter 32	No Sherlock Holmes	112
Chapter 33	Playing Pi	115
Chapter 34	Catnapping	118
Chapter 35	Follow-up	125
Chapter 36	Whose Fingerprints	129
Chapter 37	Who Cleans?	133
Chapter 38	Cleaner Isn't Mr. Clean	137
Chapter 39	Blackmail or Whatever Works	138
Chapter 40	Advice Needed	141
Chapter 41	The Burglary	144
Chapter 42	Who's Not Dead?	147
Chapter 43	Midnight Madness	150
Chapter 44	Revelations	152
Chapter 45	Gotcha	155
Chapter 46	Sleep Deprivation	157
Chapter 47	Facing the Dean Again	159
Chapter 48	Tickets for Prints	163
Chapter 49	Detectives R Us	165
Chapter 50	Marigold	167
Chapter 51	Blackmail Works	176
Chapter 52	Casing the Joint	177
Chapter 53	If It Walks and Talks Like a Duck . . .	181
Chapter 54	Sleepwalking	183
Chapter 55	Asking Marla	189
Chapter 56	Moonstruck	192
Chapter 57	The Dean Is Missing	194
Chapter 58	Rebecca	200
Chapter 59	Last-ditch Effort	202
Chapter 60	Dead Men Don't Tell	209
Chapter 61	Loose Ends	213
Chapter 62	Interrogated	218
Chapter 63	Chasing a Rat	221
Chapter 64	Dr. Conway	231
Chapter 65	Helena's Secret	236
Chapter 66	The Dean Is Awake	241
Chapter 67	Interrogating Regina Whales	243
Chapter 68	Missing Link	245
Chapter 69	One More Suspect	247

Chapter 70   Tailing the Druggie..250
Chapter 71   Wrong Turn..254
Chapter 72   Who Are You?...255
Chapter 73   All's Well..258

Epilogue..263

PROLOGUE

THE CRASH OF steel doors shutting and the clang of a lock being turned woke Samantha to a whirring noise that sounded like a buzzsaw; she saw unending darkness. She had to be dreaming! Sure that her eyes must still be closed, Samantha blinked them open again to the same pitch-black night. Forcing open her mouth, she inhaled a breath of putrid, chemically tainted air and screamed. Only the awful sound of her terrified voice reverberated in the narrow space where she lay, making her body rigid with terror. It had to be a nightmare. Forcing her arm upward, her hand banged against a hard metal surface. Feeling along the sides, with fingers that were numb from the cold, she knew that her prison was a rectangular box. Shouting out against the darkness, Samantha heard her voice bounce back, taunting her futile efforts to escape. Time was immeasurable in that place, with no light, no watch, and no person to affirm her existence. Pounding on the top of her prison only produced a hollow sound. Surrendering to utter despair, she closed her eyes against the darkness and wept in rage against whoever had imprisoned her in this, her last resting place.

CHAPTER 1

Full Moon

THE LANKY INTERN in surgical scrubs leaned his tall frame against the emergency entrance railing, his auburn hair hanging in greasy curls. The whisper of crepe soles on the terrazzo warned the doctor that someone was coming, and he straightened up.

"Ian, what are you still doing here?" The tiny nurse in an old-fashioned crisp white uniform looked up at the doctor.

"Paul Cormorant, the intern who was supposed to take over at 8:00 p.m., didn't show up. He's just lucky that I'm not reporting his sorry ass to the staff physician."

"Oh, Ian, didn't anyone tell you that Paul received a call from his family today?"

"Why am I the last to be informed, Marla?"

"We didn't know until the chief resident sauntered into the lounge."

"So what's the big emergency that kept Paul from showing up for his shift?"

"His grandmother in Manhattan was taken ill and rushed to hospital."

"Will she be all right?"

"No. The old lady died of a heart attack in the ambulance," Marla sighed. "It's really hard when you're a doctor to lose a family member like that."

Deflated, Ian no longer felt anger, only an overwhelming exhaustion. "They say lack of sleep can make a doctor more dangerous to his patient than whatever ails him. I'm beginning to believe that."

"Why don't you go . . ."

Wailing sirens reverberating through the open bay doors prevented any further conversation. The paramedic jumped onto the gurney and began to pound the chest of patient being driven at a dangerous speed toward the nearest trauma room. The biker still clad in the leathers that bore the gang insignia was leaking a thick black gooey liquid onto the floor as the other paramedic steered toward a short stocky doctor clad in surgical greens. At his side was a taller, pimple-faced teenager looking totally baffled as he watched the drama unfold.

"Stop!" the emergency staff doctor halted the rush.

Lifting his blotched red face, the emergency technician continued pounding the chest of the limp biker and croaked out an exhausted, "Why? You jumping up and taking over?"

"He's dead. All you did was speed up the process." The doctor motioned for the kid at his side to help, and they turned the patient, exposing a large bullet hole in his back.

"Damn" was followed by words usually only heard on a ship. "How the hell was I supposed to know," moaned the paramedic.

"Live and learn, isn't that right, Carson?" the emergency doctor turned to the kid at his side for affirmation.

"Right, Dr. Cleaver."

"How many times have I got to tell you, Carson? Just call me Dad. I know I'm not your father, but I've been raising you for the past five years. Doesn't that give me the right to the title?"

"The dean doesn't like it when he hears me call you Dad. He is my father."

"Yeah, well, I'm married to your mother now and took you on too. Figure that gives me some privileges."

"Sure, Dad. Glad I ran into you in the hospital. The dean has always wanted me to go back to school and follow in his footsteps. This sure makes a career in medicine a lot more interesting."

"Well, your father is basically a paper-pushing administrator now. Can't expect that to be too inspiring if he wants you to follow in his footsteps."

"Nope. And thanks for the loan of the suit, Dad."

"No problem. We keep extras in the emergency department for those whose clothes we have to cut off. Can't send them home nude, now, can we?" Dr. Cleaver's chest heaved in a brief guffaw at his own joke.

Ian noticed that Marla's dimpled smile had disappeared, and she was staring at Carson with such a look of hatred that it shocked him. The pallor of her face made Ian wonder if Marla was about to faint when she turned and walked away.

Dr. Cleaver eyed his exhausted intern and said, "Ian, go look in on the patient in 4B while I take care of this guy. There's a fifty-four-year-old female patient having chest pains. Just don't go sending her home without a full workup. We don't want a repeat of last month."

Ian's six feet three inches made him tower over almost everyone in the hospital. Dr. Cleaver was barely five feet tall, making it impossible for Ian not to lock down on the doctor who was in charge of the emergency department when he was so much shorter than Ian. But the senior staff doctor's warning sent a shudder through Ian's body as he remembered the blunder he would rather not be reminded of. He was just grateful that it hadn't been his mistake.

One detail made Ian wonder if he might have made the same mistake since the electrocardiogram tracing of the twenty-nine-year-old guy who worked in a bottling factory, loading and unloading cases of beer, hadn't shown any abnormalities. The intern on duty that night had interpreted the chest pains to be a classic case of pulled chest muscle resulting from the manual labor the guy did every day. It was only as the ambulance came screaming back into the entrance later that night, and the emergency staff recognized the man's face, that everyone jumped to it. But it was too late. The paramedics had turned up the paddles until they left burn marks on the guy's chest, but to no avail.

Like all the other doctors, Ian had been forced to sit through the rehashing of the incident as the authorities went through a long grueling enquiry into the man's death.

Looking for Marla, Ian had to race down the hallway to get her before someone else needed a nurse. "Dr. Cleaver asked me to look in on a female patient in 4B. She's experiencing chest pains. Don't suppose you want to give me a hand?"

Although it was phrased as a question, Marla knew that she was expected to play guard as he examined the patient.

"You need sleep, Ian!" Marla said.

"We better see to her. Wouldn't want our patient getting too worked up." Ian trudged heavy-footed along the marble tiles that made the long corridor glisten under neon lights, passing several closed curtains and a few partially opened ones that revealed anxious patients staring hopefully at the pair passing them. They returned to their downcast solitude as they realized they still had to wait.

Striding quickly to the far side of the unit and into the partially glassed in cubicle, Ian smiled at the middle-aged overweight woman with frizzy gray hair and a pallid complexion that gleamed with beads of sweat. Gulping air through her mouth like a fish out of water, the patient exhibited typical symptoms of a heart that wasn't pumping efficiently enough to carry the fluid away from her edematous feet and hands. It didn't take a cardiologist to figure out that the woman wasn't going home that night.

Ian picked up the chart tucked under the end of the bed, glanced over the pertinent details, and then stood watching the florescent green trace of the cardiac monitor making endless beeping noises. There was definitely an irregularity in the wave that even the greenest of interns would pick up. Adopting his most persuasive bedside manner, Ian smiled and spoke soothingly to the woman, "Hello, Mrs. Morgan. I'm Dr. Ian McLintock. You've been having some chest pains?"

"You don't look old enough to be a doctor. Where is the doctor that came in to see me a few minutes ago?" The heavy jowls sagged in a petulant look as the woman sulked over having a new doctor whom she suspected was a student.

"Dr. Cleaver was needed in another room. And I'm not as young as I look." *Getting older by the minute,* Ian thought rudely to himself. He just didn't have the energy to put up with a cranky patient, no matter how sick she was.

"Dr. McLintock is one of our senior interns, and everyone knows that the closer a doctor is to graduating, the more up-to-date are his skills. So you are getting the best there is, Mrs. Morgan." Marla almost bounced as she spouted Ian's virtues.

Ian glared at Marla and harrumphed from deep in his chest rather than try and tell her that the more she protested and spewed out a list of his virtues, the less the patient was likely to believe what she was saying. And, from the look the woman was giving him, Marla's affirmations did not appear to be helping his image.

"Unfortunately, Mrs. Morgan, what you see is what you get tonight. There have been several MVAs and . . ."

"What's an MVA?" she demanded.

"Motor vehicle accident," explained Marla.

"Oh. Well, I have chest pains." Mrs. Morgan clutched the wrong side of her chest as if to convince them.

"So I see," murmured Ian as he placed the stethoscope on her ample bosom and listened. He knew what he was going to hear from the machine tracings but felt that Mrs. Morgan was one old-fashioned woman who wouldn't trust his diagnosis without him going through certain motions, needed or not. "Dr. Cleaver wrote down instructions for medication. All we can do now, Mrs. Morgan, is wait until we have a bed available in the hospital." Ian was quickly writing instructions on the chart so that he could leave. Marla was quite capable of handling the situation from here on in.

"I have to go home," wailed the woman as her voice rose to an earsplitting pitch.

"You need to stay here." Ian felt the flush of anger rising up from his neck. *Don't argue with a heart patient*, he reminded himself.

"But my daughter is getting married tomorrow!" The woman proceeded to pull back the covers, exposing large pale thighs as she attempted to stand.

"Whoa, there now." Marla grabbed the woman's arm with the IV line trailing from a bag hung on a rolling stand.

Ian grabbed the woman's legs and rotated her quickly back into bed. "Mrs. Morgan, you can't leave the hospital. You are having chest pains for a reason. Your daughter will understand."

Enormous tears rolled down the woman's jowls as she began sobbing hysterically. "Give her a shot of morphine now," whispered Ian.

Taking Mrs. Morgan's swollen hand into his, Ian ran his fingers over the woman's arm to distract her while Marla injected the contents of a syringe into the IV line. Within minutes, the woman's head flopped back on the pillow as she struggled to keep her eyes open. "Relax, Mrs. Morgan. We're going to call your daughter, and she will tell you that arrangements can be made for the wedding party to come to you."

"Oh. You are so kind." Mrs. Morgan's doe brown eyes gazed at Ian with a drugged admiration that experience told Ian that it would turn to wrath as soon as the woman woke the next morning to find herself confined to a hospital bed instead of sitting in a church listening to her daughter utter wedding vows.

Marla followed Ian to the corridor, where they could discuss the patient without being overheard. "Keep an eye on her, Marla, and let me know if she takes a turn for the worse. She does appear stable, and there seems to be a break in the onslaught."

Marla nodded almost absentmindedly while Ian studied her face. The look of hostility had gone, and Marla's cheeks had a healthier pink glow. "Do you mind me asking why you dislike the dean's son so much?" Ian asked.

"I can't talk about it now, Ian. Maybe later when I've thought it over. Okay?"

"So that's why you disappeared so quickly. I was beginning to wonder if it was something I had done."

"No, and no! Could you just give me some time, Ian? It's very difficult for me to talk about Carson."

"Don't mean to pry. I have to have a break before the next barrage of traumas. Hope the rest of the crazies have retired for the night. It's hard to have compassion for idiots who are responsible for their own misery. People really are damn stupid. Half that happens to them wouldn't if they used an ounce of common sense."

"Oh! You are grouchy. This isn't the first time you've pulled a double shift, Ian. Why are you so tired tonight?"

"And still hung over. Nothing like a tequila sunrise to keep the old head hammering for the next twenty-four hours."

"What's a tequila sunrise?"

"Believe me, Marla, you don't want to know. Went to Steve's stag party last night. Hell no! Two nights ago now. Maybe I wouldn't have gone if I'd known that I would have to pull a double shift. But there is no way I could tell Steve, who has been my best friend from freshman year, that I couldn't attend his last hurrah especially when I'm going to be his best man."

"Dr. Tragalar is getting married? Who caught Stevie Wonder? This woman must be either a miracle worker or damned good in bed to get Dr. Steve Tragalar to pop the question."

"I've only met Angela once, and believe me, she could get any man to follow her to hell and back." It was the look of hurt on Marla's face that made Ian realize that her ego was wounded.

"And what does this Angela do for a living? Model, act, or something more mundane like nurse?" The sarcasm in Marla's voice was obvious. She had been one of a bevy of young nurses who had been thunderstruck by Dr. Tragalar, but to no avail. Steve seemed to be one of those "dedicated" doctors who appeared oblivious to all the nubile young nurses, seemingly intent on dedicating himself to the surgical residency that everyone expected would go to him.

"Steve didn't tell us. In fact, he is rather private about his fiancée and their relationship. She could be a transvestite for all we know." There was a glint of laughter in Ian's eyes. Then he decided he had better mollify Marla's ego. "Believe it or not, Angela is not nearly as beautiful as you or half the women of this hospital. It's just that Steve finally found his intellectual equal. As he said to me, sex is only a very small part of the relationship. Important, but what do you do for the rest of the time if you don't have anything in common, especially if the woman is a walking dodo? And you know Steve never had trouble getting any woman he wanted."

"Oh!" Marla was stunned speechless.

Ian wondered if he had only made the situation worse by inadvertently hinting that Marla wasn't intelligent enough to hold the interest of Steve. Using the strained silence, Ian glanced at his watch and said, "I've got to get some shut eye." Marla's dark eyes seemed to be like a bottomless liquid well that could have hypnotized Ian if he had stood there staring into them for much longer.

"In your regular spot, Ian?"

"No, in the doctors' lounge. Just give me a shout if anything happens. Otherwise, I'm going to end up telling a patient where to go, how to get there, and that I will help pay the freight."

CHAPTER 2

The Locker

*I*AN DIDN'T EVEN remember closing his eyes as he laid his head onto the hard leather cushion of the sofa except that the dream he was having was interrupted by a weird cacophony that kept hammering away in the background. Unwilling to open his eyes, Ian swore and thought I'm too damned tired to care. But the strident noise wouldn't stop. Finally, as he blinked against the glare of neon-ceiling lights, he recognized the sound. Not one, not two, but the sirens of three ambulances pulling into the circular drive were wailing in the night. "Shit, damn, hell," swearing wasn't going to make them go away. He just hoped it sounded worse than it was.

Several hours later, the old railway clock donated to the hospital by some long forgotten benefactor began bonging out midnight. A glance down at his surgical greens splattered with blood and other unidentifiable bodily fluids made Ian's empty stomach give a sickening roll. Despite his hunger, thoughts of food nauseated him as he headed toward the shower for the fourth time that night.

It would have been for the fifth or sixth time except earlier that evening he had pronounced two people dead as they were pushed through the emergency bay doors.

It hadn't been as bad as he expected, considering that there was a full moon on a holiday. It had been worse. The sounding of the old clock marked the end of the nightmare as, mysteriously, the flood of patients stopped. No amount of cold water could banish the fatigue that haunted Ian that night. Ian hit the stainless steel button that automatically opened the door to the reception area, where he saw Marla filling out forms for the last few patients. Ian stood in front of Marla until she looked up, and then he said, "I'm going to my secret hiding place and don't disturb me unless it's a plague."

"Oh, aren't you the funny one?" But Marla made no attempt to ask where his "secret hiding place" was. In extreme circumstances, the overhead paging system that they tried not to use at night would reach wherever he managed to conceal himself. She also knew if Dr. McLintock didn't get some sleep, he would become dangerous to his patients. Still curious as to his destination, she watched as Ian trod down the dreadful lime-colored corridor and rounded the bend that led to stairs going down to the basement where the pathology labs were located.

Despite the fact that he didn't look back, Ian felt Marla's eyes following him. She didn't have a clue where he was headed, only that he would have to pass the morgue before coming to the entrance to the maze of tunnels that ran underneath the hospital. At the lowest level of the hospital, Ian found himself gagging at the stench of the peculiar mixture of chemicals and decay that seeped out of the autopsy room down the hall.

Sleep deprivation does strange things to the mind, and Ian wondered if he was one step away from hallucinating when he saw a young strangely clothed intern waving at him from the end of the corridor. *What the hell does he want,* Ian thought. But the man looked panic-stricken, and out of force of habit, Ian followed the intern until he saw where he was headed. What kind of emergency could be in the morgue?

This had to be some kind of joke. But Ian was too tired to think so he followed the doctor through the shiny stainless steel doors into the pungent smelling room where two mounds covered with white sheets lay on ancient gurneys that had been retired from patient transportation and relegated to use for transporting the dead. The shocking sight was a reminder of just how busy they had been in emergency and how many DOA's they'd have that night. It was only the frigid temperature of the morgue that allowed them to store the overload of corpses out in the open before the backlog of bodies in the drawers could be shipped off to the funeral director designated by the next of kin.

The only empty spot was the metal stretcher that was used for autopsies. It bristled with levers for lowering and raising various sections to make pulling the human body apart less onerous for the pathologist whose task was to diagnose postmortem what had really killed the person lying beneath his scalpel.

The sight of the weighing scales where each organ was measured turned Ian's stomach as he remembered the long hours spent in anatomy class, wondering if he would ever make it past the worst part of medical training.

Suddenly, he realized the intern he had followed was out of sight. Taking the steps two at a time, Ian raced up to the gallery that overlooked the operating table. The all too familiar memories of the rank smell and the nauseating feeling of looking down on the autopsies performed for the crowd of student doctors and nurses above caused an involuntary shudder to pass through Ian's body as he fought the urge to turn around and flee the place. It was bad enough during the daytime when it was inhabited with live pathologists, but in the dim shadows of night, the place took on aspects of a Freddy Krueger horror movie.

Ian realized, as he glanced around the few elevated seats at the very back of the balcony, that there was no place anyone could hide. And why would the intern want to conceal himself when he seemed so desperate for Ian to follow him? After taking a sweeping glance around the glaringly white-tiled walls below, Ian raced down the stairs, leaving the empty amphitheater behind. It had to be a practical joke played by one of the guys who wanted to show the nerd of the class that he could be rattled.

Just steps away from the exit, Ian was startled by a scream that came from the wall of morgue slabs where the bodies were kept cool. Instantaneous terror made his spine stiffen, and every hair on his body stood straight on end from the goose bumps that covered his flesh. Ian would have been halfway down the corridor except his body seemed to be locked in a catatonic state and refused to obey his commands. *Get a grip*, he yelled at himself as he worked to unlock his muscles from the stark horror that had frozen them in place.

It had to be part and parcel of the joke someone was playing on him. He knew his reaction would give whoever was playing the prank fodder for the gossip that would circulate the ranks of the interns for weeks to come. Inhaling deeply, Ian told himself that the shriek did not seem to be close by but seemed to be muffled by a thick barrier. Also, old buildings like this hospital, whose original foundations were laid during the Civil War, were notorious for settling as the ancient ground gave way underneath. And what sounded like a human wail was probably the rubbing of nails together as the sub-floor sank into the tunnel that ran below the new part.

Or was he just hearing things? Anyone would be jittery as hell if they were as tired as he was. Ian knew the fatigue that had plagued him all night was catching up to him, giving him cold fingers of panic in his gut. The feeling of impending doom, that someone or something was in the morgue with him, waiting and watching, was ludicrous. He wasn't scared, but he might as well make a dash for the door anyways.

Suddenly, a wail that had to be human jarred the deathly cold stillness, and Ian recoiled in terror. *Get the hell outa here, dammit,* he told himself. But some sense of duty kept him rooted to the spot where he stood and he realized it had to be someone yelling in terror. But there were no breathing people in the room, just a whole lot of cadavers. Impossible! To make a sound, you had to be alive! It had to be someone locked in one of the drawers.

CHAPTER 3

Shock

RACING ALONG THE wall yanking open each drawer and flipping up the sheet to stare down at the gray lifeless bodies, Ian strained to hear the sound again. But there was only an eerie stillness shattered by the continual bang as he opened and closed one drawer after another until he was convinced that he needed to make an appointment to see the department shrink.

Working his way along the second wall, Ian finally heard something. It sounded like someone weeping. Tracking the noise to the end of the last row of drawers that served as the built-in filing system for bodies, Ian came to a drawer and hesitated. The last thing he wanted to do was open a slab and find that somehow a live person had been imprisoned in the icy cold refrigerator compartment. A cough made him jump.

Clicking the lever to open the lock, Ian slowly slid the drawer open and flinched as he saw the white shroud covering the body move. Hesitating before the nightmare that trapped him, Ian began slowly inching the drawer to its fully open position before lifting the sheet to see tear-filled eyes staring up at him.

A plump middle-aged woman dressed in a hospital uniform lay staring up at him with startled pale green eyes as if she was as incredulous as Ian to find him leaning over her.

"What in god's name are you doing in a locker in the morgue?" Ian bellowed.

"I don't know," the woman sobbed. "I just woke up, and it was freezing cold, and I couldn't move, and it was so dark that I couldn't see, and I thought for sure I'd been buried alive."

He thought he had seen everything is this gd hospital in this gd hick town that passed itself off as a city, but this took the cake. If he had any doubt about the reality of the situation, it disappeared when the woman grabbed his arm with such force that it felt like she was going to break the bone. Ian used his smoothest bedside voice as he tried to get her to loosen her death grip on his arm. "You'll be all right," he murmured soothingly as he tried to pry her fingers from his flesh. Despite the reassuring words, Ian found that the harder he tried to step away, the fiercer her grasp became on his arm.

The ordeal of waking up to the blackness of the refrigerated slab was something Ian didn't ever want to experience, but voicing compassion for the woman's situation had only reinforced her panic. Forcefully pulling his arm out of her clutches, Ian said, "I need to use the phone on the wall to call for some help."

"Don't leave me!" she wailed and began a kind of keening that grated on Ian's nerves.

"You need help, and I can't do it alone," he said, striding quickly over to the phone hanging on the wall next to a large assortment of knives, saws, scalpels, and other cutting devices. They were neatly hung on pegs of a large wooden organizer one would be more likely to find in a garage or abattoir, but not a morgue.

The woman's keening turned to hysterical sobs. They filled the room with an irritating echo that banished the terror Ian had felt earlier. Instead, it made him want to rush back over and choke the woman to stop the nerve-racking sound.

CHAPTER 4

Answer the Damn Phone

THE LENGTH OF time it took for someone to answer the phone in the emergency department wasn't helping Ian's already foul mood as he listened to the nonstop rings and hoped that the idiot who played receptionist hadn't decided to go hide and sleep.

"What?" snarled Joshua's sleepy voice.

"At least say emergency room, you idiot," yelled Ian. He wondered how the ward clerk had managed to get, let alone keep the job that required organizational skills and tact that were as foreign to Josh as brain surgery.

"That you, Dr. McLintock?" The snuffle of a cold came across the phone. Ian had to remember to disinfect the receiver before using the nursing station phone the next time.

"Who the hell do you think it is? The tooth fairy?"

"So watcha want, Doc?"

"Get someone to take over the desk for you. Then get Marla, a stretcher, and as many blankets from the warming cabinet as possible. Then hurry your sorry ass down to the morgue as fast as you can get here."

"Someone got put on a slab that's still alive?" Even though he had to be one of the stupidest clods in the hospital, Ian never ceased to be amazed at how many times Josh seemed to sense what was happening without being told. A regular Radar O'Reilly was their Josh.

"Shut up, Josh. Tell no one. You hear?"

After hanging up, Ian went over and began rubbing the icy hands of the woman still lying in the open drawer. The act of kindness stopped the god-awful moaning and carrying on of the woman. It was amazing someone from the staff hadn't heard her earlier in the day.

The cold seemed to suck the heat from Ian's body, but he didn't want to attempt to lift the woman out on his own, mostly because she would be dead weight and unable to help him. The urge to giggle came back as he thought of her as "dead weight." He really needed to get some sleep, or he would end up telling a family member that their loved one died and then break into hysterical laughter. Ian could visualize himself being dragged off to a padded room on the psych ward for such an inappropriate response.

It felt like an eternity waiting for Josh and Marla to arrive. Suddenly, Ian realized with a shock that he didn't even know who the woman was. "What's your name?"

"Samantha Rutledge. But all the cleaning staff calls me Sam or Sammy."

"How on earth did you ever end up in a drawer in the morgue?" Ian regretted immediately the harshness of his words, as if the woman were responsible for her predicament.

Samantha began weeping again with intervening hiccups. "I don't know!"

"Can you remember what you did today?" Hell it was tomorrow already; the watch showed that it was 4:00 a.m. *Better not to confuse the woman,* Ian thought as he waited patiently for her to answer.

A faraway look in the woman's gray eyes gave him the impression that she really wasn't sure. But she had to remember something.

"Tell me the last thing you remember, even if it's going home from work on your last day."

"Oh. I remember that all right. It was my husband's birthday, and I picked up a cake from the cafeteria. He has a real sweet tooth." Samantha came close to smiling at the memory.

"Then what do you remember?" prompted Ian.

Samantha had a slight blush on her icy white cheeks. *Christ, don't tell me you laid the guy,* Ian thought. "Do you remember coming in to work this morning?"

After several minutes, the puzzled look in the woman's eyes gave way to a kind of eureka look. "Yes. I remember changing into my uniform at the locker."

"Then what?"

"I started the same routine I do every day. I got my cart from the locked cupboard and began collecting the garbage from my areas."

"What is the last thing you remember?"

A sad look of utter desolation made Samantha's eyes and mouth droop. Tears welled up making the green iris look almost blue in the neon lights of the morgue. "I don't know. It just stops, and I can't remember what happened before I ended up here."

The sound of wheels whispering down the corridor alerted Ian to the arrival of Josh and Marla. Prying his hand out of Samantha's grasp, he said, "I have to go and open the door, or they can't get in."

Ian propped the double doors ajar with the bolt while Marla wheeled the gurney into the morgue, Josh several steps behind. "Don't see why I had to come too," he grumbled.

"I need another man to help lift this woman out of the locker."

Josh jumped as he saw Samantha's hand gripping the side of the locker. "Suffering succotash! You weren't joking, were you?" muttered Josh as the reality of the situation hit him.

"Quit your yammering and come give me a hand."

Josh walked slowly to the side of the drawer almost as if he suspected they were going to stuff him into the locker and close the drawer. "Get the lead out, Josh. The woman is suffering from hypothermia."

The sarcasm galvanized the ward clerk into action, and he lifted on one side while Ian struggled on the other side of the hefty woman who, as Ian had suspected, was so cold as to be unable to assist them. After bumping her on the ledge of the drawer, they managed to get her onto the gurney where Marla began unfolding one after another of the warm blankets onto the woman. Samantha reacted to their warmth by having severe chills and shaking so badly that Ian thought she would rattle herself to death.

"Let's get out of here," muttered Marla, who was obviously very spooked by the idea of finding a live person imprisoned in the morgue.

"You go ahead to the emergency department, Marla. I need to talk to Josh for a few minutes."

Thrusting his lower lip out in a petulant look that had comic proportions, Josh clearly resented staying behind. "What do you want to talk to me about?"

"This has to stay a secret. Is that clear, Josh?"

"What are you saying? That I am a blabber mouth?"

"Someone spilled the beans about that guy who came back with the heart attack."

"There were ten people on duty that night."

"And we all know who went out and got drunk as a skunk at the After Hours Tavern."

"It wasn't me, and you can't prove it."

"Maybe not, but this time there are only three of us who know what happened here. You, me, and Marla. I know Marla won't talk and I won't. So if anything gets out, we'll know who has loose lips."

"You can't keep this a secret. Everyone's bound to find out sooner or later."

"We're going to make sure that it's later, much, much later. Do you hear?"

"Can I go now? This place always gave me the creeps, and now it scares the hell outa me."

"Okay, but just remember. No one finds out about this. The hospital administration will make a settlement with Samantha for keeping quiet. We all know how that works, so anybody finds out and we're gonna come after you. Maybe let you find out what it's like to have a short siesta in one of the morgue drawers." Ian felt ashamed that he'd stooped to such a low level in trying to scare Josh, but the look on the ward clerk's face told him that he had hit on the ultimate threat.

"You wouldn't do that."

"Like I said, if I hear anything got out, make sure you leave the hospital if you don't want a little taste of what Samantha Rutledge experienced."

Josh hurried out into the corridor and almost ran toward the emergency department. Ian felt a malicious desire to laugh, except he still had to make the phone call to the head honcho of the hospital. This was one incident that had to be dealt with at the highest levels of management and quickly to start damage control. If Ian knew anything about the place and the way it was run, he would lay odds that the hospital lawyer would be at Samantha Rutledge's bedside in less than an hour.

CHAPTER 5

Facing the Dean

*O*NLY THE EXTREMELY hard chair and Brandi's continual walking to and fro in the Dean of Medicine's office kept Ian from nodding off. Staring through bleary eyes that threatened to close of their own accord, Ian gawked at the secretary's impressive six-foot voluptuous body as she flashed him a reassuring smile before bending at the waist to get a paper from the bottom of a filing cabinet. This movement raised the already brief miniskirt up high enough to expose the bottom of a curved buttock that peeked out from a black lacy thong.

Waltzing with the folder in her hand over to the desk, Brandi puckered her collagen enhanced lips into a moue and said, "He should be here any minute now, Dr. McLintock."

If he hadn't been so exhausted, Ian knew that he would be fighting for self-control in the face of such a provocative display of female anatomy. But the twenty-eight-hour nonstop stretch had done to his libido what an ice cold shower could never do—it seemed to have killed any response to the luscious lady in front of him. In fact, Ian could have sworn that twenty naked-dancing Madonnas would not have gotten a rise out of him.

His speculation on the state of his masculinity was put to rest as the carved mahogany door opened and the towering frame of the Dean of Medicine lumbered into the room. He paused in front of Ian and shook his shaggy mane of curly gray hair. "Hear someone's been up to practical jokes in the hospital. Well, you'd better come in and tell me about it, Ian . . . , isn't it?"

Following the bulky figure only partially camouflaged by the expensive cut of his Armani suit, Ian wondered at how a medical man could let himself get to such a gargantuan size, knowing all the health problems carrying around such excess weight could cause. But the head of the medical school did not seem to exhibit any of the symptoms his weight might engender. *Stop diagnosing the bastard,* Ian told himself. *You are off duty now.*

"Sit. You must be exhausted." Ian had been waiting for the dean to insinuate himself into the leather chair that didn't look like it would accommodate a man of the dean's size.

"Thanks. It has been longer than I anticipated . . ."

"Right. I remember what it was like." The dean cut short Ian's explanation. "Let's get right to business, Ian. What's this I hear about you finding a live person on the slab in the morgue? Don't they keep the place locked up when nobody's there? We're going to have to look into the useless excuse for security we have running around the hospital. They cost more than they're worth. We could hire a bunch of boy scouts who'd do a better job."

Ian had lowered his head so his chin was resting on his arm propped against the armrest of the chair and was fighting to keep his eyes open. He didn't want a damn lecture on hospital security from this stuffed shirt.

"Well! Let's hear all the dirty details." The dean must have seen that Ian was about to fall asleep, and his gruff voice shocked Ian back into consciousness.

"There's not much to tell . . . ," Ian summarized exactly what had transpired in the early hours of the morning, including his conversation with the lawyer, Richard Lucresfeld (nicknamed Tricky Dickey by the hospital staff), who had taken charge of Samantha Rutledge.

Peering at Ian through the triangle made by balancing his fingertips together, the dean stated, "I'm getting the feeling you aren't telling me everything, Doctor!"

Ian hesitated, unsure what the dean was getting at.

"How in the blue blazes did you end up going into the morgue at that time of the morning anyways?"

"Oh!" The dean had asked the one question Ian was not prepared to answer. "I was just walking down the corridor." It was the truth.

"But why did you go into the morgue?"

"Some intern was ahead of me and motioned me to follow him." It sounded crazy to Ian's ears, even if it was the truth. As he sat watching for the dean's reaction, he was surprised to find the man turn an odd gray color. Then he harrumphed as if something had caught in his windpipe.

"You expect me to believe this? Who was this intern and what was he doing down by the morgue at that hour of the morning?"

"I don't know. He disappeared after I went into the morgue."

"Did you hunt for him? He may be the person responsible for this poor woman being in there." The dean looked a little less like he was about to faint, but his color still concerned Ian, especially since the man was so overweight, the typical heart attack waiting to happen.

"Quite frankly, I forgot about the intern as soon as I heard the sound of someone weeping."

"Are you telling me you made no attempt to find the young man who led you into the morgue?"

"Yes, sir. I felt that Samantha was suffering from hypothermia and needed immediate attention."

"Just how many people know about this?"

"Just Marla, Josh, me, the lawyer, and now you."

"Let's keep it that way, shall we?" The dean glared at Ian.

"No problem. Josh knows his job is on the line, and the rest of us understand the code of confidentiality."

"So it's just this Samantha . . . you said Rutledge, that we have to worry about?"

"The lawyer took care of her."

"Go home and stay there for a couple of days. We can't have the patients thinking all interns walk around with a five-o'clock shadow and so stunned from lack of sleep that they can't walk straight."

"Thank you, sir. I'm on my way."

"You don't talk in your sleep, do you, Dr . . . . ?"

"Not usually. But I don't have a roommate anyways."

Ian felt the dean's eyes on his back as he tried to walk a straight line out of the office. Sleep deprived! Ian headed to the nearest washroom and stared at himself in the mirror. Holy shit! He really could scare a patient in his present state.

As he stumbled out of the hospital, Ian couldn't help wonder what had upset the dean. Sure it was one of the worst pranks ever played on anyone, but nothing to have a heart attack over. It wasn't until Ian told him about the intern motioning him toward the morgue that the dean got upset. He couldn't help wondering why?

Before he realized it, Ian was standing at the main entrance to St. Cinnabar, feeling like he had been sleepwalking since he didn't remember getting from the Dean of Medicine's office to the impressive winding staircase that led down to the street. But he did have the distinct feeling that someone had been walking behind him. As he left the building, Ian turned suddenly and glanced back, but there wasn't anyone there. Then he saw the two elderly women approaching the Versailles-type flight of steps that led up to the entrance of the hospital. Ian recognized Helena as the most powerful force behind the Women's Hospital Auxiliary. But the petit black-haired woman was a stranger to Ian. It was the dark brooding look on the woman's face, as if she had suffered tremendously during her life and was putting up a good front that intrigued Ian. But he needed to get home before he started hallucinating from lack of sleep. *Whoever the woman was, she was not important to him or so,* he thought.

CHAPTER 6

Guess Who's Surprised

FROM THE FIRST time she met Helena DuCarthenson, Rebecca had a strange feeling of déjà vu. As the newest member of the Women's Hospital Auxiliary, Rebecca was being given a guided tour of the establishment.

All Rebecca knew about the head of the Women's Hospital Auxiliary was that Helena's husband had died leaving her with more money than she could spend in ten lifetimes. Once Helena had moved to Slatington from Boston, she had never let anyone forget about her previous status as a member of one of Massachusetts's oldest and wealthiest families.

Drained from concealing the bitterness that lay just beneath the surface, Rebecca pushed the idea from her mind that Helena might have something in her background that she was hiding. Rebecca was sufficiently acquainted with basic psychology to know that she could be projecting her own secrets onto this other woman.

Living up to her reputation for being fanatical about the historical significance of old buildings, Helena droned on about the past of the hospital. "This place dates back to the end of the Civil War but is not listed anywhere in the War Office archives from that time."

"The building doesn't look that old," commented Rebecca. "In fact, it looks as if it was built much later than that. It has almost a European flavor to its structure."

"Quite right. The upper part of the hospital was added on to what was called the Negro medical camp. Even though the blacks were fighting the South, they weren't ever treated by the white surgeons in the army. You probably don't know this, Rebecca, but the original hospital consisted of a central structure where the apothecary, kitchen, laundry, and surgical services were located. Built to withstand bombardment during the Civil War, underground tunnels fanned out like spokes on a wheel connecting everything else. Not that anyone ever attacked them since the Negro medical encampment wasn't listed as part of the army."

"How interesting," murmured Rebecca as she tried to suppress waves of anger.

"Yes, but one of the white officers was severely wounded and was about to have his leg amputated when a former slave of his told him that the black medical men were saving the limbs of soldiers with wounds like the officer's. So the officer had his former slave and several soldiers transport him to the black encampment where the 'doctor' saved his leg. Not that Negroes were ever allowed to attend the medical schools of that time. Apparently, the black man had been a slave to a surgeon and learned the trade from his master."

"Oh?" Rebecca said, suddenly more interested in the history of the hospital. "So how did it get to be so important?"

"This officer became a General, and his family was quite wealthy. So he took over the Negro encampment and put white doctors in charge. But he was smart enough to use the skills of the Negro doing the surgery. Of course, no white man would be caught dead going to a Negro medical man. But as long as the person in charge was white and the Nigger was listed as his assistant, they could get the best care possible and still say they went to a white doctor."

"Interesting, very interesting to learn things haven't changed much in these many years. Lots of black soldiers helped liberate the camps in Germany at the end of the Second World War. But very few were ever given credit for their part in the liberation of Europe."

"Well, you couldn't do that 'cause then they would get uppity and expect to be treated the same as us. But the building has even more interesting facts attached to it. When the Surgeon General agreed to preserve this site, the people of the city decided that it would be appropriate to have a European architect design the new building that would be added on," Helena stated in one long-winded breath.

Waving a heavily ringed hand proudly at the building and spouting off like a brochure for a tourist attraction, as if she had an entire tour group instead of one elderly woman beside her, Helena continued describing the difficulties encountered by the architect in preserving the original foundation while not compromising the integrity of the stone and cement tunnels that had survived the Civil War.

Too bad the original hospital hadn't been bombed into oblivion, Rebecca thought while smiling sweetly at her escort. It didn't matter. She made the proper unenthusiastic murmurs as she followed her elegantly dressed companion up the circular staircase into the hospital. Staying a step behind her guide, she felt like an actress playing a part on some bizarre stage.

So engrossed in her own importance and the upper class clipped tones of her own voice, Helena babbled on, completely oblivious to her companion's lack of interest. Nor was she aware that she was leading someone so consumed with hatred that even the tight smile on her face was difficult to maintain.

The nurses and doctors hurrying along the corridors looked too young, as if they had skipped directly from grade school and were part of a masquerade party. Rebecca didn't need anyone to tell her it was a symptom of old age. A glance down at the diamond on her wrinkled age-spotted hand reminded her just how old she was.

"Everyone was so happy to hear that you are joining the Women's Auxiliary," Helena continued as she led the way to the second meeting of the month.

"I'm the one who should be grateful that they welcomed me with such open arms," Rebecca murmured.

"Now, now. You have so much to offer, and we are always on the lookout for fresh blood."

This was a small backwater community that had steadfastly refused to move ahead in the area of human rights. It was only her enormous wealth that opened the doors of this group of women just wide enough to let Rebecca penetrate the elite high society. Resenting bitterly that wealth had opened the doors for her, Rebecca reminded herself that she had her own agenda. And she was using these women just as they were catering to her in hopes of wrangling a substantial donation to the hospital. They had already given her everything she needed to know right down to which tunnel connected to each part of the hospital.

But Rebecca couldn't help notice that everyone was going about their business as usual. It reminded her of the day her husband Sam died. The world ended for Rebecca at that moment. The grief was so intense that she couldn't even cry but stood dry-eyed at the bedside waiting for something. Then she heard laughter in the corridors, and the nurse and orderly came to take his body. They hadn't even looked sad. Sam was nothing to them and everything to her. It was then that the rage began to boil up inside her.

She had slowly begun to let go of the anger when she had come across the letter locked away with Sam's papers. Suddenly, the madness returned, and she had no choice. She had been propelled to this city to find the man responsible, to get revenge. The sudden influx of twenty student nurses all trying to pass them en masse in the narrow corridor startled Rebecca from her black reverie.

Looming ahead of them was the glassed-off portion of the cafeteria that was reserved for special meetings. And Helena had finally stopped talking. Rebecca was afraid her face betrayed her thoughts and decided she had better keep up the silly banter expected of a new member of the auxiliary. "This part of the hospital is especially nice, letting in the lovely spring sun. Will we be selling daffodils at the fund-raiser?" she asked.

"Oh yes, I'm so glad that you reminded me. Yes, and we are adding home crafts as well. If we are going to sit on those hard chairs all day, we might as well offer the staff and visitors a choice of goods. Some people are wonderful about buying flowers, but others . . ."

"Of course, not everyone loves flowers," murmured Rebecca.

"Well, we're almost there. You'll be delighted to know that we've asked the dean to speak to our lunch group today."

Rebecca stopped dead in her tracks. She had not expected to face the man so soon!

Helena turned as she realized her companion was now several feet behind her. "Is something the matter? You look frightfully pale. Do you want to sit for a moment? I can get you a glass of water."

"No. It's just a bit of angina." Making motions as if she were placing a pill under her tongue, she tried to cover her reaction. "I'll be fine now."

As they walked into the private lunch area where the other members were already seated, Rebecca stared at the huge man standing at the head of the table. There was nothing she could do but take a deep breath, smile at them, and take her seat. But as soon as the meeting was over, she would call that stupid man, Reggie Johnson. As a private investigator, he was not worth one-tenth of what Rebecca was paying him.

CHAPTER 7

Unidentified Intern

STUMBLING INTO THE apartment, Ian halted as he eyed the persistent blinking of his answering machine and his unmade bed. Pushing a button, he listened to the voice mail as he stripped naked and pulled the covers around his body, leaving half the mattress exposed. It was the third or fourth message that he vaguely remembered as he passed out.

The shrill ringing of the phone roused Ian from what felt like a very short nap. *Damn, why hadn't the machine picked up?* It was several minutes before he saw that the alarm clock had gone off, and it was twenty hours after he had laid his head down.

A painful throbbing in his temples felt like an overdue hangover had just hit. Snatches of weird dreams came back as Ian dressed. A nightmare in which he followed that same peculiarly dressed intern, only this time it wasn't into the morgue but down a gloomy overgrown path that led to a yawning grave. He had looked down and recoiled at the sight of skeletal remains with bits of dried flesh and wispy hair that lay in the bottom of an open grave. Even more sinister were the two intact eyeballs that had stared back at him.

The terrifying memory brought bile up his throat and almost made him vomit on the spot. Even anatomy classes hadn't made him lose his cookies. But the grotesque corpse in his dream threatened to. Then he remembered another detail. The bones of the arm pointed straight up at him, almost accusingly. What the hell did that mean? Usually, Ian attributed nightmares to having eaten too late at night. But this dream was different, almost prophetic. Maybe he would try and find the book on the meaning of dreams that his sister was always consulting.

A glance at the bulletin board beside his bed reminded Ian that he had a special session to attend today at four o'clock. Leaping out of the bed and padding across the cold tiles into the bathroom, it wasn't until the spray of the shower had pounded him for several minutes that Ian began to feel cleansed of the hideous images from the nightmare. When he looked at his watch again, the hands seemed to have jerked forward in one leap, and Ian scrambled, still damp, into his clothes and hurried out the door, grateful that he'd learned to get dressed on the run.

It was a fast day, filled with catch up since he had missed almost two days, and patients had been discharged and admitted apparently en masse. Struggling to read through the new charts, it was four o'clock before he knew it and had to race down the corridor to slide into the meeting on time.

Entering the amphitheater just as the lights were lowered and the slides were being projected on the wide screen at the front, Ian slid into a seat next to another intern. A former roommate from medical school, Frank Woo, nudged him. "Cutting it a little close, aren't you?"

"Gentleman, do I have your attention?" The staff physician had obviously overheard the whispered conversation.

"Ol' bat ears himself," muttered Frank directly into Ian's ear.

"Shhhh!" Ian gave his friend a tap.

As the lecture droned on, Ian looked around for the intern he had followed into the morgue. Every nationality was represented in this oversized lecture hall. Sitting at the back gave Ian a bird's-eye view of the other interns, but he couldn't spot anyone wearing the old-fashioned suit that the man wore the other night. Bored with what he had already researched because of a case that came in through emergency, Ian busied himself by studying each person row-by-row starting at the front. The guy had to be here because this was the most important lecture of the year, with several questions on the exam based on what Dr. Flangelieu was droning on about at the front while pointing at pertinent cells projected onto the screen.

Most of the doctors were not Anglo Saxon, coming from every background and nationality imaginable. Skipping over Andy, Jacque, Uri, and several other interns of various nationalities, Ian immediately dismissed them since the man he saw outside the morgue was definitely Anglo Saxon. He also knew that after subtracting the twenty-five females, that left only ten possible candidates. One was too tall, one was too fat, and one was too short. The rest had distinctive features like jet-black hair, a long hooked nose, and a leg that was obviously prosthesis.

The two left were dressed in the trendiest clothes that must have come directly from New York. No one in the audience bore the slightest resemblance to the man Ian had followed into the morgue.

"What cells are being used in experiments to 'cure' diabetics?" Dr. Flangelieu eyed the audience and then barked out, "Dr. Ian McLintock?"

"Islet of Langerhans cells, sir."

"You were paying attention?"

"Yes, sir."

The lecture continued on, and Ian stopped searching for the person who was obviously not present. Maybe he was wrong. Maybe the guy was a visitor or some other health care worker. Why had he assumed the guy was an intern? There were no answers, and the more he thought about it, the more his head throbbed. The pills had long worn off, and the headache was returning with a vengeance. Maybe he had a brain tumor and was imagining things? *Oh, shut up,* he told himself. Everyone knew that doctors were the biggest hypochondriacs. It was the stress of going without sleep and then going overboard getting more than twenty hours at once. Everyone knew it took weeks to recuperate, and Ian knew he just had to wait this out.

Finally, the lecture was over, and taking advantage of being at the very back of the lecture hall, Ian was grateful he could escape before the others. He headed toward the room of a patient he admitted three days ago, hoping the guy hadn't been discharged yet. Dr. Lester Conway was a retired doctor and veteran of Second World War who loved to have company.

"Wait up, Ian. What's the hurry?" Frank Woo strode alongside Ian.

Their friendship had begun even before they shared rooms. Although they were from entirely different backgrounds, Ian found himself drawn like a magnet to the cheerful Chinese medical student. Frank Woo was able to laugh at everything, finding something funny in every crisis. The guy had an infectious grin and easy manner that helped Ian when he began to feel that he had made a mistake in pursuing a career in medicine.

With marks at the top of his class, Frank had not endeared himself to the other students as he set a new and higher benchmark that forced the others to buckle down and study. It didn't help that Frank made even the most difficult of their courses seem easy. The others grouped together to study in an attempt to topple Frank's status in the class. Ian could not ignore the snide remarks of their classmates who attributed Frank's success to his Chinese heritage. Besides, Ian had drawn Frank as a roommate and knew only too well how hard Frank studied to keep his standing in the class. And that Frank's father, a doctor, expected Frank to stand first in his class.

More than once Ian had been grateful that his old man owned a hardware store in a small town in Connecticut. His father had been so proud that Ian had even been accepted to medical school that he didn't even question his ranking among the other would-be doctors. And Ian was careful never to tell him that he was second only to Frank Woo.

Things would have been different if Ian hadn't overheard some of the guys planning to play a trick on Frank. Instinctively, Ian stopped them with the threat of going to the authorities. After that, Ian no longer had to worry about being included in the fraternity or any of the activities that would keep him from studying. He was a persona non gratis and, as a result, spent a lot of time with Frank and the other nerds of their class.

It had really irked him at first to be excluded from the in-group, but it had paid off. Because he refused to go along with what people now recognized as bullying, Ian had maintained an average that gave him a chance for one of the few residency openings at the hospital.

"You're awfully quiet, Ian. How's it going?"

"Okay. I'm just a little tired. How're you doing, Frank?"

"Not bad. But I did hear they've been keeping you busy. And you look stressed to the max. What's this rumor I hear going around the hospital?"

"I don't know. Who's been gossiping?" Ian asked.

"One of the interns said that a patient got put on a slab in the morgue, and it turned out they weren't dead?"

"Christ almighty. Who the hell told you that? If I get a hold of the idiot, they'll be lucky if they aren't suspended for a month." It took every ounce of self-control to keep his reaction to scornful derision while Ian felt like the earth was being ripped out from under him. He knew he had to do damage control real fast.

"Whoa, here. Aren't you overreacting a little, Ian?"

"It's the same thing every day, Frank. Some idiot gets bored with nothing to do and decides to start a rumor. Well, some of them can be downright vicious. If I hear of anyone repeating what you told me, they will be in big trouble."

"Forget I said anything. Hear you've been working long hours. Pulled a couple of double shifts?"

"Yeah. I got stuck covering for Paul Cormorant when his grandmother died. You aren't suggesting that I'm just being miserable from lack of sleep?"

"Nah. I know better than that, Ian. Got to run. Give me a call when you have a spare minute." Frank laughed at what they both knew was almost nonexistent.

Ian wondered how even that much information had got leaked. He would have to have a talk with the ER clerk, Joshua.

That night he cornered Marla when there was a break in the ER. "Let's go into the lounge so we can talk privately."

"What's up, Ian? You have that look in your eye like you want to strangle someone."

"Someone leaked out that there was a live person in the morgue. And there are only four of us that know about it."

"Well, you know it wasn't me, Ian!" Marla looked like she wanted to hit him for even insinuating she might be party to such gossip.

"Of course, I know you wouldn't tell anyone. So it has to be Joshua!"

"Maybe not."

"What do you mean?"

"Samantha has been turning up at the ER almost every second night since it happened. Since she can't tell anyone what happened, she asks for you, Ian. The other interns refuse to call you in just for her, so I end up dealing with her."

"So what are you saying?"

"I need some help with Samantha. Someone may have overheard us talking and got a gist of what happened but didn't realize it was Samantha you found. You are the only other person who knows. Would you take a turn with her?"

"Sure. It's the least we can do for the poor woman. I don't know what I would do if I woke up in pitch-black on a refrigerator slab in the morgue. In fact, they probably would have had to lock me up in the psych ward for a while. Guess the settlement didn't help when she consented to sign the nondisclosure clause."

"Probably the worst thing she could have agreed to. What she really needs to do is tell everyone what happened to her, not hide it," Marla sighed with relief, knowing that Ian had agreed to deal with Samantha the next time she appeared in the emergency department.

Ian hated having to keep his mouth shut too. But all hell would have broken lose if it had gotten out that a live person had been put on a slab and locked in the morgue. There was one old geezer who had insisted that someone sit with his body for twenty-four hours after he was pronounced dead before they could release his earthly remains to the mortuary. After discovering Samantha, Ian had become acutely aware of the problems that would arise if even one patient were to find out.

"Okay. The next time Samantha Rutledge shows up in the ER, call me at home if you have to. We have to stop the rumors before someone figures out the truth."

"Thanks, Ian. You look bushed. Why don't you find a place to put your feet up, and I'll call you if we need you."

"Did anyone ever tell you that you're an angel?"

The dimples in her cheeks deepened as Marla tried to suppress a smile. "Only after a shot of Demerol. Get out of here before another ambulance pulls in." Ian felt Marla's eyes trained on his back as he headed toward his secret passage.

CHAPTER 8

Tunnels

*I*AN DOUBTED THAT he would ever make it though medical school let alone actually set up practice one day when an old black porter who seemed to belong to a bygone era had taken an interest in him.

The strange kinship that developed began one day as Ian noticed this elderly porter pushing a stretcher down the long sterile hospital corridors. It was difficult to guess the man's age, but his walk was typical of a man experiencing serious foot pain. Ian had waited until the man delivered his patient before confronting the porter. It was a touchy situation since Ian knew next to nothing about the porter but could appreciate the agony reflected in the man's face as he took each step.

"Shouldn't you have someone look at that foot?" Ian asked.

"Can't afford to, and what business is it of yours?" The cocoa face was still almost wrinkle-free although the man's crinkly hair and beard were a mass of tight snowy curls, and his hands gnarled with age.

"Medicine is my business," Ian had stated bluntly, facing down the old porter.

"You don't know anythin', white boy. I've been around here for more years than I can remember, and most of you young whippersnappers are more'n likely to kill a body instead of curing them."

Ian recognized the truth when he heard it but had no intention of trying to cure the man's ailments by himself. He would present the problem as a hypothetical case to one of the senior staff members and use them to outline a cure.

Suddenly, he realized he didn't even know the man's name. "I'm Ian McLintock, from Connecticut. What's your name?"

"Moby White." The man grinned from ear to ear exposing perfect pearly white teeth. "Always thought it amusing to be a black man named White."

"Pleased to meet you, Mr. White. So will you let me see what's making you limp?"

"Can't stand formalities. Friends call me Mo. If you're going to be perusing this poor black body, you might as well call me Mo too." And he sat, slowly taking off his right shoe. The toes he showed Ian looked like they had been frostbitten, they were so mottled.

"Are you diabetic, Mo?"

"Don't know. Haven't seen a doctor in years," his thin belly rolled with laughter as he finished by saying, "except to run from them with my stretchers."

"Would you come with me to the teaching room? There's equipment there that I need."

"I don't know why I trust you, boy, but lead on and I'll follow."

That began the long friendship that finally ended when Mo dropped dead one day from a heart attack while wheeling a patient back to his room. It had been too late to save his toes, but Ian managed to get the best internist on staff to take a look, and they got the man's blood sugar under control. By way of thanks, Mo had shown Ian the maze of underground tunnels and several shortcuts that helped him when he was late for a class.

He had occasion to thank Mo that year. Ian found one classmate exceptionally nosey. Normally, he would have avoided the guy, but Roger Inkster made a point of beating Ian to each lecture and plunking himself down in the chair that Ian had unofficially adopted as his own. Ian knew it was childish to let that annoy him, but he couldn't get over the fact that Roger deliberately sat wherever Ian did as if by occupying his place he would get better marks.

Whatever the reason, Ian finally admitted to himself that he had to fight back or go crazy. So Ian would wait for Roger to leave a lecture ahead of him. Then Ian would take off down one of the underground passages Mo had shown him. When Roger arrived for at the next classroom, Ian would be sitting in the seat he preferred much to Roger's annoyance. The way Roger stared at Ian with the bewildered look of a little kid who had just lost a race almost made up for all the suppressed rage Ian felt since the beginning of the petty competition. But the best part was that no matter how many times Ian beat Roger to their next destination, Roger refused to acknowledge the fact and ask Ian how he managed to do it.

Thinking about Mo and Roger, Ian almost forgot to duck as the tunnel dipped down under rough-hewn crossbeams in the oldest part of the hospital. The air stank so bad that Ian would have suspected there were decaying bodies nearby. But he knew that wasn't possible and that it was just the mold and mildew so prevalent in the cramped underground space that never saw the light of day. Even breathing was difficult in places where the ventilation had been blocked off by recent construction overhead.

Finally, he reached the newer section that let him walk upright once again. Up the stairs and to the right, he spotted the door to the old stairwell. It was usually locked, but the skeleton key that Mo had given him just before he died opened all the old locks.

It amused Ian to think that not even the hospital administrator could get from one end of the hospital to the other as fast as he could.

The patient Ian wanted to check on was a retired physician who had had a mild heart attack. The man had made a fast recovery and was waiting for a place in a retirement home. In fact, Dr. Lester Conway would have been able to return to his own home except that he was a widower and had let himself deteriorate after his wife's death to the point that he probably would have died if he hadn't been brought in for a myocardial infarction. But bed rest and the proper medication had minimized the damaged caused by the heart attack.

Ian reached the man's room and was pleased to discover that Dr. Conway was snoring away. It was as he hoped. The patient next to Dr. Conway had been sent home, so Ian pulled the curtain around the empty bed, made himself comfortable in the Cadillac chair, and put his feet up.

Despite his attempt to clear his mind and dose off, his brain churned with the events of the day. Just as Ian thought, he had finally cleared the mental decks, the problem of who had put Samantha Rutledge in the morgue popped into his head gnawing away at his brain like a cancer.

Nothing he did, nothing he thought of, seem to help banish the issue of how a cleaning lady could come to work one morning and end up on a slab by the end of that same day and not remember a thing about it. Someone had to have done it. Someone must have seen something.

Give it a rest, Ian ordered himself. But he just couldn't shake the horror of finding a live person in that place. Ian fell asleep despite the turmoil in his brain and was drifting in and out of a dream state when suddenly he was jolted awake by the sound of heavy footsteps on the terrazzo floor as someone entered the room.

CHAPTER 9

Eavesdropping

"**HOW ARE YOU** tonight, Dr. Conway?" a low gravelly voice that sounded as if it belonged to a much older man reverberated in the small room.

Ian recognized the voice of a fellow intern, Louis Parker, a Texan and ex-military who had gotten through college on a veteran's scholarship. Unfortunately, he seemed to be one of the dumbest wanna be doctor in the class. Frank Woo had been assigned to tutor the guy, but Ian knew from their conversations that Frank was about to give up on him.

"Can't stand formality, and I'm retired. So how about calling me Lester? And the answer to your question is 'bout the same as yesterday. At my age things don't change much, no matter what you do." The rustle of bedclothes as Dr. Lester Conway roused himself from a sleep made Ian wonder why Lou hadn't just let the man sleep and come back later.

Ian thought about how Lou, as everyone called him, had done a stint overseas during the Desert Storm. As a GI, he had been given a heads up despite his lack of academic brilliance. The resentment of his preferential treatment only exacerbated the tension between Lou and his classmates as he struggled to get through medical school.

There was a class pool on how long the guy would last with no one taking the bet that Lou would make it through his year. It wasn't just that the guy was dumb, he might have killed a patient if Frank had not been with him and caught Lou's mistake.

"How are the nurses treating you, Dr. Conway?"

"They are the sweetest young things. Why, if I was your age, I'd be chasing them all over the hospital."

Ian had sat in silence too long and was embarrassed to get up and leave, so he sat with his eyes shut and figured if they discovered him behind the curtain, he would just let on that he was still sleeping instead of eavesdropping on the conversation. Besides, Ian was curious as to how Lou dealt with his patients when there was no one around peering over his shoulder.

Lou did the run up of questions that were required of all patients, and Ian was impressed with the guy's bedside manner. He definitely knew how to talk to people, if he just wasn't so dumb.

"So what do you see with all the lights flickering on the monitor there, young fella?"

"There doesn't appear to be any anomalies."

There were more rustlings, and Ian heard the sound of two barefeet hitting the cold hard terrazzo. "Damn, these tiles are cold."

"Why are you getting up?"

"Wanna show you something, young man, and can't do it lying down. Now you see the wave as it goes up and then dips down again?"

"Yes, sir."

"Well, right about here if you look hard you're gonna see an extra little bump that most people would miss. Do you see what I mean?"

Ian could hear Lou leaning over the patient to get closer to the florescent green tracings. "Now wait till I am still again. All this moving is disturbing the wave. Now do you see it?"

"Yes, I do!" The amazement in Lou's voice was unmistakable.

"You know, son, I was healthy as a horse and worked fourteen hour a day until my wife, Jessie, died. Many a patient of mine complained of a broken heart when their mate passed on. Never had enough sympathy for them until it happened to me. I really believe that's why I had my heart attack. Lost my best friend when Jessie died, and I just didn't want to go on without her."

"That's terrible. I'm so sorry, Dr. Conway."

"It's Lester. And don't be sorry. The only way you miss someone that bad is if you had a damn good marriage, and I would wager that ours was one of the best. You're not married, are you?"

"Nope. Couldn't ask the woman I loved to wait while I was away, and when I came back, she had gotten married."

"Used to think depression caused a lot of heart attacks when I was younger. Now those specialists agree with me. They say you have less chance of surviving an infraction if you are really down in the dumps, and they only had to get some highfalutin specialist to waste lots of money to discover what I always suspected."

"I saw that report. It just sounded like common sense to me."

"You know how I'm doing, son. So, how're you doing, Doc?" asked Lester. "Is it still as grueling to be an intern as when I was your age?"

"Worse, I think. Each year they discover so many new things that the textbooks just keep getting thicker and thicker."

"It was a real bugger when I got accepted at the end of the war—on the GI bill, you know."

"You were in the military?" The acute interest in Lou's voice was unmistakable.

"Did a stint in the South Pacific before they dropped the bomb on Hiroshima. Hell of a thing those A bombs. But it saved a lot of lives."

"I'm an ex-marine. Only action I saw was during the Desert Storm. People don't think we were really in combat, not like you."

"War is war, kid. Once you've seen arms, legs, guts blown to kingdom come, nothing is ever the same. I know what you mean, kid. I had a lot of patients who were in Vietnam. Never could reach some of them. They were too far-gone, and nobody appreciated what they went through. My wife used to get mad at me when something on the news would stir up old memories, and I would have those nightmares again. She used to say, 'Lester, it's been forty years since the war ended. Let it go.' But I couldn't stop the memories from flooding back.

"Even medical school was a nightmare for me. I left grade ten to sneak off and sign up. Lied about my age so I wouldn't miss out on the war. When I came back from overseas, I had to finish up so I could graduate and then go on to college. If it hadn't been for this Jewish kid, Izzy, who started tutoring me and a couple of the other guys on the GI bill, I would have been done before I started. He was smart and real nice too. If it wasn't for Izzy, we woulda flunked outa medical school. We were that dumb."

"Yeah, I've got a tutor too, but I'm not sure it's gonna do me any good."

"Listen, kid, I'm stuck here for a while. You wanta come and talk to me just bring those medical books. Some things don't change."

"You mean it?"

"Sure do. I'm so bored instead of lying here I could eat grass. How about tonight? I might not know some of the new stuff, but that kid Izzy taught me how to study, and I never forgot."

"Do you still keep in contact with this Izzy guy?"

"Naw. He died the year we graduated."

"What a waste. Finishing four years of medical school and dying. Gee, I didn't realize it was getting that late. I'd better get going. See you tonight. And thanks."

"No thanks necessary. You're doing me a favor, kid. And I owe it to Izzy to help someone else."

Ian could see under the curtain the spring in Lou's step as he walked out of the room. He couldn't help wondering what happened to Izzy that he died just as he finished medical school. It was something Ian hadn't thought much about . . . That after years of grueling education, it could all end without ever getting a chance to set up a medical practice and recoup the money spent on his education.

"You can come out now," the raspy voice yelled.

"Didn't mean to eavesdrop." Ian felt a blush rising from the roots of his hair.

"If you got any more guys like him, I'd be more than willing to help them out. It's better than sitting here waiting for God."

"What happened to the guy Izzy, who tutored you?"

"It's a bit of a mystery . . ." Lester was interrupted as Ian's pager went off.

"Damn! Guess I've got to go too."

"Don't forget, young fella, you got any more boys that need help, you send them around to see me. Least I can do to repay Izzy."

"I'll keep you in mind. Maybe I'll come myself."

"Well, skedaddle or somebody's gonna be after your ass."

CHAPTER 10

Promotions

HOW THE COLLEGE basketball recruiters had let Ian slip through their fingers was a mystery to Marla. The guy was six feet three inches at least and had the slender build and cat-like movements of a natural-born athlete. She remembered someone telling her that he had been offered a position on one of the better college basketball teams but turned it down in favor of medicine. She would never understand why. The guy would have been a multimillionaire by now with all the advertising promotions offered to successful athletes. But Ian had a warm, gentle personality that was not suited to competitive sports. He fit the mold of a doctor as far as Marla could see.

It was the way he disappeared down a set of stairs that she figured led nowhere that always astonished her. But she knew that he had made friends with one of the oldest and most reclusive employees of the hospital. Mo had a lot of secrets, and most of them went to the grave with him. But Marla would have loved to know what he did tell Ian before he passed on, especially since their hospital had a rather little known history as a confederate hospital built to treat wounded southern soldiers.

"What are you staring at, Marla?" Emma's voice startled Marla out of her daydream.

"Just wondering where Dr. McLintock was off to."

"He is one gorgeous hunk of a man, isn't he? Suppose you have your eye on him?"

"No. Ours is strictly a professional relationship. Doctor and nurse."

"Sure, Marla, and my mother is still a virgin." She gave a deep throaty laugh. "But if you aren't interested in him, guess you wouldn't mind if I took a run at him. He's still a free agent last time I heard."

"Go for it, Emma. Like they say, all's fair in love and war."

"I would, but I see the way he looks at you. And you seem to be totally unaware that the guy is stuck on you."

"Don't be ridiculous, Emma. Dr. McLintock is married to his work. He doesn't have time for a girlfriend right now."

"That's what they said about Stevie Wonder. And now he's going to tie the knot. Bet there are a lot of women kicking their asses for letting him get away. Just remember, Marla, if you don't try, you'll never know."

"Advice for the lovelorn? Not meaning to change the topic, Emma, but have you heard any more news about who they are going to hire to replace Crystal? She was the best manager we ever had. Too bad she had a breakdown."

"Word has it that they are going to try to fill the position internally. Why don't you put your name in for the job? You would make a great boss, Marla."

"Yeah, I could see it now. You would expect me to give you every holiday and weekend off because we're old friends and former classmates."

"No, I wouldn't. I'm not so immature that I would expect favors just because we're friends. Besides, I know that you would be a better boss than some idiot that they might hire from out of town. Why the administrators look down their nose at homegrown talent in favor of someone from a big city or another country is beyond me."

"I think the men regard an accent as a mark of a high-class person."

"Don't make me say what I think of those crass idiots and male chauvinists on the hiring panel. Promise me one thing, Marla."

"What's that?"

"That you will put in your application for the job. You can always turn it down if you decide you really don't want it."

"I'll think about it. But if you're so eager for someone in the hospital to get the promotion, why don't you apply for it, Emma?"

"Lack of qualification for one reason. And my husband would leave me if I ended up staying late all those nights the job inevitably begets."

"There are always ways around the late nights, Emma. You know that any job can be delegated. Look what has happened since Crystal went on extended sick leave. We're doing the work she used to do."

"So you'll put your name in for the job then?"

"Okay." Marla laughed. It was true that she could do the job. In fact, she was doing most of the administrative part already and had been surprised at how easily she managed what had seemed to be a monumental task for Crystal.

"Damn! Another ambulance making a beeline for us. Why do they have to put the siren on for the last fifty feet coming into the hospital? Are they afraid we won't notice them? Well, it's back to work." Emma headed toward the emergency-parking bay.

CHAPTER 11

Dead Man Walking?

THE EARLY MORNING sun blazing through the southern-facing pane of glass heated up the blanket wrapped around Ian. Opening one eye a slit and peaking at his watch, he did a double take, sure that his watch had stopped sometime during the previous evening. It couldn't be 8:30 in the morning. He felt like he had just laid his head on the pillow. With the sheet wrapped around his body, Ian dashed to the shower and did a once-over with the lather to rid himself of any lingering sleep-induced body odor.

Sliding into the clothes flung over the back of the chair, he took the stairs two at a time and jogged down the street to the hospital. He had to make the weekly Morbidity and Mortality meeting.

Once inside St. Cinnabar, he slowed down to a fast-paced trot that made his footsteps on the old marble terrazzo tiles echo through the corridor. Racing around the corner, Ian had to dodge a laden food trolley being pushed by Sally. "Whoa, there, Doc. What's the big hurry?" she yelled at his disappearing back.

"Sorry. But I'm late," Ian yelled as he headed toward the large dark oak double doors of the auditorium which were already shut. The hinges squeaked noisily as he opened one door just wide enough to slide into the conference room. Someone had just dimmed the lights, and the first slide of what looked like a lengthy presentation had just been projected on to an oversized white sheet that was substituting for a screen.

Ian wondered if the light-fingered nutcase that was wandering St. Cinnabar had stolen the real screen, forcing the tech staff to improvise. Fatigue made his brain shove it to a far dark corner labeled moot questions. The darkness of the room allowed him to close his eyes until the slide presentation was over.

"You sleeping?" Andy Sutton poked Ian.

"No. I listen better with my eyes shut!"

"Likely story. They say one of the cadavers got up and walked away, missing the Morbidity and Mortality lecture." The long low chuckle resonated down the back aisle.

"Somebody is having a real blast spreading rumors again. Thought you were too smart to swallow some smart ass's gossip."

"You sure it's just gossip?"

"I'd bet my career on it." Ian suppressed the rage he felt. Whoever leaked out the information had done a good job of spreading it without giving any details.

"I suppose you don't believe that there's a ghost that walks the halls down by the morgue either," sneered Andy.

Cold fingers gripped his spine as Ian suppressed the terror he felt. "What dork started that tall tale?" Ian tried to put as much sarcasm into his voice as possible.

"It wasn't me. And if you ask some of the staff doctors, this specter has been haunting the corridors of St. Cinnabar for some thirty years. So if it's a lie, it's a long-lived one." Andy laughed at the irony of his statement.

At the front of the lecture hall, the professor stopped and gave a long cough. Dr. Renard was too polite to center out any intern, but he was obviously ticked at having a discussion being carried on at the back of the theater.

"Meet me at the doctors' lounge when this is over," whispered Ian.

"Sure. So you believe there is a ghost."

"Ssssh. Do you want to get us thrown out?" Ian felt impatient for the discussion to end. He had to know what this apparition looked like.

CHAPTER 12

Haunted Halls

*I*AN CLOSED HIS eyes again and listened to the surgeon explain what went wrong in an operation that should have had a successful outcome. *Why don't they just say the patient was allergic to the damn anesthetic and be done with it,* Ian thought as the discussion droned on. The head of anesthesiology explored all the various avenues of responsibility. *Why can't the man admit that the patient wasn't checked for what was an extremely rare and inherited defect?* Ian wondered. The man died, and there was nothing they could do, except trace all relatives of his and check them for the same allergic response to that particular drug. Then the guy's death would not be totally in vain. It would at least help others survive.

The long dark tunnel stretched out in front of Ian, and he saw the strangely dressed doctor beckoning him to follow. But his feet felt like they were encased in cement, and he couldn't move. *Where is the man going?* Ian wondered. Suddenly, he felt a sharp nudge. Ian woke with a jerk as Andy got up to leave.

"It's bad enough to sleep through the lecture, but, man, you were starting to have some kind of weird dream." Andy stared at Ian. But Ian was not about to tell Andy about the nightmare he had been having while sitting up in the middle of an auditorium full of doctors. When the last doctor marched past him, Ian got up and followed Andy out the door.

"Coming to the lounge?" Patrick Fitzroy's grin was surrounded by a mass of freckles.

"You headed that way too?" *It was a dumb question,* thought Ian. They were all headed to the informal meeting they had after one of these sessions unless they had patients or rounds to attend to.

"The guys are meeting to plan the next baseball game. There has to be some time when we have nine of us free."

"Don't count on it, Pat. Last time we played the student nurses, they had twenty players to our seven."

"We still won."

"I suspect they took pity and let us have that last run."

"No way. Men are stronger than women."

"We had two female interns on our side. How do you explain that?" Ian knew Pat was a male chauvinist, but liked him anyways. The women all adored him and would never suspect that he harbored such antiquated opinions.

"Pat, have you ever heard a rumor about a ghost walking the halls late at night?" Ian knew that Pat was a pragmatist and would put an end to the hoax Andy was trying to put over on him.

"Here at the hospital, you mean?"

"Yeah! Where else would I be talking about?"

"As a matter of fact, the guys were discussing it about three weeks ago. Seems like no one had seen this ghost for a long time. Then, three doctors saw the same specter walking the halls down by the morgue three nights in a row."

"Were you talking to Andy?"

"Not recently. Why? What has Andy got to do with this?"

"If you guys are pulling my leg, I'll get even if it's the last thing I ever do." Ian felt his face flush with rage.

"You brought this up, Ian. Not me. If you don't believe me, go ask Dr. Histane, the pathologist. The interns said he almost shit himself when he got called in late one night. He saw what he thought was an Intern waiting for him outside the morgue. When he reached the doors, there was nothing there, just a spot of real cold air. Nothing scares that man, but he called in another doctor to stay with him while he did the emergency autopsy."

"Cold-blooded Histane got scared? You've got to be joking."

"Hell no. The man was the laughing stock of the hospital. Apparently, the other doctor he called in was so pissed off at being dragged out of bed to babysit the Head of Pathology that he told everyone who would listen and some who wouldn't. There wasn't a doctor or nurse in the hospital that didn't know."

"That must have been embarrassing."

"The guy ended up hiring a special technician to be on call late at night so he wouldn't have to be alone in the morgue. So, if Dr. Histane believes there's a ghost walking the corridors, you can bet your bottom dollar there's something to the rumor."

"But psychics have been known to use holograms to project an image into thin air."

"Can you imagine anyone with that much intelligence working in a hospital? They'd be making more money duping the public with fortune-telling. Come in and ask the guys about it." Pat opened the lounge door and waited for Ian to go in ahead of him.

"I wondered if you would make it," Andy commented as Ian pulled up a chair.

"Pat was telling me about the hospital phantom. Sorry, I didn't believe you, Andy."

"What I couldn't figure out was why you got so mad? Did you think I was lying to you?"

"Yeah. I thought maybe you guys got together and decided to tell me a real whopper. But I guess I'm just a little paranoid from lack of sleep."

"Anyone who can sleep sitting up during a Mortality and Morbidity lecture with those guys arguing has to be sleep deprived." Andy turned to Pat for support.

"I agree. I was wondering who was snoring in the back row. You're just lucky, Ian, that they were yelling so loud that they couldn't hear you down front."

"Okay, okay. But I want to know more about this so-called ghost. What does he look like? When and where does he appear? According to you, Pat, he has been seen down by the morgue."

"Yeah. Everyone who has had the guts to admit seeing the guy says he is always in the corridor outside the morgue. Is that where you saw him, Ian?" Pat stared with his cornflower blue eyes and waited.

"What makes you think I saw some frigging ghost?"

"Because you got so mad. That's why. Right, Andy?"

"Yeah, man. You practically leapt down my throat. Even if we were playing a practical joke, you wouldn't get that angry. So tell us what happened."

They had attracted the attention of the other interns, and now the whole gang was waiting for Ian to explain. "Okay, so I did see what I thought was an intern dressed in strange clothes down by the morgue. When I followed him into the morgue, he had disappeared."

"What was he wearing?" Pat prompted Ian, while the others waited.

"The more I think about it, the more I realize his suit was something from the fifties, maybe earlier. Real old-fashioned."

"What did the guy look like?" This time Andy egged him on.

"Real young. Scarcely old enough to be in medical school, except he had a stethoscope hung around his neck. That must be why I thought he was an intern." Ian finally answered one of the questions that had been bugging him.

"Sounds like the ghost all right," piped up Midgie. The shortest doctor in the class, Michael had been nicknamed Midget and then Midgie. With good humor, he lived with the handle although he would have preferred Mike.

"How do you know?" demanded Ian.

Midgie walked over to the wall of bookshelves and pulled a yearbook from 1950 off the shelf. Flipping through the dusty volume, he stopped at a page with pictures of all the students from that graduating year. "Did he look like this?" Midgie shoved the page under Ian's nose.

"Geez! Yeah. Dr. Isaac Steinman! Nickname Izzy. This is the guy that died just before graduation."

"How did you know that?" Andy leaned on Ian's shoulder and studied the photo.

"One of the patients on ward seven was a classmate of this kid. Anyone mind if I take this yearbook with me?"

"Naw. Aren't you going to stick around to help plan the game?"

"No. I want to check something out. Just let me know what night you decide on. Either I will be available, or I won't." Ian rushed out the door and forced himself to slow to a trot as he headed toward Dr. Conway's room.

The annoying ping, ping, ping of his pager stopped Ian in his tracks. He was on call and knew that although the page might be something totally stupid, he couldn't ignore it just in case someone was in urgent need. Stopping at the nearest nursing station, he dialed the number and heard Marla's voice. Normally level headed even under the worst circumstances, Marla's voice had a high-pitched quality about it that made her sound close to hysteria. There had been an explosion and that meant burn victims.

"Okay, I'll be right there." Dr. Conway and the ghost would have to wait. Ian did not relish the scene he would be about to witness and could only hope that it sounded worse than it was.

CHAPTER 13

Endless Emergencies

*I*AN SPRINTED TO reach the elevator doors before they closed. The stench of smoke, probably from one of the other people on the lift, who had just had a cigarette, triggered the awful memory of burn patients who had flooded the emergency department more than a year ago. Some idiot had thrown a homemade Molotov cocktail into a school in the lower east end. The kids had been the worst part of the fire.

Everyone had pulled through except for one fireman who had gone back in to look for a student whom everyone thought was still in the building. It turned out the kid had played hooky and had gone home early, and the man had rushed back into the death trap for nothing.

Marla had been on duty when the guy was wheeled in with burns to most of his body. Despite the gut-wrenching situation, she had continued talking to the man as they cut away his gear until they found a patch of skin where they could inject morphine. It seemed like yesterday to Ian as the image of Marla calmly explaining everything to the poor man.

"We will have to intubate you so we need to know your next of kin, sir."

"I'm going to die, aren't I?" The man could scarcely croak out the words; his throat was so burned from smoke inhalation.

"That's not why we need to know your next of kin. Once we put the tube down your throat, you won't be able to talk." Marla was good at lying to patients, and it was a standard policy not to tell someone that they didn't have a good chance of making it.

"Don't lie to me. I know I'm dying."

"Sir, we need to know your next of kin."

The man's eyes filled with tears. "It's not necessary. I am talking to my family." Marla was stunned to realize that she had been working on her father who had been so badly burned that she didn't recognize him. Ian remembered pushing her down onto a chair before Marla fainted.

"Dad!" With immense courage, she held back the tears for the sake of her father while the staff doctor called for another nurse. Then he sent Marla out of the room until the rest of the procedure had been finished.

Marla had known that in order to allow her father to breathe they would make a lateral incision in her father's chest to stop the burned thoracic skin from tightening like a vise that would eventually stop his chest and lungs from expanding.

From that day, whenever burn victims arrived in the ER, the staff went out of their way to prevent Marla from having to deal with them. Eventually, she told everyone that she had to either quit the department or face what everyone else had to. But it was still the only time Ian saw Marla lose the distance required by a medical professional.

CHAPTER 14

Isolated

*T*HE QUESTION WHY someone had drugged her and put her in a cadaver drawer in the morgue plagued Samantha. At first, it seemed right to sign the agreement. The hospital lawyer, Mr. Lucresfeld, had been so kind. He had insisted that she could call him by his first name, Richard. He had explained how it was in her best interests to accept the hospital's generous offer of compensation for what had happened to her.

Unsure of what to do, Samantha would have preferred to talk to a lawyer since she had difficulty understanding the complicated document Mr. Lucresfeld had pushed in front of her. She was still shaken by the ordeal and confused by the sedative Dr. McLintock had given her. Finally, Samantha had asked to talk it over with her husband first.

At first, Larry was furious that he had been called from work. It wasn't until much later that Samantha wondered if her husband had even missed her when she didn't come home from work that evening.

Samantha remembered only too clearly the obsequious tone Larry used when he asked the lawyer, "Would you leave us alone for a minute, Mr. Lucresfeld?"

Even as she watched him looking over the numerous pages, Samantha wasn't sure Larry knew what he was reading either. Confused and pressured, Samantha relied on Larry to decipher the legal agreement. But once he heard the amount of money the hospital was willing to pay, he wasted no time convincing Samantha that she didn't need her own legal representation. He shrugged off the trauma of the experience, saying to Samantha, "You weren't hurt. Hell, with this much money we can buy a house, a new car, and still go on a vacation."

Samantha had tried to explain to her husband the misgivings that plagued her. But, unable to find the words to explain the gnawing feeling, she meekly said, "Larry, it just feels wrong, no matter how much money the hospital is willing to pay me."

"Shit, I'd be willing to lie on a slab all night long if they wanted to give me this much money. It's not as if someone tried to murder you!"

But Samantha wasn't so sure that someone hadn't tried to kill her. It was all so terrifyingly strange. "So you think it was someone's idea of a bad joke?" she asked her husband.

"Yeah! Who have you pissed off lately?"

Samantha cringed at the word "pissed." "No one!" The tears streamed down her cheeks.

"Look, Sammy, it's not like we'll ever get another chance for this much money. Just ask the doctor for some tranquilizers. You'll get over it."

It hurt even more to think Larry passed off the incident as nothing and had no sympathy for how she felt. Sniffing back the rest of her tears, Samantha had agreed, saying, "Just pass me the damn pen, Larry."

She signed the document, and Larry had snatched it before Samantha could change her mind and rip it up. Then Larry went to find the hotshot lawyer Richard Lucresfeld. When he returned, Larry helped Samantha get dressed and took her home.

It was as he drove away from the hospital that Samantha finally figured out what had been bugging her about the document she had just signed. She had agreed not to disclose the details of that night to anyone. If she did tell anyone, they would have to return the money in full. Now she cried hysterically as she thought about Larry, who listened but didn't understand how traumatic it had been, locked in a box, not a shred of light, increasingly less air to breathe, not knowing where she was, or if she would ever get out alive.

Now she couldn't tell anyone else what happened! It was too late, and when Samantha asked her family doctor for tranquilizers as her husband had suggested, the doctor refused to give them to her unless she could explain why she was so agitated.

Somewhat simpleminded Samantha took the secrecy clause very seriously. It prevented her from telling her family physician what had happened, with the result that she had returned home empty-handed. The well-stocked liquor cabinet provided some relief until the night Larry went on the midnight shift. As her husband walked out the door, lunch-bucket in hand, Samantha snuggled down in the bed, a large glass of Irish cream in hand as she watched the talk shows. By two, she couldn't keep her eyes open and turned off the light.

Scarcely had she fallen asleep when the scrapping of something in the walls woke her. Opening her eyes, the stifling darkness reminded Samantha of the morgue drawer. Scrambling to turn on the bedside lamp, she knocked it over. It took several panicky moments before she got the light on. By then her heart was racing, perspiration streamed down her face, and she could hardly move with terror.

She couldn't endure another night alone. Determined to find someone she could talk to, Samantha threw on the slacks that were draped over the back of the chair and tucked her nightgown into them. Sliding into a bulky sweater that hid the fact that she had no bra on, Samantha dialed for a taxi and asked the dispatcher if the man would come up to the apartment door to get her.

It seemed like an eternity before the cab driver buzzed the apartment, and Samantha let him in the main entrance. Once she was safe in the car, the driver treated Samantha with kid gloves, fearful that she might faint or bleed in his taxi. Turning into the circular drive at the emergency entrance, the cabbie made sure that he escorted Samantha inside and handed her over to the receptionist.

For once the waiting room was not packed with people and Samantha demanded to talk to Dr. Ian McLintock and no one else. The triage nurse smiled sweetly and insisted that Dr. McLintock was not available.

Samantha began weeping and gulping for breath as the nurse rolled her eyes and said, "Follow me. I can't promise you anything because we have had a major explosion, and the emergency staff are all busy. But if you will wait in here, I will ask Dr. McLintock to see you as soon as he is free."

The extremely small room had nothing in it except a triangular bench in the corner covered with a thin cushion. Sitting down, Samantha wondered why the room was so bare. But she didn't care. At least she wasn't alone at home, and the lights were on. Samantha wasn't sure how long she had been nodding off, body bent against the corner of the wall, when the door swung open.

CHAPTER 15

Consoling Samantha

"WHAT ARE YOU doing here?" Ian muttered the words before he could stop them coming out of his mouth. Of course, he knew exactly why the poor woman was in the psychiatric assessment booth.

"My husband, Larry, is on midnights, and I'm too terrified to stay alone. My doctor won't give me tranquilizers unless I tell him what is upsetting me. And I can't because of the agreement I signed." Choking sobs stopped the rest.

Sitting beside Samantha, Ian put his arm around her shoulder and felt the loose flesh, unencumbered by female undergarments. It didn't take a rocket scientist to figure out the poor woman had been too terrified to take the time to dress properly, that she had thrown clothes on over a night gown. "Do you have a friend who can come and stay with you?"

"No!" Anything else Samantha wanted to say was muffled by heartrending sobs.

"Let me give you something to help you calm down, and then we can talk." Ian left Samantha with several small boxes of tissues and went in search of Marla.

He found Marla in the room with one of the burn victims. Despite the brave front, Ian could see the tension in Marla's body. So he went back out the door and found another nurse at the station. "June, I have to have Marla help me with this patient. Would you mind going in and taking over with the burn patient?"

June screwed up her face in disgust. She was one of the least tactful nurses on staff, and Ian hated putting the guy in her care. But he was telling the truth.

"What's so important that only Marla can handle it?" There was a hint of something haughty in her words.

Instead of giving in to his fury, Ian just restated what he knew was the truth, "Marla is the only one here who can handle this patient." He waved to the observation camera trained on Samantha in the booth.

"Oh! Why didn't you say so?" June stomped off toward the room with Ian in her wake.

Once Marla came out into the corridor, Ian put his arm around her and said, "How are you doing?"

"I'm fine. You didn't have to do that, Ian. I'm over my father's death."

"I didn't do it for you. I need you somewhere else." The clean scent of her freshly washed hair was having an erotic effect on Ian. The warmth of Marla's shoulders under his touch was very sensual. He pulled back and said, "Samantha turned up in emergency again, and she's too terrified to go home alone tonight."

"Can't blame her. I wouldn't want to be alone in the dark either after what happened to her. And she can't tell anyone because of that jackass Richard Lucresfeld."

"Don't blame him. He was just following hospital policy. Apparently, it was her husband that talked Samantha into signing. I've written orders for a tranquilizer. Would you go and sit with her until she's calmed down? There's no point in trying to talk to her while she's still in hysterics."

"For once I'm grateful to someone for showing up in the ER. June wouldn't have moved her butt to help any of us if you hadn't come along and asked her to."

"Glad to hear I've been of use to someone tonight. How did you make out? The paramedics brought in an MVA, and I didn't get involved with the guys from the factory explosion."

"It wasn't as bad as we first thought. Lucky, those guys were shielded by the wall." Marla managed to make eye contact with Ian so he knew that, although she dreaded dealing with burn victims, she had managed to cope. "Christa came in and handled the one guy who had third-degree burns. So I just had arms and hands to bandage. It could have been a lot worse."

"You know that you don't have to always be on the front line." Ian watched as Marla blushed and changed the subject. She obviously didn't want to bring up her father's death again.

"I'll get two coffees and use Samantha as an excuse to put my feet up for a while." Marla walked toward the vending machines and then carried the cups toward the observation cubicle.

Ian opened the door for her and then turned toward the lounge. He needed some time to collect his thoughts and knew that Samantha would talk nonstop for an hour once the drugs took effect. At least she would be able to get some of it off her chest. But who would put a middle-aged cleaning woman on a slab in the morgue? Just as Ian thought he had put the incident out of his mind, there she was again. Whether he wanted to or not, he was being forced to face the puzzle again and had no choice but to try and figure it out, if for no other reason than to help Samantha get over the shock.

CHAPTER 16

Accidental Casualty

*T*HE RUDDY TINGE of dawn made a pink pool on the hospital corridor as Ian finally found a free moment to look in on Samantha. Opening the door to the observation room, Ian discovered Marla still sitting with her. With a subtle wave of his hand, Ian signaled Marla to come out so they could talk in private.

"It's too bad that you had to spend the whole night with her." Marla's drooping eyelids and pinpoint irises betrayed how exhausted she was.

"It's been quiet, and I really felt sorry for Samantha. She hasn't been coping, and to make matters worse, her stupid husband has offered her no support or sympathy at all. Larry was only interested in how much money the hospital paid his wife to keep quiet."

"Some men are like that."

"Huh! Some?"

"Shall we leave that discussion for another night? I just want to know what Samantha told you."

"Not much. She was really spaced out on the drugs you prescribed, muttering about her grandchild and how she almost didn't live to see it born. Then she just sat and stared into space for about an hour. But she was a good excuse for me to get off my feet for a while. June usually raises hell if she thinks she's working harder than someone else. With Samantha needing counseling, well, you get the picture, Ian."

"Yeah. Glad she provided a break for you. Now I've got to try and get her to sort this out. We can't have Samantha Rutledge showing up in the emergency department every time her husband is on midnights."

"Good luck, Ian. I have a feeling you are going to need it."

"Thanks a lot." Ian laughed as he watched the sensual sway of Marla's slim hips as she walked toward the nurses' lounge. He had never thought about asking her out before now. Marla had broken up with her fiancé after her father died. The jerk couldn't cope with a girlfriend who needed some TLC herself. Even as Ian thought about what it would be like to take Marla in his arms and let him touch her soft lips and softer breasts, he squelched the image. It never turned out well if you dated the people you worked with, no matter what they showed on those dramas on TV.

Opening the door, he startled Samantha, who had been nodding off. "How are you feeling now?"

"Better. That nurse, Marla, is so nice. Stayed with me the whole time."

"Yes, she is a top-notch nurse. But I need to talk to you about this. We have to figure out what you are going to do when your husband, Larry—isn't it, is on night shift."

Samantha started to sob again and then stopped just as quickly. "We moved here so that Larry could find a job. And I left all my friends back in Seattle. I have no one to stay with me."

"What if you were to work the same shift as Larry?"

"You mean come into the hospital for midnights?" There was a look of stark terror in Samantha's eyes.

"Guess that wouldn't be such a great idea after all." *How dumb can I be?* Ian thought. The woman had been imprisoned within the hospital morgue.

"Well . . . if I could work in the emergency department maybe that would be all right."

"How's that, Samantha?"

"I know the woman who works nights here. Kim Christianson is her name. She might trade with me if I explained to her that I was afraid to stay alone when Larry is on midnights."

"And you would be okay working midnights here?" Ian couldn't believe the woman would even consider it.

"Larry could drop me off, and this department is always busy. I wouldn't have to worry about being alone—ever. Kim said that if she has to take out the garbage that the security guy goes with her."

"So that's your solution!"

"Oh, thank you, Dr. McLintock."

"Don't thank me. You solved your own problem. Now I would like you to tell me everything you can remember about the day you got put in the morgue."

Samantha's doe eyes filled with tears again. "It is really important to help you get past this, or I wouldn't ask."

"You mean if I face it, then I can get over it?"

"Sort of. Can you do that? Tell me everything you remember, beginning with coming in to work and changing into your uniform?"

"I'll try, Dr. McLintock." There was a long hesitation while Samantha appeared to be stealing himself for the ordeal. By the end of an hour, Ian had learned only a few things, including the fact that Samantha had run into her friend from the cafeteria who catered the board meetings. And that day had been the scheduled meeting of the governors of the hospital. But Samantha couldn't remember anything after that.

By eight o'clock, Ian had listed the name of every person Samantha could or should have talked to during a normal day at work. Then he suggested that she phone her husband, Larry, at work to pick her up from the hospital. Ian stayed long enough to fend off the husband's fury at being diverted from his normal early morning routine of breakfast with the guys from work in order to pick up his wife.

As far as Ian was concerned, Samantha should have stayed in Seattle and let the jerk find work elsewhere without her. Ian really couldn't fathom how any woman would put up with a Neanderthal like Larry. But he was not a middle-aged frumpy woman, terrified of being alone.

"Thank you so much for everything, Dr. McLintock," Samantha gushed as she followed her husband out of the hospital.

Ian waited until the car had pulled out of the circular drive before leaving. He would have to wait to follow up on some ideas buzzing around his head, not that he had a hope in hell of cracking the case. But he wanted to help Samantha come to terms with the trauma she had endured. And that would only happen if he could find some reasonable explanation for what had happened to her.

CHAPTER 17

Lost and Found

*T*HE FEELINGS REBECCA kept in control brewed like a pustule beneath the surface waiting to burst forth. If only her husband, Sam, hadn't died, if only she hadn't decided to sell the mansion, she would never have found it. And she would have continued believing that her brother had died of natural causes. Now she knew the horrible truth, the cover-up that had robbed her brother of vengeance, of justice, for what they had done to him.

But the enormous rambling monstrosity of a house that lay empty except for the servants who tiptoed around her was unbearable. The staff were almost like family, only they weren't. And there were the embarrassed silences every time Rebecca ran into one of them as they stood silently waiting for her to speak, not knowing how to deal with the widow in mourning.

She waited until they had left for the day or retired to the servants' quarters before letting herself weep. The tears had been kept in check since she was a child. But the memory of watching her parents marched by Nazis into the two long lines that led to the foul-smelling chambers boiled to the surface. It was such a long time ago. Why had the memories surfaced again? The nightmare that was her life in the concentration camp.

Even now Rebecca wondered why she had been spared while everyone she loved had died. If she had known how, she would have killed herself. Mature for nine, she was very pretty, and the commandant's wife had picked her out to work for her in their kitchen. Naive or maybe just in denial, she had been ignorant of her parent's fate. It was sheer luck that the grandmotherly woman who cooked for the commandant's family had trained her so well that she became indispensable to the household.

She would have remained ignorant of what happened until the day the camp was liberated if only Rebecca had not incited the jealousy of the commandant's daughter.

With all her clothes confiscated upon arrival at the camp, she had nothing to wear but the uniform handed out to everyone who did not get marched off.

Unwilling to have her serve the family in those rags, the commandant's wife gave the cook some clothes for Rebecca to wear. They were too large and hung on her pathetically thin frame, but they were pretty. And like any young girl, Rebecca reveled in the new skirt as she swung around the kitchen, showing off for the cook.

Suddenly, she heard a shriek and saw the commandant's daughter fly at her in a rage. Tearing at the clothes, Gretchen screamed, "Take it off! The commandant will send you to the ovens where your parents went." Gretchen yanked the dress, ripping the buttons and tearing the material off Rebecca's thin body.

Defending herself with her arms over her face, she was sure that Gretchen would have scratched her eyes out if the commandant's wife hadn't walked into the kitchen and seized the dress. "I gave it to the girl. We can't have her serving the men naked, and the other clothes were not good enough!"

"I don't want to see her wearing my clothes!"

"The clothes are too small for you, Gretchen!"

The memory of Gretchen still clawing away at her, screaming obscenities, calling her a dirty Jew were fresh in her memory as if it had happened yesterday. She could not forget the rest of the scene. The commandant's wife had pulled Gretchen out of the kitchen, yelling at her, "Stop now! We'll get some other clothes for her."

Stunned, Rebecca had stood frozen with fear and shock until the cook pushed her into the pantry at the end of the kitchen, where the tins of food were stored. She remembered sinking to the floor in utter despair, too stunned to cry for her parents.

The cook closed the door on her, and then she followed the commandant's wife out of the kitchen, her heavy footsteps echoing on the wooden floor. The voices resonated through the thin walls as she heard Anika's soothing voice trying to placate the spoiled Gretchen.

Her mother answered the cook, saying, "I'll get the girl some other clothes. Don't worry about Gretchen. She has her dirty little secrets too and won't tell the commandant because, if she does, I have some things to tell him that Gretchen doesn't want him to know."

Dead, burnt up in the ovens. Rebecca knew then what caused the stench coming from the smoke stacks. But that first day in the camp day when her parents joined the two lines of men and women who were marched away never to be seen again, she had believed that they were taken away on another train to work in the farmer's fields or labor in a factory making munitions for the war. Now she could no longer hide from the truth.

Gretchen left her alone after that because her mother threatened to tell the commandant something so awful that Gretchen kept her distance; the looks of sheer hatred was the only weapon used to intimidate the kitchen helper.

For years Rebecca had managed to keep the memories locked away, smoldering beneath the surface. Her wedding to Sam had been idyllic except for that unbearably sad feeling that marred the joy. Everything in life had been tainted with the sorrow of the past. But she managed to make her husband happy. He had been born in the States and never experienced the wrenching misery of survival in a camp. Sam had cautiously gained her trust and then her love when she did not want to love anyone.

Rebecca could never forget the day she met Sam. She had only been liberated from the camp a year and in Slatington for three months when her brother Izzy died under mysterious circumstances. His death had been the final blow. Unable to face life alone, Rebecca had been standing on the bridge waiting to jump when the car had pulled up.

The most handsome man she had ever seen pleaded with her to come down. She hadn't jumped because she couldn't hurt this dark-haired man with the kind eyes. Once she was safely in his car, Sam would not let her go. He told her that once you saved someone's life, you were responsible for them from then on. She didn't know whether to believe him, but he was the only person who cared whether she lived or died. And for him, she decided that life was bearable.

Now Sam was dead, and she had sold the mansion, moving back to where she and her brother, Izzy, had spent a few happy months together. With the wealth Sam left her, Rebecca had no worries. But she had no happiness either. She would have endured the rest of her life in silence if she hadn't made the discovery that changed her forever.

The day was dreary with rain that pelted against windows that reached from floor to ceiling, framing the black billowing clouds that raced across a bitter cold sky. It was almost as if the weather reflected her foul mood. But she had decided the time had come to choose what she would keep and what she would sell. She found it in the dusty attic, long forgotten amidst the antiques shunted out of sight.

At first, Rebecca stared at the steamer trunk, shocked to see that it was still where Sam had stowed it when he helped her clear away Izzy's belongings after the funeral. It was like some nightmare that she had had. It could not be real, except there was the trunk with his initials.

Steeling herself, Rebecca opened the case and began rummaging through the pitiful belongings of her brother. Then she saw it, tossed almost as an afterthought onto the medical school jersey with the letters Izzy had earned in the four years he studied at Slatington's medical school.

Curious as to why he had kept that particular letter, she opened it and saw that it was addressed to her! But she had never seen it before even though it was dated ten years after Izzy's death. As Rebecca read, bitter tears streamed down her face. She knew Sam had hidden it from her to spare her the pain of reliving Izzy's death. But now she knew why and how he died, and she raged against the injustice.

The emptiness was replaced by a need to revenge her brother's death. No longer an empty shell, Rebecca had a reason to live, an obsession that stopped her from ending everything and joining her husband, Sam, in death.

CHAPTER 18

Encounter

*S*LIDING OUT A side entrance of the emergency department for a coffee break, Ian realized that he was beginning a new shift without puzzling over Samantha Rutledge. Relieved to find himself putting the incident behind, Ian strode quickly down the corridor to the vending machines where a snatch of a conversation taking place just around the bend caught his attention.

A brief glance gave Ian the impression that a woman was pushing her husband down the corridor in a wheelchair until he saw that the elderly matron was wearing the distinctive green and yellow smock of the Women's Hospital Auxiliary. And she had stopped the Dean of Medicine who was passing by calling out his name, "Dr. Whales, you must remember Dr. Conway?" The woman had a smile frozen on her face, but her eyes glinted with something akin to hatred.

When the dean seemed to be stumped, she prompted him with, "He was in your graduating class of 1950."

Without missing a beat, the dean gave his best performance as he recognized the volunteer uniform the woman wore and surmised that she was probably a member of what the board members referred to as the multimillionaire widow's club. A lot of money was raised by these women, and even more was donated as they tried to whittle down the formidable income tax they had to hand over to the IRS every year.

"It has been a long time, Dr. Conway. But I am always glad to run into a fellow alumnus. And I am surprised that I haven't met you yet, my dear woman. I thought I knew every lady in our formidable volunteer roster." Waiting for the woman to answer, the dean betrayed his impatience to move on despite his bonhomie by rocking back and forth on his feet.

"Rebecca Cornwell. I've just moved here two months ago after my husband passed on. Everyone in the group has sung your praises, Dr. Whales."

"Call me Chester, dear woman." The dean appeared to be acquainted with Rebecca's history, probably from his wife's involvement with the Women's Hospital Auxiliary group.

Standing on the sidelines, Ian would have guessed that Rebecca's husband had left her filthy rich from the attention she was getting from the Dean of Medicine.

"It's so nice meeting you, Chester. I was just mentioning to Dr. Conway that it would be so nice to have all the doctors come back for a reunion."

Dr. Conway added, "This lady has it all planned out. I just wasn't sure you would remember me, Chester. We've both changed a lot over the years. In fact, I'm positive that I wouldn't have known you if Rebecca hadn't run into you and introduced herself."

"Of course, I remember you, Dr. Conway. It was such a small class that year. With all the men sent overseas and so few returning home."

"Chester is the Dean of Medicine at the hospital," Rebecca added for Dr. Conway's benefit.

"So you made out real well for yourself. I remember when Izzy and you were competing for the same place on the surgical team. We all had a bet going that Izzy would be selected. He was, but then he died."

The reaction of the dean could not have been more bizarre. The man turned red and then a gray white color that made him appear to be on the verge of fainting. "It is really nice seeing you again, Dr. Conway. I would spend more time chatting, but I am late for a meeting." The dean rushed off down the corridor like the devil was at his heels.

Ian was intrigued by the dean's reaction to the name Izzy. What puzzled him even more was the blatant dislike on Rebecca Cornwell's face as she watched the retreating back of the dean. Why did this woman hate Chesterton Whales so much?

Just as Ian was about to head back to the emergency department, he saw Helena DuCarthenson, head of the Women's Auxiliary, coming around the corner. As soon as Rebecca saw Helena, she wheeled Dr. Conway in her direction. "Helena! How nice to run into you. Have you met Dr. Lester Conway?"

The woman's cheeks showed a tinge of scarlet as if she was embarrassed to run into them. "Oh! No, I don't believe I know Dr. Conway. You seem to have taken him under your wing, Rebecca?"

"Dr. Conway has been most helpful in filling me in on the background of St. Cinnabar. The hospital has had some most unusual occurrences in its long history."

It was Lester Conway who looked embarrassed now. "That was just between the two of us, Rebecca dear."

"So what tales have you been spinning, Dr. Conway?" There was a hard glint in Helena's eyes. "We should get together and discuss them since I, too, am quite intrigued with the history of this hospital."

"I really don't know that much about the history of St. Cinnabar. Rebecca is exaggerating."

"But I am really interested if you don't mind me coming and having a talk with you, Dr. Conway?" There was an insistence in Helena's voice that she would not take no for an answer.

"Of course! But I really am a bit tired right now. Rebecca, if you wouldn't mind, I would like to return to my room."

"Certainly, Dr. Conway. I have been thoughtless to keep you going. You should have told me earlier that you were getting tired."

"I will be looking forward to our little chat, Dr. Conway," commented Helena as Rebecca pushed the wheelchair down the corridor to the elevators.

"I just met Helena when I joined the Women's Auxiliary. But from the moment I saw her, I felt as though I had known her before. Have you ever had that happen to you, Dr. Conway? You know how you can meet someone and feel like you knew them in a previous life?"

"But you couldn't know Helena," Dr. Conway's voice quivered as though he had been upset by the meeting.

"I'm not sure about that," replied Rebecca. The feeling that she knew Helena was stronger now that when she first met the woman.

"It's commonly referred to as déjà vu. It usually happens when one visits a new place for the first time and feels as though they have been there before. But I've never heard of it happening with a person."

"Neither had I until I experienced it with Helena. It makes me wonder if we did meet somewhere before?"

"That is quite impossible!" Dr. Conway sounded upset enough to make Rebecca wonder.

CHAPTER 19

Friends and Acquaintances

ANOTHER DAY PASSED before Ian found time to track down the people who Samantha said she usually ran into during a normal day's work in the hospital. Contrary to what she had told him, Ian discovered that Samantha had many friends throughout the hospital. All the cleaning staff described her as a warmhearted woman who would do anything for anyone. Not a single person had anything bad to say about Samantha.

But the strangest thing was that none of them remembered seeing her on the day that she ended up in the morgue. Ian was about to give up locating anyone who could help pinpoint the movements of Samantha that morning when he ran into Sally from the cafeteria, wheeling the "catering" cart to a special meeting. Ian had the habit of teasing Sally by attempting to steal one of the squares from her cart.

"Don't even think it!" Sally warned Ian as he approached her.

"Why don't we get cookies and squares like this in the cafeteria?"

"Because you aren't a member of the board or the president of the hospital or . . ."

Ian didn't let her finish, "I get the picture. Lowly interns don't count. We just work endless hours saving lives and get no thanks in the end."

Sally had that look in her eye. "Too bad, it isn't the day of the board meeting."

"Why's that?" Ian picked up on the sarcasm in Sally's voice.

"If it was, I could offer you a cup of really high-priced coffee, thanks to the Dean of Medicine."

"Does he still get special coffee?"

"Of course. The phenomenal salary he pulls in isn't enough. Special blend of coffee brought in just for him. One thermos for the rest of the board and his own person carafe that he doesn't have to share. Disgusting, isn't it?"

"Are you in the habit of giving away the Dean of Medicine's special coffee?" Ian wished it was the day of the meeting because he would like to know just how good this coffee was, if it got laced with something other than just ground coffee beans.

"One day I gave every drop of his coffee away," Sally said in a very pleased manner.

"You've got to be kidding, Sally. What happened?"

"I ran into Sammy and offered her a cup. The dean had been particularly nasty to her when she cleaned his office the week before, and I wanted to settle the score. So after Sammy got her cup full, I poured the rest of his special blend down the drain and filled the carafe up with regular coffee. He never even noticed!"

Ian had to stifle the excitement he felt as he asked Sally, "What day did you do this?"

"Oh, let me see. It had to be more than a week ago. Can't remember exactly."

"It's really important, Sally. Try to remember."

"Don't tell me the old bastard's raising a stink about it now? I'll have to ask Sammy. It was the next day that she got so sick that she took time off from work. Strange, what happened to her." Sally looked at Ian and waited, expecting him to fill her in on the details.

"Can you look up the date on the catering list in the office?" Ian didn't want to pressure the woman, but he really wanted her to confirm what he already suspected.

"Silly me. Of course, I know. They hold the board meetings every third Monday of the month."

Speechless, Ian just stared at the woman.

Finally putting two and two together, Sally demanded, "Why did you want to know, Dr. McLintock?"

"Just curious, that's all. By the way, did Samantha tell you why she was off sick?"

"No. That's what's so odd. Sammy and I have been good friends ever since she started working here. She usually tells me everything. Then all of a sudden she clams up like aliens abducted her. I even asked her if she had been raped." The pink bloom of embarrassment flushed the caterer's cheeks as if just saying the word was a sacrilege.

"And what did Sammy say?"

"She was stunned for a minute or two. Then said that she didn't think so. That isn't something you would forget, is it?"

"Not likely. Just give Sammy time. Sometimes patient confidentiality forces us to keep silent. And we just have to bear with it." Ian had ignored all the openings Sally gave him to tell what happened. Since she had been forthcoming with her information, he felt he owed her some explanation for not saying anything about Samantha. Sally understood about patient confidentiality, but not why her best friend refused to confide in her.

Sammy had signed the contract and was not breathing a word of what happened to anyone. Ian understood why the woman felt like she was going mad. Not only had she locked in a morgue wondering if she was going to die, but now she couldn't tell even her closest friend about it. Ian wondered how much the hospital lawyers paid to buy her silence.

"Do you suppose . . . ?"

"Do I think what, Sally?" Ian knew he was considering it, but he didn't want to put the idea into the woman's head. He wanted to know if she had drawn a similar conclusion about the coffee.

"Do you think someone put something into the dean's coffee and that's what made Samantha so ill?"

"It's not likely, but I would prefer that you don't discuss this with anyone else."

"Who am I likely to tell? If the old bastard found out, he'd have me fired on the spot."

"For switching the coffee on him? I don't think that the Dean of Medicine would be so petty and mean-spirited, Sally."

"You haven't heard some of the stories I have then. You remember the one secretary he had before the blonde bombshell he has now. Well, some say that he tried to seduce her, and when she refused to have sex with the old goat, he let her go."

"That sounds like malicious gossip!" Ian was stunned at the hatred in Sally's voice.

"Gossip my eye. It's the gospel truth. Even heard the poor dear hasn't been able to find another job because the dean won't give her a reference."

"That's hard to believe."

"You don't have to take my word for it. Just ask anyone. They'll tell you. And the dean's wife, the one that works for the Women's Hospital Auxiliary. Well, she isn't his first wife. She started as his secretary. Heard the woman figures her husband is about to replace her too and that's why she is haunting the halls of the hospital, trying to keep tabs on hubby. But I heard it's not the sex she cares about. She just likes being Mrs. Dr. Dean and wants to keep her position in the community. Won't do like the first Mrs. Dean and leave in a huff because hubby is banging the latest secretary."

It was Ian's turn to feel the heat of a blush that went from his throat up to his hairline. "I've got an appointment, Sally. Thanks for telling me about Samantha. Talk to you later." He knew she was grinning ear to ear at his discomfiture and watched as he hurried away. That was just more information about the dean than Ian really wanted to know.

Now he began to wonder if the dean's wife knew about her husband's affair with his secretary. That would be the logical explanation for why someone would want to dope the dean's coffee. Ian made a mental note to find out if the dean's wife was volunteering in the hospital that day.

CHAPTER 20

Gossip

THE DOCTORS OF the graduating class of 1950 were the topic of hospital gossip as word spread that they were going to have a reunion at the end of the term. What made the event so newsworthy was the guest speaker, the Dean of Medicine, who was also a member of that graduating class. Suddenly, the man who held the tight reins of authority over the medical school had his true age revealed much to his chagrin and the general shock of his colleagues. There were a few people who would have guessed that Dr. Chester Whales was that old and that the medical institution had allowed a man of his age to continue holding one of the most prestigious positions in the medical school.

Comments about what dye he used to keep the color in his hair and who his plastic surgeon was raged about in the eternal grapevine of gossip that kept the drudgery of hospital work interesting for those at the bottom of the ladder.

When the staff doctor in the ER congratulated Dr. Whales on the upcoming event, the dean responded with an abruptness that bordered on disgust. Turning his back on Dr. Cleaver, the dean walked swiftly through the department, looking quickly in each curtained stall. It was obvious that he was searching for someone.

Marla was embarrassed as the dean intruded on a pelvic exam. "What can I do for you *Dr.* Whales?" The emphasis on *doctor* was to reassure the woman lying on her back was in one of the most delicate situations that most females hate to find themselves in, especially with a strange male barging in on them.

"Ah, nurse Strafford. Can you tell me where that bright young intern Dr. Ian McLintock is hiding?"

The surprise at finding the Dean of Medicine searching for one of the lowly interns was enough to make Marla laugh. Instead, she bit her lower lip and stared at the man. Several seconds passed before she was sufficiently composed to say something. "I'm not sure. But I think this is one of Ian's lieu days for covering the compassionate leave given to Dr. Paul Cormorant when his grandmother died."

"So he's not here?"

Biting her tongue this time, Marla wished that she could say, "Duh. Isn't that what I said," to the most pompous ass that ever walked the corridors of the hospital. There were several incidents that hardened Marla's opinion of the man standing in front of her, not including his rude entrance into the examining room without any regard for the feelings of the patient. Finally, she responded once more with, "I am not sure what Dr. McLintock does on his days off, Doctor."

"When you do see him, would you tell Dr. McLintock to stop around my office?" Leaving as briskly as he entered the cubicle, the sound of his heavy footsteps retreating down the terrazzo hall left Marla feeling more than a little steamed.

"Sorry about the intrusion, Mrs. Planter, but that was the Dean of Medicine. He is one of those doctors from the old school that feel nothing is sacred."

"Oh! The Dean of Medicine. How wonderful!"

Shaking her head, Marla realized the woman was one of those females who would strip naked for anyone, if he said he was a doctor.

CHAPTER 21

In a Snit

*T*HE DEAN WAS not having the best of days as he left the ER in a huff. There was something afoot, and he meant to find out who was behind it. Except that he knew most people hated him and that he would be the last person to find out what was going on in the hospital. The only reason the fiasco over the cleaning lady was brought to his attention was because of the man who found her, one of his interns.

The dean would have dismissed the incident out of hand, attributed it to the overactive imagination of a sleep-deprived doctor working too many shifts in a row. But he couldn't ignore it, and the fact that it had taken place made the hair on his neck stand on end whenever he thought of it.

Most of the older staff knew about the tragedy that had happened the year his class graduated. Izzy Steinman had died under mysterious circumstances, and although Chester had never seen him walking the corridors of St. Cinnabar, there were enough credible accounts to shake him to his core, especially when the intern Ian McLintock described the medical student who was reputed to haunt the hospital in exact detail.

And lately, Chester had been having nightmares about being buried alive. Even his normally frigid wife, who cared more about her standing in the medical community than their marriage, had suddenly become solicitous. It was the last thing he wanted—renewed interest from Regina, whose bed he had not shared for the past two years.

She had taken to crawling in next to him, trying to console him as if he were a child having night terrors. It was so ludicrous that he would have laughed, if he hadn't been so terrified. Despite his repugnance at having his wife lying next to him again, he had to admit that just having a warm live body next to his had helped him get some rest.

A heavy hand on his shoulder made the dean recoil. "Whoa, there, Chester. Aren't you the jumpy one today?"

Dr. Reginald Hammersmith was one of those infuriating people who were always in a good mood, and his bonhomie really annoyed the dean, especially today with everything going wrong.

"Don't like people sneaking up on me, damn it!" he growled.

"I didn't sneak up on you, Chester. Lighten up. Heard through the grapevine that you are like a bear with a sore paw. So what's up? Or, maybe, what's not?" The guffaw came from the belly. Maybe it was Dr. Hammersmith's specialty that made him see humor where most men didn't. But he was the most sought-after urologist in the city and had been able to indulge his extravagant tastes, thanks to his unequalled popularity.

The dean was among the very few of Dr. Hammersmith's colleges who knew that he owned two mansions, one of them on a remote Greek island and several deluxe cars of which the Mercedes was his favorite. It was this opulent lifestyle that irked the dean as much as being confronted about his masculinity. "I don't have that problem, Reg."

"Well, your wife seems to think there's something not quite right, Chester?"

The dean's face turned a purple color, and he sputtered for a few moments until the words finally got choked out. "And what the hell has my wife been doing talking to you?"

"Said you have been unable to sleep. Having nightmares. Waking up screaming, and woke everyone in the house, including the maid that sleeps in the attic."

"Shit! That bitch never could keep her mouth shut."

"So what's wrong, Chester? We go back a long ways. You can tell me."

"And you can go to hell!" The dean left so fast that the urologist was left scratching his head.

The dean needed a release and hoped that Brandi was in a randy mood today. Usually, he made his trysts with his secretary elsewhere so that there was not even a ghost of a chance of being caught with his pants down. The thought of Reg considering him having *that* problem made the dean laugh. That was the least of his worries. Now, with the thoughts of the long legs and the shapely bottom of his secretary perpetually tilted upward as she filed in the bottom drawers of the filing cabinet, the dean discovered a newfound spring in his step as he hastened toward his office. With any luck, Brandi would consider the chance of being discovered doing it in the dean's office an aphrodisiac and would get a bigger boost out of their union than usual.

CHAPTER 22

Why Didn't I Stay Home?

*I*AN HADN'T PLANNED on coming in to the hospital that afternoon, but the results of his investigations so far had yielded some rather surprising information, and he knew that the only way to confirm what he suspected would be to try and sneak out some object that the person had touched. He hadn't worked out in his mind how he was going to do that but knew from experience that if you played with a problem long enough, the solution usually dropped into your lap when you least expected it.

He was halfway to the volunteer office when Marla saw him. "Ian! I thought you had the day off."

"I do, but there was something I had to check out, so here I am. What did you want, Marla?"

"It isn't me. The dean came barging into the ER this morning looking for you. Told me to tell you to drop into his office if I saw you. So I am telling you. Okay?"

"Yeah. But what could he want?"

"Beats me. But rumor is running rampant through the hospital that he has been acting really strange lately. Someone even heard him chewing out his friend Dr. Reginald Hammersmith in the corridor this morning."

"Just what I wanted on my day off, to go see the beast."

"It's not that bad, Ian. Maybe it's got something to do with Samantha?" The rest remained unspoken between them.

"You're probably right. Guess I'll go beard the lion in his den and get it over with."

"Beard the lion in his den? How quaint."

"An old saying of my grandmother, meaning you . . ."

"I know what it means."

"Since it is my day off, I'd better get going, or it will be time to turn around and come back in again. Thanks for agreeing to help, Marla. I really appreciate it."

"You're welcome, *Doctor*." Marla was not used to being thanked by one of the interns, and Ian picked up on the irony in her voice.

CHAPTER 23

Connecting the Dots

THE REAL POSSIBILITY that Samantha had been drugged because she drank the coffee intended for the Dean of Medicine really worried Ian because it threw a whole new light on the situation.

If what Sally had said was true, it would make sense that the Dean of Medicine had been the real target. Although he couldn't prove his theory, Ian was convinced that because of Sally's attempt at revenge, the dean had drunk regular coffee instead of his special blend from his carafe. Then he adjourned the board meeting early, which meant that Samantha, who had drunk just one cup of the dean's special blend of coffee, was summoned to clean up before the drug had a chance to take full effect.

Feeling tired and maybe a little pompous at having drunk the dean's coffee, Samantha sat in his chair at the head of the table. When the person who was expecting to find Dr. Chesterton Whales in a drugged stupor showed up, they found Samantha in the boardroom. Maybe they thought that she was the intended victim if they didn't know the sex of the Dean of Medicine? Perhaps they thought Samantha was dead and felt compelled to hide her where no one would look? In the morgue, she might have been processed as a John Doe?

Ian had to laugh at himself. A female John Doe. But the situation was not funny. Sammy Rutledge was almost killed by mistake. That meant the Dean of Medicine was still in danger. But who could hate the man enough to want him dead?

With nothing more than vicious gossip to go on, Ian felt compelled to see the dean. Steeling himself for the encounter, Ian turned around and headed to the administrator's office.

CHAPTER 24

Unexpected Company

AS THE KNOB turned in Ian's hand, the door swung at him with such velocity that he barely escaped being slammed in the face as he jumped to one side. But he was not entirely spared as a woman stormed out of the Dean of Medicine's office, tears streaming down her face and muttering, "I'll get the salacious old bastard."

Even in her haste, the woman had enough presence of mind to grab Ian to stop him from falling over, scraping his hand with a key in the process. "Sorry," she whispered before breaking into a run down the corridor.

What the hell was that? Ian wondered as he continued on into the secretary's outer office. Brandi was nowhere to be seen. Ian walked over to the mahogany door and was about to tap lightly on it when he heard a chorus of moans. Putting his earflap against the panel, he could hear the secretary's voice shouting, "More! More! Faster! Faster!"

Then there was a silence. "Did you lock the door?" No mistaking the dean's timorous voice.

"Of course, I did," the secretary gasped.

Ian stood stock-still and thought, *No wonder the woman was so upset.*

When the grunts and gasps began again in earnest, Ian knew the dean no longer suspected anyone was there. Tiptoeing out the other door, Ian stopped long enough to flip the metal flap in the doorjamb so that once he closed it, the door would automatically lock.

Ian had never met the dean's wife and wondered if she was the woman who almost knocked him over in her rush to leave the office. She had a key, so that explained how she got into the receptionist's area if the outer door was locked. If Sally was right and the dean's wife knew about her husband's affair with his secretary, she could have decided to check up on them and then decided not to break in, wanting to wait for a more opportune time to wreak revenge on her husband.

That would be the logical explanation for why someone would want to dope the dean's coffee. Ian made a mental note to find out if the dean's wife was volunteering in the hospital the day Samantha ended up in the morgue.

The whole affair made it crucial that Ian warn the dean about his coffee. But there was no way Ian would ever admit that he overheard the dean and his secretary going at it in his office. Even the thought of facing the man sent a blush up on Ian's face. *How the blue blazes was he going to deal with this,* he wondered as he headed out the door.

CHAPTER 25

Who Drugged the Coffee?

THE ELDERLY WOMAN who was secretary of the Women's Hospital Auxiliary was one of those characters that left a lasting impression on everyone she came into contact with.

Ian had met the grand dame in his first year of medical school when Matilda Smith joined her husband in throwing the biggest and best party their well-staffed mansion and small fortune could muster. Best of all, Matilda got drunk, flirted, and danced with all the guys including Ian. She even made an improper suggestion, which he politely ignored, given her condition.

Her husband had died shortly after that party, and Matilda had thrown herself into the Women's Hospital Auxiliary. After so many years, Matilda had been given charge of orienting new volunteers. So Ian was in the habit of seeing her as he made rounds through the hospital. He admired the woman for her youthful outlook.

In retrospect, Ian suspected that Matilda wasn't that drunk the night she propositioned him since she continued to flirt with him whenever their paths crossed.

If anyone knew what was happening behind the scenes in the hospital, Matilda would. So he deliberately went in search of her. He needed to find out who the lady was that was "helping" with the board members tea the day Samantha disappeared.

It was eerie that just as he was thinking about her, Ian saw Matilda coming down the corridor from the cafeteria alongside another blue-haired lady whose fingers were covered in diamonds. Ian watched Matilda as she walked with a floating elegance learned only at exclusive finishing schools.

When the other volunteer veered down another corridor, Ian seized the opportunity to saunter nonchalantly up to Mrs. Smith. Matilda turned her elegantly coiffed head and studied Ian with such intensity that, flinching slightly under her studied gaze, Ian faltered and then tried flirting with the woman. "Mrs. Smith. I haven't seen you in so long that I thought you had found yourself a new husband and left us."

As they approached the Women's Auxiliary Canteen, Matilda continued to stare at Ian, her dark green eyes flashing from under carefully applied false eyelashes that looked natural until one got too close. Matilda gave a little snort of disgust as she flipped her long perfectly dyed auburn hair. "He'd have to be pretty darn good in bed for me to give up my freedom and compromise the fortune the good doctor left me."

No subtlety there, thought Ian. That was why he loved Matilda; she called a spade a spade and didn't care who she shocked. "Your ladies help out the catering part of the cafeteria every time the board meets, don't they?"

"They aren't my ladies, but yes, they do try and ease the burden placed on the kitchen staff. Why did you want to know, Dr. McLintock?" A glint of suspicion darkened her eyes as she stared at him.

"The woman in charge said that there was some item left behind and wondered if I could find out who was helping that day."

"Why didn't *this woman* just call up the Women's Auxiliary Office and ask?"

"Uh, because, uh, there was a problem. You really don't want to know all the mundane details, Mrs. Smith, do you?"

"You are hiding something, Dr. McLintock, as sure as God made little green apples."

"Why would I be hiding anything, Mrs. Smith?"

"Call me Matilda, and I'll call you Ian. Can't stand all this formality."

"Okay, Matilda. There is nothing to hide. Believe me."

"Not in a million years, but I will give you the woman's name anyways. She is no younger than me, but they say she was left quite a lot of money by her husband. Much more than me. You aren't looking for a woman to keep you, are you, Ian?"

The rush of heat reached his cheeks, and Ian couldn't do anything to stop himself.

"That's what I like about you, Dr. Ian. You blush like you've never made love to a woman before. I know I shouldn't tease you, but what else is there left for a woman my age. No red-blooded young man would even glance my way. So I have fun flirting with all you young doctors. And you look a lot like my husband when he was your age."

Ian knew he was blushing again and hated that this woman could make him so uncomfortable. "You were going to tell me who the volunteer was, Mrs. Smith."

"Oooh. Back to Mrs. Smith again. Maybe I won't tell you, Ian."

"Matilda, tell me her goddamn name. You've had your fun at my expense."

"Mrs. Rebecca Cornwell helped out the day of the board meeting. Now tell me why you want to know."

"Can't tell anyone. Had to sign a confidentiality agreement."

"You expect me to believe that, young man."

"You can call the hospital lawyer, and he will tell you that I am bound to an oath of secrecy."

"I will find out what is going on, you can count on that!" Matilda looked at him with the stern look of a woman used to getting her own way.

"Thank you for the information, Matilda. I have to get back to the emergency department. There were ambulance sirens just a few minutes ago, so I expect they will need me."

"Saved by the siren? I will see you around, Dr. Ian McLintock, and the next time you won't escape so easily."

Ian made a mental note to avoid Matilda every time he saw her in the corridors of the hospital. If anyone could get information out of someone, he was positive that she could, just by the sheer force of her personality.

It was several hours later before Ian finally got a chance to write down everything he had discovered since the night he found Samantha locked on a slab in the morgue. He shrugged and looked at the list he made.

Someone had doped the coffee destined for the Dean of Medicine on the day of the board meeting? Sally was on catering duty that day and gave the dean's coffee to Samantha, who later ended up drugged and on a slab in the morgue. Sally poured the rest of the special coffee out and filled the dean's thermos with regular coffee, thus preventing him from also being drugged. Although Sally had done it with malicious intent, she had probably saved the dean's life.

Ian knew there were holes in his theory. But if Samantha had gone up to clean the board office and ended up comatose in the seat usually occupied by the dean, the person who found her might have thought

Samantha was dead and hid her in the most logical place to put a dead body—the morgue.

He could only draw one conclusion. Someone had slipped a potentially lethal dose of date rape drug into the dean's coffee. The lab work confirmed that it was in Samantha's blood. The fact that the Dean of Medicine hadn't drunk it did not change the fact that he appeared to be the intended victim.

This brought up the next point. Why would someone want to drug and/or kill the Dean of Medicine? Since Ian had inadvertently overheard the sexual encounter between the dean and his secretary, Ian couldn't help wondering if the dean's wife knew about his affair with Brandi. And if she did, would the dean's wife be sufficiently jealous to try and kill her husband?

The malicious gossip circulating about the Dean of Medicine's wife, Regina, led Ian to believe that she was almost as ditsy as the man's secretary. Somehow, the idea that Regina had enough brains to plot such a complicated manner of killing her husband was ludicrous. The woman just wasn't smart enough. The whole thing had been carefully planned so that whoever did it would have escaped detection if Ian had not found Samantha before she succumbed to hypothermia in the morgue.

And what if Samantha had not been given the dean's special brand of coffee when Sally made an attempt to thumb her nose at the dean's pomposity?

It felt like he was going around in circles, getting no closer to the truth, and Ian was worried that whoever made the first attempt would try again. And the next time, they might succeed in killing the dean.

There was also the problem of how that person got their hands on the drug. It pointed to a medical professional. Anyone else might have difficulty unless they purchased it on the street from one of the pushers. But who was it? A throbbing headache forced Ian to put everything on hold.

CHAPTER 26

Who's Who of the Auxiliary

IT WAS ALMOST three o'clock in the afternoon before Marla had a chance to go for lunch. Carefully choosing a seat in the far corner of the cafeteria in an attempt to find peace and quiet, Marla was startled to see the Women's Hospital Auxiliary were converging on the long table on the other side of the pillar that partially hid her.

No sooner had the group settled themselves and began talking when Sally, the catering specialist for the cafeteria, appeared with platters of finger food and crustless sandwiches.

Despite her semihidden position behind the post, Marla couldn't help notice that the women all wore plenty of diamonds on their wrinkled age-spotted fingers as they raised the dainty food from the center of the table onto glass plates. Not knowing the value of their rings, Marla made an educated guess that the jewelry sported by these women was enough to buy and sell Staten Island.

And her efforts to ignore them were futile since Marla could not help but hear the polite bantering among the ladies as they shuffled little stacks of multicolored fliers around the circle. Dead center and facing each other were two matrons who were doing battle for control of the group. The one woman was a familiar face around the hospital, being the wife of the Dean of Medicine. But the other short dark-haired lady dueling for top gun of the auxiliary was a stranger.

The words, "Now, Rebecca, this is the way we've always handled an affair like this," drifted across the divide. The new contender for leadership, Rebecca, answered the challenge with, "Then it's about time you had a change."

Another comment from one of the women on the end of the table as she addressed the dark curly haired Rebecca jogged Marla's memory.

There had been gossip going around the hospital for several weeks about the power struggle going on between the two women who loved to pull strings whether through volunteer work or by making strategic donations to the appropriate department.

Marla remembered one of the nurses saying that the newest member of the auxiliary was the widow of a pharmaceutical mogul, whose wealth equaled that of all the other women combined.

"We'll have to get someone to find everyone listed in the yearbook," one voice cawed through the jumble of voices competing for attention.

Suddenly, there was a thudding of a gavel as another faceless voice ordered, "Silence. We'll never get anywhere with everyone talking at once. Leila, you begin with your ideas, and we will work our way around the circle."

"Why does she always get to go first," whined a cracked voice.

That did it. Marla almost choked on her coffee and decided that if the woman heard her snort, they might figure out what she was giggling about. Stifling the laughter that shook her, Marla wondered if she had better get up and move before she lost control. Another comment made her decide that she couldn't sit there with a serviette over her mouth, and she began to pack up her lunch. Just as she was about to get up, a hand on her shoulder made her jump.

"Sorry, Marla. Didn't mean to startle you." Ian had a tray. "You aren't leaving yet, are you?" He was blocking her way.

"They're having a meeting of the Women's Auxiliary, and I didn't want to disturb them," Marla whispered.

"Oh, good. Will you do me a really big favor and tell me the names of these infamous ladies?"

"Huh? Why on earth would you want to know their names, Ian? Besides, you probably already have met most of them."

"Humor me, okay?"

"I don't understand, but I guess it wouldn't kill me to finish my lunch down here."

Pushing his tray toward the center of the table, Ian nudged Marla so that the pillar no longer hid her. "Name each one and who they belong to."

"Aren't you the pushy one? Why the sudden interest in the Ladies' Auxiliary?"

"I can't go into detail right now, but I promise I will explain later, at a very expensive restaurant."

"Only if I get to choose."

"Agreed. Now start with that little woman with the dark hair and eyes."

"Her name is Rebecca Cornwell and is the newest member. Apparently, from hospital gossip, her husband was a pharmaceutical mogul, who died a couple of months ago. The poor woman couldn't face living in their mansion alone, so she sold it and moved to Slatington."

"Is she the one that has them in such a tizzy? Sally said that this Rebecca has them all trying to outdo each other."

"All except the woman with the bottle blond hair and facelift. You must know Regina Whales from the parties given at the dean's house?"

"No. Can't say I've ever met the woman. So that is Mrs. Dr. Dean Whales the second. She looks like she's keeping the plastic surgeons in Mercedes."

"What do you mean, the 'second'? Was the dean married before her?"

"Can't tell you who filled me in, but apparently, she was the dean's secretary until the first wife found out about the office affair and walked out. She got promoted to wifey number two."

"Well, aren't you a fount of information. I thought I was supposed to be filling you in on who's who."

"You are, Marla. I didn't know what she looked like. How do the two bottle blonds get along? It surprises me that Helena DuCarthenson hasn't tried to wrench control out of the hands of Mrs. Whales the second."

"Regina."

"What?"

"Her name is Regina Whales. And Helena DuCarthenson is not a bottle blond. It's natural. And she's the widow of a Boston Industrialist with more money than anyone at that table, except for Rebecca Cornwell. Rumor has it that Helena has taken Rebecca under her wing. But I figure she's just keeping tabs on her competition. Helena wouldn't want to give up control of the group. Especially to a newcomer, no matter how much money she has."

"Meow. Shall I get you a plate of milk, Marla?"

"I resent that! I'm not being catty, just giving you the facts," said Marla as she gave Ian a shove.

Ian laughed and said, "I'm only kidding!" He had already gotten the information he came for but enjoyed the sensual warmth of Marla's slim body pressed close to his so much that he wouldn't for the world stop her. And since she was making moves to leave, Ian stopped teasing Marla so that she would stay.

CHAPTER 27

Reunion

LATE AFTERNOON, SUN poured through the dirty windows of the hospital corridor and reflected off the worn marble tiles. Just as the dean was rounding the bend in the long hallway, he almost knocked over the petit woman who had just moved to Slatington. This was the second time in less than a day that he saw the widow of that pharmaceutical tycoon. And there was definitely something about the woman that disturbed him. Even so, Chester Whales chuckled to himself whenever he thought of what he had heard through the hospital grapevine. Mrs. Cornwell had set the Hospital Auxiliary on its ear by volunteering and then proving that she had more money than all the other ladies put together.

The dean smiled at the woman who had brought in several huge donations that were matched by the estate of her late husband and murmured seductively, "Mrs. Rebecca Cornwell, what a pleasure to run into you again. And I almost did, didn't I?" The dean chortled at his little joke.

"Looking forward to the upcoming reunion, Dr. Whales." The woman smiled sweetly up at his face.

Controlling the rage he felt every time he was reminded of the class reunion, the dean cleared his throat and said pleasantly, "You have no idea, my dear lady. And I hear that you have thrown yourself into the organizing of the event. What a wonderful addition you have made to the Ladies' Auxiliary. I have heard absolutely marvelous things about you," *and a lot of really catty ones, too, from my wife,* he thought.

"It's my pleasure, Dr. Whales, just knowing you will be getting together with your classmates after so many years. What a splendid idea to reunite men with such a history of accomplishments. My dear Samuel thought highly of the medical profession and said that he would have loved to have become a doctor if circumstances had been different."

"I'm sure your husband would have made an outstanding contribution to the medical profession, especially since he was such a gifted pharmacist." The dean wanted desperately to escape from the woman but counted the money she would contribute over the years as more important than his momentary discomfort at being reminded of the upcoming event.

"Well, I know how busy an important man like you must be, so I won't keep you, Dr. Whales."

As the tiny figure disappeared in the direction of the volunteer office, the dean breathed a sigh of relief. He couldn't help wondering what Helena DuCarthenson had told Rebecca Cornwell about the history of the hospital and his part in it. Nothing, he hoped. But he knew that he would have to confront Helena and remind her once again that he had some information that would ruin her standing in the community if it ever got out.

It didn't matter that it had been stolen during a burglary several months earlier. He was sure that Helena didn't know that. Otherwise, she would have confronted him with the information she had about him. It was a deadlock that had forced them to continue in peaceful coexistence as long as each kept the other at bay with the information they knew would ruin the other. It was not the happiest of circumstances, but Chester had learned to live with it.

CHAPTER 28

Warning

IT TOOK A while before Ian got enough courage to face the dean. With so many women expressing sheer unbridled hatred for the man and Ian's suspicions, he felt that he had no other choice than to warn him about the coffee. As Ian walked in the door, Brandi flashed perfect white teeth in a seductive smile and asked, "What can I do for you, Dr. McLintock?"

Ian hoped he was reading something into the tone of the secretary's voice that wasn't there. But he wasn't too sure. "I would like to talk to Dr. Whales if he can spare me a few minutes."

"You just make yourself comfortable, Dr. McLintock." Brandi swayed on her spike heels that accentuated the tilt of her rear end as she walked into the dean's office. When Brandi returned, she said, "He's rather busy, but if you can wait, he will see you."

Ian was beginning to feel more than a little uncomfortable as he remembered the passionate encounter he had overheard the other day. It didn't help that the dean's secretary bent over at the waist each time she got a file from the cabinet. And most of them seemed to be located in the bottom drawer, giving him a good view of Brandi's frilly tight panties.

Finally, the mahogany door swung open, and the dean said, "Ian. What can I do for you, lad? Come on in."

Once seated opposite the Dean of Medicine, Ian regretted coming. How could he tell this man that someone had tried to drug him? The seconds ticked by as Ian tried to decide how to begin or if he should just make up some excuse and leave. He certainly couldn't tell the man the gossip Sally had relayed to him.

"Out with it, boy. What can be that hard to talk about? Got a young woman in the family way?" Wink, wink.

There was no way he could stop the surge of heat rising from his chest and flushing his face. Ian was even more upset that he showed how much the dean had upset him. There was nothing to do but say it. "No, sir. It isn't about me, sir." Ian felt so angry that the dean suspected him of having problems with an unwanted pregnancy that the vein in his forehead throbbed painfully.

"Well. That leaves the rest of the world if the problem isn't about you."

"This is difficult to say, sir. But it concerns you."

"Me?" The dean glowered at Ian with a menacing look that made Ian wonder exactly what the professor of medicine was hiding.

"Maybe I had better clarify that, sir. Samantha Rutledge and you."

"Who on earth is Samantha Rutledge? Quit beating around the bush and spit it out, man."

"Samantha is the woman I found in the morgue locker."

A look of relief spread across the dean's face. "Oh. That poor woman. I had forgotten her name. How is she doing? I take it you have been doing some posttraumatic follow-up with her."

"I hadn't planned on it, sir. But with the agreement, she has no one else to talk to."

"I understand. You are one of our best doctors, Ian. And I have made sure that that is noted on your record. Keep up the good work."

For a moment Ian thought, the dean was going to send him on his way, assuming that Ian was milking his involvement in hopes of gaining one of the limited residencies open to the interns. "You don't understand, sir."

"What exactly don't I understand, young man. Come on. Spit it out."

"I think you were the intended victim, not Samantha Rutledge."

"That's preposterous. How could you possibly come to that conclusion?" The dean's face lost the ruddy color it usually had and took on a pallor that made the man look several years older.

"It involves several people, and I need your word that you will not take action against any of them," blurted out Ian.

"You know I can't promise that if they are responsible for putting that woman into a locker in the morgue."

"These people didn't put Samantha into the locker. That I can assure you. Now, can I have your solemn promise not to fire, prosecute or otherwise take action against these individuals? If my theory is correct, what they did saved your life."

"In that case, yes, I promise that anything you tell me will not be used against them."

"Thank you."

"Now for heaven's sakes, man, out with it."

"You have a special coffee brought in during the board meetings for you. On the morning that Samantha disappeared into the morgue, the woman from the cafeteria gave your coffee to Samantha and replaced it with the regular coffee served to the board members."

There was a steely glint in the dean's gray eyes that showed he was annoyed. No, Ian saw from the glare that the man was angry as hell. The heavy silence filled a long void in the conversation as Ian waited for the blast that didn't come.

"And . . . ," prompted the dean.

"After the board meeting, Samantha Rutledge, who had drunk the coffee meant for you, came in to clean up and sat down in your chair. At least, that's what I think happened."

"Do you have any proof of this?"

"Only the woman from the cafeteria's word that she gave Samantha your coffee. After that I am guessing what happened."

"Who is this woman that works in the kitchen?"

"I would rather not say, sir. Since you did promise that there would be no repercussions."

"Who drugged the coffee then? And why did this Rutledge woman end up being put in a drawer in the morgue?"

"Unfortunately, I don't have the answers to those questions. But supposing that whoever came into the boardroom expecting to find you unconscious found Samantha instead, he or she may have been compelled to cover their tracks. They may have even thought that Samantha was you."

"Poppycock. Everyone knows who the Dean of Medicine is."

"Or they may have thought she was dead and felt the safest place to hide a dead body was in the morgue." Ian almost giggled but coughed. He hadn't been getting enough sleep, and he was going to laugh at the wrong time.

"There is something in what you say. So you have come to warn me. Is that it?"

"Yes. If I am right, then you are still in danger."

"And what am I supposed to do? Hire a food-and-drink taster like the kings of old?"

It was funny, but Ian dug his nails into his leg and waited for the giddy feeling to pass.

"Is that what I am supposed to do? I really find the idea that there is someone sneaking around the hospital intending to drug or kill me preposterous."

"It does sound unbelievable, sir. But after a lot of soul-searching, I felt that I had to warn you just in case I was on the right track."

"You did a toxicology screen on that woman, Samantha Rutledge, didn't you?"

"Yes. Of course, sir."

"And she wasn't just drunk or high on street drugs?"

"No, sir, she had a potentially fatal dose of the date rape drug in her body. The cooling effect of the morgue slab probably saved her life. But she doesn't know how close she came to actually dying."

"My word. You didn't tell me this the first time you talked to me."

"At that time, I had no idea that you might have been the intended victim."

Several harrumphs echoed in the oak-paneled room as the dean, looking pale and shaken, seemed to be searching for something more to say.

"I know what a busy schedule you have, sir, and I'm expected down in emergency, so if you don't mind, I'll leave now."

"Of course. And thank you for coming to tell me. You know we have an open-door policy. Anything else that you find out, please do not hesitate to come and inform me." The dean rose and shook Ian's hand.

The cool, wet clasp of the older man's hand revealed just how shaken he was by Ian's "suppositions." But at least the old man hadn't laughed Ian out of his office or suggested he consult with the staff shrink.

CHAPTER 29

Tracking the Special Blend

TOO MANY DAYS had already passed since he had found Samantha in the morgue. If Ian was going to find anything to help ferret out the person responsible, he knew he had to see Sally as soon as possible. Even so, it might be too late.

Picking the time that the catering team ran carts around to various departments for meetings, Ian spotted Sally coming back into the hospital cafeteria with her empty catering cart. She looked like she was going to go directly into the inner sanctum of the kitchen without speaking to him. Desperate for some clue as to the identity of the person who doped the coffee, Ian motioned for Sally to join him, where he sat at a table by the exit. "Sit down and take a load off your feet, Sally."

"I have a bone to pick with you, Dr. McLintock!" Sally's face was red with fury.

"What's happened?"

"The dean has been scrutinizing everyone on staff. Fortunately, the next board meeting isn't for another week, and I managed to switch with Jessica. Did you a half to tell him about the coffee?"

"The bastard!" Ian swore long and loud. "He gave me his word that there would be no repercussions."

"And you believed a man like that? He is so ambitious that he would walk over his own mother to get where he wanted to go."

Ian stared at Sally. "Aren't you just a tad cynical?"

"No. But I find the whole lot of you doctors extremely naive, except for the ones that are hell bent to be top dog in the department."

"That is not fair, Sally."

"Grow up, Doc. Life is not the fairy tale you guys live, going to high-class private schools paid for by your wealthy parents, then onto an

Ivy League college and then sauntering into the hospital where you expect everyone to bow and scrape toward you because you got an MD after your name."

"Are we that bad?"

"Not you personally. But a lot of them are. The official joke going around asks what the difference between a doctor and God is?"

Ian knew he should be able to come up with the punch line but was momentarily baffled.

Laughing, Sally said, "God doesn't think he's a doctor."

Groaning over what was one of the oldest jokes going, usually told by disgruntled nurses, Ian stared at Sally before asking her the question that had plagued him all day. "Did you wash the Dean of Medicine's special carafe after the last board meeting?"

Sally blushed a bright red and said, "Of course!"

"Tell the truth. It is really important, and I won't squeal on you."

"No! We were rushed off our feet that day, and I knew it wouldn't be used until the next meeting."

Ian grabbed Sally and gave her a kiss. "You are an angel. Now get me that carafe but put these gloves on first."

"You are mad. What do you want with the carafe?" Suddenly, her eyes lit up as Sally began to see what Ian was after.

"You think that whoever doped the coffee might have left their fingerprints on the container?"

"You are as bright as you are beautiful, Sally."

She blushed, took the gloves from Ian, and went through the doors to the food preparation area. In a few minutes, she returned with a shopping bag. "Get this back to me before the next meeting, or I'm toast."

"Don't worry, Sally. The dean will have his special carafe even if it isn't this one."

CHAPTER 30

Investigation

IT WAS ONE thing to get his hands on the coffee urn and another to get a useable set of prints. Medicine was his specialty and not forensic science. But Ian knew the first item on the agenda was to make sure the container was safe, locked up in his cupboard in the staff lounge. There wasn't time to do anything else as his pager began the incessant beeping. But Ian didn't bother to call the number; it was the reception area of the ER, and he was heading there anyways.

By ten at night, Ian just wanted to go home, but he had promised to stay an extra hour for Crawford. The man really owed him now. Fortunately, it was quiet, and Ian decided to use the opportunity to visit the hospital basement, where the dispatch office for the portering services was located.

The place looked like a dungeon with its drab-colored walls, no windows and furniture discarded from other departments. But the two men manning the phones that night were having an animated conversation, taking advantage of the unusual lull to discuss the latest ball game.

"Well, look who's slumming, Jake? If it ain't, Dr. Ian McLintock himself lowering himself to pay us a visit. What's up, Doc?" The obese red-headed man gave a long belly laugh over his imitation of Bugs Bunny.

"Now is that any way to greet the man who pulled your ass out of the fire?" Ian asked. Jake had staggered into work one night, drunk as a lord after breaking up with his latest girlfriend. The supervisor who never set foot in the hospital in the evening picked that night to show up. Taking pity on Jake, Ian put him on a gurney and connected up an IV line. Then he called the manager and told him that Jake had been rushed into emergency with a severe case of Montezuma's curse. The manager never bothered to ask what Montezuma's curse was.

"You ain't never gonna let me forget that night, are you, Doc?"

"What happened, Jake? You never did tell me why you didn't make in to work that night." The man sitting next to Jake was as skinny as Jake was fat. Rogers's elbows looked as if the bones might poke through his skin at any moment.

"Just mind yer own friggin' business, Roger."

"It's our little secret, right, Jake?" Ian winked at the dispatcher. Then he slapped a fiver on the counter and said, "Why don't you go to that new coffee shop they opened up next door and get us three coffees and some doughnuts."

Roger lifted his bony butt from the padded swivel chair, palmed the money, and made a slow flailing progress to the exit.

"Geez, Doc, watch what you say in front of Roger. He's got the biggest mouth going."

"I know. Just so you remember and don't tell him anything we talk about tonight, okay?"

"Right. You don't squeal, and I don't squeal."

"You remember that muscular kid that worked his way through high school?"

"Geez, Doc. That could have been any of a dozen kids we hire each summer. Can't you narrow it down a bit?"

"His name was common, like George or Dick or Harry?"

"I hate guessing games. What did he end up doing once he finished school? That might give me a clue who you're talking about."

"Oh. Sorry. Haven't been getting much sleep lately. He went through the police academy and was hired by the city police."

"You mean Harold! Geez, why didn't you say so, Doc?"

"Do you have a number or address for Harold. I need to get in touch with him."

"Well, that depends on what you need to talk to Harold about. The hospital has strict policies about giving out employee phones and addresses. They might fall into the hands of a serial murderer or stalker, if you get my drift."

Ian could feel the anger mounting as Jake stonewalled him. The big red-haired ape was going to make him pay for referring to the night he wanted to forget. But Ian had to have Harold's address.

Standing with his fists clenched in his pockets, Ian listened to the huge railway clock ticking away the seconds, wondering how to outsmart the dispatcher. Finally, he said, "I wouldn't want you to break any hospital rules, so why don't I give you my cell phone number and you can give Harold a call and tell him to phone me. I am sure there is no written policy in the hospital manual against that, is there?"

Stymied by Ian, the dispatcher flipped through the rotor wheel of his index cards and stopped. Then he slowly began dialing a number, a sly grin on his face. Ian knew that Jake figured the guy would be out. But there was a surprised gleam in Jake's eyes that told Ian someone had answered the phone.

Holding the receiver out for Ian to grab, Jake pretended to be busy as he shuffled some papers. "Hello, Harold?"

Harold's voice was so loud that anyone in the dispatch office could hear without trying. "Yeah. Who's this?"

"Dr. Ian McLintock. Listen, Harold, I need a favor, but I would rather not discuss it over the phone."

"Do you want to come here, Doc? I only live two blocks from St. Cinnabar."

"Give me your address, and I'll be there in half an hour." Ian scribbled down the numbers on a scrap piece of paper that was lying on top of the dispatcher's desk. Then he hung up and said, "Thanks, Jake. See you around."

"Aren't you gonna wait for your coffee, Doc?" There was a real disappointment in the man's face.

"Oh. One of you guys can drink two coffees, can't you? I would stay, but this is really important. But I will come back. Promise."

Jake looked like a kid who had his favorite toy taken away. Ian made a mental note to return as soon as possible and shoot the shit with the guys. He needed to keep Jake and Roger on his side. Especially with all the weird things happening around the hospital, he might just need someone to cover for him.

CHAPTER 31

Fingerprints

*T*HE TINY BACHELOR apartment where Ian had found Harold Tredmore was closer to the hospital than he had expected, and he immediately wondered how Harold managed to get his hands on such prime real estate. Most places this close to St. Cinnabar were snatched up by nurses or medical students and then passed on from one person to another when someone left. The other surprise was to find Harold hobbling around on crutches.

"Hey, Doc. I don't know what you want to talk to me about, but I am sure glad of the company. Want a beer?"

"Sure." Ian couldn't help staring at the cast-encased leg with endless pencil and pen autographs scratched on it. "What happened, Harold?"

"Got sideswiped by an idiot running a red light."

"He must have hit the police cruiser hard?"

"Wouldn't have left a mark on me if I had been in a car. But I am one of the elite motorcycle cops they still put out on the streets."

"Ouch! Lost a bit of skin, I'd imagine."

"No. I was lucky. The leathers saved my skin, but I had a compound fracture so I'm off for at least three months and getting bored as hell. So what can I do you for, Doc? I got time on my hands so anything you want you got."

"Only some help getting fingerprints off a coffee urn. But that might pose a problem if you aren't working?"

"No problem. Ever since I was a kid, I wanted to be a detective. Even got my own fingerprinting kit, thanks to my mom. She blew the budget and got me the top of the line stuff for Christmas three years ago. Once I get the prints, my sarge will get them done for me."

"You must be in tight to have the sergeant willing to run errands for you."

"He's my uncle, and Mom has been hysterical ever since the accident. So Uncle Charlie has been bending over backward to placate her. My dad served thirty years on the force and died a month before his retirement. So, you can figure out that my mother wanted me to do anything but become a cop. It was my Uncle Charlie who encouraged me to stand up to Mom. She almost disowned her brother the night they brought me into the hospital. Fortunately, she realized it wasn't his fault."

"So you come from a long line of policemen?"

"Yeah. Grandpa Cirrus was the epitome of the Irish cop. Even got a picture of him in the old uniform and round helmet-type hats they used to wear."

Ian wandered over to the artificial fireplace and examined a sepia-toned print that looked like a picture from an old Keystone Cop movie. Next to it was a more recent picture of a man that could be none other than Harold's father, the family resemblance was so acute.

"This is your dad?"

"Yeah. He had just graduated from the academy. Mom gave it to me when I was in grade one and had to do a show-and-tell. I was so proud of him." There was a long embarrassed silence as Harold stared at the photo.

"You are the spitting image of your old man. Your mom must be really proud of you."

"Yeah. But she says she'd rather have me alive than a hero."

"Can't blame her." Ian wandered over to the sofa, sat down, and took a long swig of beer. It tasted good.

"So why do you want me to dust this urn for fingerprints? It's not something a medical doctor is usually interested in."

"Unfortunately, I can't tell you that, Harold. It has to do with an incident in the hospital, and the persons involved all had to sign a confidentiality agreement when the lawyers settled."

"Sounds really intriguing. But I've got to admit that you are a real lifesaver, Doc. I thought I was going to go off my skull sitting here watching gd soap operas. No wonder housewives end up with nervous breakdowns."

"So, if I have some other things for you to do, you might be interested?"

"Like a PI? Yeah, man! I always liked detective stories. Hoped I would get to do more of that stuff when I joined the police force. Found out it is a hell of a lot less glamorous than I anticipated, except the ladies are all super impressed with the uniform. Hell. Here I am flapping my gums. How you doing? Got the nurses all lusting after your body?" Harold gave a deep belly laugh.

"Unfortunately, I have been too tired to notice. Seems whenever one of the other interns has a problem, I get to pull a double shift."

"Ouch. Nothing like a twelve-hour shadow to turn the ladies off?"

"Get kind of grouchy too. They are starting to say that the difference between me and God is that God doesn't think he's a doctor."

Harold looked like he was going to roll onto the floor; he was laughing so hard. Ian didn't think the joke was that funny especially since he made up the first part just to entertain Harold. But Ian understood why some men become stand-up comedians. It was nice to have an appreciative audience.

"So do you have this coffee urn with you, Doc?" Harold asked after he stopped laughing.

Ian handed him the shopping bag, and Harold started hobbling toward a desk.

"What do you need? Can I get it for you?"

"Sure, there's a case that looks like a fishing tackle box. Just bring it over and set it on the coffee table. We'll have to wait until after Sunday dinner to get these run through the police bank."

"Why Sunday?" Ian could not see any sense in waiting three days.

"Uncle Charlie and I have a standing invitation for Sunday dinner at Mom's." Harold saw the question mark in Ian's eyes. "Uncle Charlie lost his wife several years ago and is an abominable cook. So Mom makes sure he has at least one real good meal a week. There is nothing that makes a man grateful like really good home cooking. I think Uncle Charlie would do almost anything after that meal."

"So are you going to drag him down to the office and have him teach you how to use the system in case you get promoted?"

"That's a good line, Doc. I was beginning to wonder what I was going to tell him. But now I don't have to think anything up."

"Your uncle wouldn't happen to like pro basketball, would he?"

"Yeah! But he has to settle for listening to the games on radio or watch them on TV if he has the night off."

"Don't suppose you noticed how tall I am?"

"Geez, no, Doc." Harold feigned a look of astonishment and rolled his eyes. "You didn't try out for pro basketball by any chance?"

"No, but two of the guys on my high school basketball team were snatched up. They tried to sign me up for college basketball, but I wanted to go to medical school and figured I couldn't do both."

"No kidding. So where are these two buddies of yours now?"

"One is on the Hornets team in Charlotte, and the other one got picked up by the Grizzlies in Memphis. Both tried out for the Lakers but didn't make the first cut, so they settled for their second choice."

"And you can get tickets from these pals of yours?"

"Yeah, as a matter of fact, I have them with me."

"Holy cow! Uncle Charlie will be outta his mind when he sees them. If Mom's home-cooked meal doesn't do it, the tickets to the games will. But I had better look at that coffee urn and see if there's anything on it worth looking at." It didn't take long for Harold to carefully brush the gray dust all around the shiny surface. He then began systematically placing the celluloid strips over the entire surface. If there was even a trace invisible to the naked eye, he would have it on one of the tiny pieces of sticky clear tape.

Ian watched as Harold carefully put the labeled pieces of colloid tape away in the tackle box and then glanced at his watch. "Got to go, Harold. Early morning tomorrow, and I haven't been getting much sleep."

"No need to explain, Doc. Just promise me one thing."

"What's that, Harold?"

"You need any more help with this case you call on me. I can get around pretty good with these crutches. Need a stakeout, and I'm your man."

Ian almost laughed except the earnest look on Harold face told him that the guy was desperate for something to break the monotony.

It was a kind of eureka moment as Ian thought about the morgue. "There is one other place where we might need prints from, but we may be too late to get any. And it's got to stay top secret." *Why hadn't he thought of it earlier?* "But the cleaning staff have probably erased any evidence. And I'm not sure how I would sneak you past the beefed-up security they've got in place at the hospital."

"If I'm good at anything, Doc, it's keeping a secret. And you would be surprised how sloppy cleaners can be. I heard of a cold case where they found prints belonging to a killer two years after the body was found. Just let me know when and where."

"You're on. And maybe I can pay you a minimum wage."

"No money necessary. You can always return the favor sometime in the future. I just need an excuse to get outa this gd apartment."

"Great! I've got your number, and you have my cell phone number so we'll be in touch. Really gotta go now."

Trudging back to the hospital, Ian couldn't believe that his pager hadn't gone off for over two hours. The dumb luck seemed to bode well for his little investigation since it had given him time to see Harold.

But the idea of trying to get prints off the cold locker where Samantha had been imprisoned stumped him. Not only had they beefed up security in and around St. Cinnabar, but Dr. Whales had also insisted on the hospital security doing an hourly check of the morgue since Samantha was found there. That meant that Ian had to find someone who would turn a blind eye if he showed up with Harold on crutches.

Ian hoped that even though he was on call that the pager would remain silent for the rest of the night as he turned the key in the apartment door and flopped half undressed onto his unmade bed. The peeping of birds outside the apartment window at 6:30 a.m. and the warm stream of sunlight prevented him from rolling over and going back to sleep. Despite his resolution to keep a low profile and hide out for most of the day, Ian discovered that he didn't need to look for trouble because it had already found him. His pager started vibrating and refused to stop, no matter how many times Ian hit the off button. Stumbling to the phone, he dialed the hospital.

CHAPTER 32

No Sherlock Holmes

*T*HERE WERE TWO ambulances butted up against the open double doors as Ian squeezed in past a group of doctors and paramedics blocking what little space there was left at the entrance. It defied any logic that people had to congregate in doorways or across narrow corridors, especially in hospitals, and then stare at you as you tried to squeeze by as if you were the one trespassing on their body space.

Neanderthals, Ian thought as he suppressed the urge to push his way through and fling people against the nearest wall.

Geez, I'm in an ugly mood, he told himself. *Get a grip or you will end up barking at some poor innocent family member.* He was halfway to the doctors' locker room when he saw June waving at him madly from her seat behind the nurses' station. *Damn, what now!* Doing an abrupt turn, Ian trudged to the counter and leaned over to hear what June had started whispering to him.

". . . and the dean is fit to be tied, so you better go see him immediately." Ian didn't ask June to repeat the part he hadn't heard, turning on his heel and marching angrily to the dean's office.

The door was open for a change, but Brandi was nowhere in sight as Ian walked into the outer office. The carved oak door to the dean's office was also wide open, and the dean was wildly pacing around like a madman. The only thing missing was the flailing of arms and the ranting. One glance and Ian knew someone had either burglarized the dean's office or deliberately trashed it.

"What's happened?" Ian asked softly in an attempt to soothe the distraught older man.

"What the hell does it look like happened?" roared Dr. Whales.

"Have you called the police?"

"No. And I'm not going to."

"Is that wise?"

The glare of furious blue gray eyes made Ian shut up. He could understand not calling in the cops over Samantha, but a break-in was different. He wondered what it was the dean was hiding. "Are you missing anything, Dr. Whales?"

"Nothing, except . . . . hell and damnation!"

"What? You did ask me to come and see you."

"They only took some snapshots and an envelope with documentation."

"Someone is blackmailing you?" Ian realized too late the shock in his voice.

"No! Dammit! It was a manila envelope with information showing that one of the cleaning staff on nights wasn't doing his job. The pictures were taken over the period of a month with a date stamp on each to show garbage deliberately left for the man on days to pick up."

"So, what does that have to do with me?" It sure baffled the hell out of Ian, what he was supposed to do about it.

"Nothing. Some anonymous person couldn't get the management in housekeeping to come down on the guy, so they must have figured that I would do something about it if I knew what was going on, as if I have nothing better to do with my time than get involved in the disciplining of lazy cleaning staff!"

Ian stood watching as the dean picked up items randomly and replaced them on the oversized desk. "Who was the cleaner?"

"Some idiot who cleans the pathology and morgue on the night shift. Name sounds like that psychologist who did bell-ringing experiments with dogs."

"Pavlov?"

"Parlo, Parlo Farnsworth," the dean spat out the name.

"You don't think he had anything to do with Samantha's being locked in the morgue on a slab?"

"Precisely! She's on the cleaning staff. The idiot probably thought she had squealed on him and decided to teach her a lesson!"

"So what does that have to do with me?"

"So you were wrong when you came and told me that I was the intended victim!" the dean yelled at Ian.

The heat rushing up from his chest was turning his face a hot crimson color. "You are right, sir. But I never claimed to have any expertise in investigation. We should have called the police in the night we found Samantha."

"No, you sure aren't Sherlock Holmes, that's for sure. So I would appreciate you forgetting any reasons you had for thinking that I might have been the intended victim instead of Samantha Rutledge."

There was no doubt that the dean was ordering Ian to drop the matter. "Certainly, sir. Will you be calling in the manager from housekeeping?"

"No! Let them fight it out among themselves. If someone went to all that trouble to send me pictures and times and dates, they've probably already told the dough head who manages the idiots who are supposed to clean the hospital. Any more incidents and I'll fire the manager. They're easier to get rid of. Like the old Chinese warlords, they used to lop off a head or two and then everyone got the message and behaved themselves, at least for a while."

Obviously, the dean was a fan of Shogun. "Shall I go then?"

"Yes, yes. Can't have our medical staff standing around while we've got patients lining up in the emergency department."

CHAPTER 33

Playing Pi

SERGEANT CHARLIE MAHONEY had not been the pushover Harold had hoped his uncle would be. With only a short time to go before his retirement and years of following the rules, Charlie was not exactly eager to run interference for Harold. But he promised to think about the problem of running the fingerprints through the department database. The major stumbling block would be the crime scene investigators, who kept a close eye on their computers.

It took two days after the Sunday meal before Harold's phone rang. "Hi!"

"Harold. I hope you don't mind, but I used those tickets to get Mosey to show you how to use the databases in the lab to track down the fingerprints."

"No, I don't mind, Uncle Charlie. It's just a shame that you gave up the chance to see the games."

"Well, your mother and I talked about this, and if this helps you get promoted off that damned motorcycle, it's worth it. She damned near skinned me alive again after you left on Sunday. I just wish I had never encouraged you to go against her and enter the police academy."

"It's not your fault, Uncle Charlie. So when do I show up and let Mosey walk me through the procedure."

"Tonight. The inspector is throwing a big shindig for all the plain clothes guys to celebrate that big drug bust, so there won't be too many around. The flatfoots that will be in the station will be glued to the Lakers game and won't care unless somebody bombs the place."

"I'll be there. And thanks, Uncle Charlie."

"Just use this chance and start studying for a promotion. I can't take much more of your mother's bitching. Even her cooking can't make up for the hassle she puts me through every Sunday."

The police station looked dreary in the misty rain that shrouded all the buildings downtown. After passing through the processing area and noticing that there was only one bleary eyed drunk in filthy tattered clothes that stunk of human excrement and one very young hooker sitting in the hallway on hard benches, Harold knew that he wouldn't get in anyone's way that night.

"You must be Harold, Charlie's nephew?" The gaunt, balding man with coke-bottle thick glasses and a long beak nose hailed him as he opened the frosted glass door that had "CSI" etched on it.

"Hi, you must be Dr. Mosey?" Harold shook the long bony hand extended toward him and thought the guy must be suffering from hypothermia to have such cold fingers.

"You must have some pull for getting those tickets?"

"Old high school friends who made it into the big league."

"NBA! They must be rolling in dough. Well, let's get started. The old man is only going to be away tonight and won't be back in until late tomorrow afternoon unless there's a high-profile homicide."

As Harold undid his tackle box and laid out the prints, he got a grunt of approval from Dr. Mosey and found himself sitting back as the elderly man ran the celluloid tape into a scanner and began pecking away at the keyboard at lightning speed. It seemed to take forever, and Harold watched as one database after another did not produce a match.

Reading the disappointment on Harold's face, Dr. Mosey said, "Unless the person has a record or was employed by a Federal or State Department, or had some reason to be fingerprinted, they won't be in the system. But every once in a while you get lucky." Just then the system stopped and the word "match" flashed on the screen.

Dr. Mosey looked startled and turned to Harold. "I don't know what this person did, but they have a file on them. Looks like the lady was liberated from a German concentration camp at the end of the war."

"Can you print out the record?"

"Yes. But I shouldn't. It appears that this was part of an investigation into suspected war criminals immigrating to the States at the end of the war."

"Why would they suspect a woman of being a war criminal if she was in a concentration camp?"

"From the information here, it says she worked in the kitchen for the prison commandant."

"But they also added that she was a Jewish prisoner who was spared because she could be used as slave labor."

"Yes. But there were a lot of lies told so that some Germans could slip into the country under the guise of refugee status."

"Even women?"

"You are too young to understand. But there were women guards at those camps, and some of them were as vicious as the men in the atrocities they committed."

"How do you know, Dr. Mosey?"

"My mother was a survivor of a concentration camp. At first, she would never tell us anything about that part of her life. Then she had a complete breakdown, and the psychiatrist told her that she had to let us know what happened to her if she wanted to get better. It wasn't until she was forced to that she started telling us what happened.

"No one could ever imagine what those people went through. And the ones who lived suffered from survivor guilt. They couldn't get over the fact that they hadn't died too. Eventually, she began to get past the need to tell us. But I will never forget the grisly details of what happened."

Harold was at a loss for words and just stared at the skeletal thin man. Then Dr. Mosey handed him the sheets of paper and said, "Whatever this woman did, she probably had good reason for it. Just remember that."

"We don't know what her role in this was, just that she handled the coffee urn. She may just be an innocent bystander."

Sergeant Charlie Mahoney walked into the lab at that moment and sensing the strained atmosphere waited for Dr. Mosey to speak.

"We found what Harold was looking for," commented the doctor.

"Great. So does Harold have the makings of a CSI? His mom is determined that her kid ain't gonna be a motorcycle cop for the rest of his life."

"He's a bright lad, and if he's willing to go back to college and take the right courses, he could work his way into crime scene investigation."

"That's great. Thanks for helping my nephew, Dr. Mosey. So are you ready to go, Harold? The Lakers won their game, and I've got to be at work for eight tomorrow. Can't sleep in like you."

"Sure, Uncle Charlie. And thanks again, Dr. Mosey."

"Any time, kid."

Harold suspected that there was a bigger story behind the fingerprints, and he was determined to find out what it was.

CHAPTER 34

Catnapping

*T*HERE WAS NO night so peaceful as the evening of the basketball game. Sprawled on the bed, propped up against a couple of monster pillows his mother had made for him, Ian wondered if the lull in the emergencies was due to the fact that the male population was glued to a television or in bars betting on the outcome of the match. Even though Ian was rooting for the Hornets, especially since Spider was playing, he knew the odds favored the Lakers. Halfway through the match, with the Lakers leading, he slipped off into a deep sleep. It was the sound of bells ringing that woke Ian.

Swearing, he searched for the pager until he realized he wasn't on call. By then he was awake, the phone had stopped ringing, and he wondered who the blue blazes was calling that late at night. There didn't seem to be any point getting undressed since he would have to be up and showered in three more hours. So Ian tossed the cushions, wrapped the sheet around his fully clothed body, and dropped back into an unconscious state. The alarm had to have rung for twenty minutes before Ian sat up, swore that if he could sleep a year he'd never catch up, and tumbled out of bed.

Fortune seemed to be against him as soon as he walked into the hospital. Each minute seemed an hour long as he faced an endless round of emergencies, as if everyone who stayed home the night before had gone out and gotten smashed up to make up for lost time.

Staring at the faux-stained glass partition that separated the doctors' work area from the porters waiting for the next call, Ian sat studying the chart handed to him by Louis Parker.

The conversation behind the divide was so intense that Ian had difficulty blocking it out. The tall skinny porter was bemoaning a trick played on someone in their department.

"That's a rotten thing to do to anyone, let alone a simpleton like Kurt."

"They should never have hired him in the first place. The guy is unstable and a real screw up. Some do-gooder social worker must have pulled strings to get the guy hired, and then nobody wanted to admit he couldn't do the job."

"That's not fair, Gil, and you know it. How can a guy do his job with his coworkers constantly picking on him? This last stunt by Finkface really topped them all. Fixing the guy's chair so he fell as soon as he sat on it. The guy coulda been killed."

"How come you're taking the side of this retard?"

"Finkface is the retard. Anyone with a normal IQ wouldn't have to pick on some dummy to get his kicks."

"Oh yeah. Well, I heard that that ghost was an intern who was killed when the joke his classmates pulled on him went wrong . . ."

Ian really didn't want to listen to any more hospital gossip, even though he felt sorry for this Kurt. It was past lunchtime, and his stomach was growling. Stuffing the patient's file under his arm, Ian headed toward the cafeteria.

Lights in the corridor leading to the central food processing area flickered as if there was a short somewhere, and the nauseating smell from the trough where the overflow of water stood stagnating almost made him turn around and head up to the restaurant-style café on the floor above. Run by the Ladies' Auxiliary, the food was definitely of a much better quality, but also a bit expensive.

The staff member working behind the counter pulled three large pizzas from the oven, and that made up Ian's mind. After purchasing several slices, he sat down to read the file. Unfortunately, there were pages and pages of barely legible notes on the patient just admitted from emergency. Louis was the only intern who had the habit of writing every minute detail just to cover his ass.

After reaching the last page, Ian had no better idea than Lou about what the guy who looked like death warmed over was suffering from. Blood work showed an abnormally high SED rate but little else. There was no history of diabetes.

The only clue noted and highlighted by Lou was that the man was ex-military and had served a stint overseas during the Desert Storm. There was a long list of vague complaints that had been attributed to PTSS otherwise known as posttraumatic stress syndrome. But Ian knew there was definitely something wrong with the guy. He was as baffled as Lou as to what it was.

Something was niggling away at the back of his mind. He vaguely remembered reading about soldiers coming back from the Suez Canal having similar symptoms. Not that Ian was old enough to remember. But he had sliced open his leg as a kid and was waiting for the family doctor to stitch him up when he pulled out one of the physician's ancient medical journals. In an attempt to get his mind off the coming ordeal, Ian had waded into the most interesting article . . . about the strange illness suffered by peacekeeping veterans returning from the Middle East so many years ago.

When Dr. Hudson finally called Ian in to get his leg sutured shut, Ian remembered how the doctor, who seemed old even then, had calmed his fears and talked to him while swiftly closing the gaping wound. It was Dr. Hudson who had encouraged Ian to pursue a career in medicine while everyone else pushed him to try out for the NBA.

Racking his brain, Ian couldn't remember the date of the journal but thought about Dr. Conway. The man was a veteran and would probably have read anything pertaining to medicine involving the military. It was a long shot, but Ian decided that if Lou could consult with the old guy, so could he.

Picking up the last slice of pizza, Ian left the cafeteria and headed toward the elevators.

When he finally reached Dr. Conway's room, the old man was snoring like a buzz saw. The second bed was empty again, and never one to turn down an opportunity, Ian pulled the bedside curtains around just far enough to hide him, then plumped up a pillow on the headrest of the Cadillac chair before putting his feet up on the bed.

There was no point in rereading the patient's chart, and Ian figured he might as well get a few minutes shut-eye until Dr. Conway woke up. He figured the snoring in the bed would keep him from going into too deep a sleep. Dozing off, he had just begun to dream when the sound of footsteps entering the room startled him awake.

"What's up, son?" The sound of Dr. Conway's voice echoed past the curtain. He too had been woken by the footsteps.

"Got a difficult case, Doc, and I don't know what to do. Thought I would get your opinion if you don't mind." It was Louis Parker.

"No problem. Keeps me mentally alert having to delve back into what I know. So what's the problem?"

Louis explained in detail the case that arrived in the emergency department and then waited for the old doctor to answer. It was a very interesting conversation as the old man, instead of telling the intern the answer, asked several more questions until Louis came up with the answer on his own.

"So it's not that serious?"

"Naw. The nurse on duty probably knew what it was all along but didn't want to destroy your ego. She probably figures you are in the library looking up the symptoms. Sit down for a while, and we can talk. Days in here can be really long."

Ian was surprised that Lou didn't mention the ex-veteran but lay his head back down and closed his eyes, confident that the two men were oblivious to his presence behind the curtain.

"You're a graduate of St. Cinnabar Medical School, aren't you?"

"Yeah. How did you know?"

"Someone was looking through the old yearbooks, and I saw the name Lester Conway. Figured it had to be you. You must know a lot about what happened in the hospital way back then?"

"Who's been spreading rumors?"

"Some of the guys were talking about the ghost that haunts the hospital."

There was a long cough as Dr. Conway hesitated. "I think I started to tell you about my friend in medical school—Izzy Steinman—last time you were here, smart as a whip and the youngest fellow in our class. His family was wealthy Austrian Jews who saw Hitler coming and sent the boy to relatives in the States. Whenever I needed advice, Izzy was the one I went to."

"What year was that?"

"Couple of years after the war ended. I was discharged early because of injuries suffered in the Philippines. Decided to go through for a doctor. Almost flunked out except Izzy took pity on us GI types. Tutored us until we started getting it on our own."

"I remember you telling me about him. That was mighty nice of him."

"Yeah, he was a really special person." Dr. Conway's voice, that normally was gruff from age, had taken on a deeper timber as if talking about his classmate had upset him.

There was a long, long pause until Lou asked, "Was he the one who died?"

Another cough and Dr. Conway's voice sounded stronger as he said, "Yeah. Real tragedy that was."

"What happened?"

"There were a couple of young bucks about same age as Izzy. Too young for the war. Got pushed through school real fast to fill the void left by the guys who went to war and never came back. Chester came from a long line of doctors and was expected to be top of the class. His old man was top surgeon in some highfalutin hospital in Boston. He was the same age as Izzy if I remember correctly."

"Should have been friends, being of an age, then?"

"You'd think so, wouldn't you? But Chester was eaten up with jealousy. He was afraid Izzy was going to beat him out for the top residency coming open at the hospital because Izzy worked harder. And he was smarter too. Didn't have any money and not too many distractions to keep him from his studies. Think there might have been anti-Semitic feelings too, coming from a wealthy old Boston family. There was another guy who was friends with him, and they bullied Izzy something terrible. But Izzy just ignored them. Guess he felt lucky they couldn't do what the Nazis did to his family back in Austria."

"What did they do to this Izzy guy?" Lou asked.

"One day we were all sitting along this long bench in the cafeteria, and Izzy opens up his lunch box. He jumps back, and we all looked. There was this human finger sticking up. It wasn't hard to figure out where they got it from, 'cause Izzy's cadaver was missing a digit during anatomy class that afternoon."

"Uugh! I think I would have lost it right there. What did Izzy do?"

"Got up and walked away. Left his lunch box and everything. Said that they were amateurs compared to the Nazis. Made all the guys sitting there real ashamed for not sticking up for Izzy except maybe they still didn't believe what had happened in Europe. Wasn't until later that we found out his whole family died in a concentration camp except for one sister. Damn shame.

"It was soon after that happened that Rebecca arrived from Europe, skinny as a skeleton, but real pretty. They shared a tiny house, and Izzy went home for his meals after that. So they had to find some other way to bother him."

"And nobody did anything?"

"Izzy didn't complain. It wouldn't have done him any good anyways 'cause we didn't know anything about bullying then. You stood up to your tormentors and became a man. At least that was what we understood. Not like nowadays."

"What else did they do to him?"

"One time, if I remember rightly, they stole his assignment. Only reason he didn't get penalized was that one of the other guys he tutored went to the dean and said Izzy had already finished his paper because he'd seen it."

"So the head of the medical school knew something was going on?"

"Yeah. But he was a friend of Chester's father. Fat chance he would side with Izzy over his friend's kid."

"So what happened? Why did Izzy die?"

"I can only guess, but I should have tried to warn Izzy. But I really didn't think they would go through with it."

"With what?" Suddenly, Louis's pager started beeping.

"You'd better see what that's about." Dr. Conway sounded relieved to be interrupted.

"It's the emergency department extension. Guess I'd better go." There was a scuffing of the chair legs as Louis got up.

Ian hoped old Dr. Conway would go back to sleep. But the patient seemed to have radar.

"That you sleeping behind the curtain again, Dr. McLintock?"

"Yep!" Before Ian had a chance to ask Dr. Conway to finish telling what the two medical students did to Izzy, his pager began the annoying buzz that didn't stop until he pressed the button to see who was calling.

"Guess you have to skedaddle too, Dr. McLintock."

"Looks like it. But I'll be back, Dr. Conway."

Ian wished that he had asked Dr. Conway what had happened to Izzy Steinman since his yearbook picture resembled the person Ian had followed into the morgue. But he still wasn't about to swallow the line that a ghost haunted the hospital and that it was the specter of Izzy Steinman that had led him to Samantha.

"Before you take off, Doc, I would like to ask you a favor."

"Sure, Dr. Conway, anything."

"There's a patient down the hallway who is dying of cancer. I know him from the war. Really nice chap who came from Newfoundland. Settled in Connecticut after the war with his bride."

"So what do you want me to do?"

"I know you're not his doctor. But Elliot is in bad pain, and the morphine they've been giving him doesn't seem to be working. I wheeled into his room and had to leave. You wouldn't leave a dog suffering like that."

"His doctor should increase the dosage."

"That's what's so peculiar. Elliot is getting as much as he can take without it killing him. I sneaked a look at his chart. So I can't understand why it's not working. If they give him any more, he's gonna die on them."

"I'm not supposed to be looking at another doctor's patient. You know that."

"Sure, Doc. But it wouldn't hurt just to take a peek in on him. Sort of hover around when the nurse gives him his injection."

"Okay. But it probably won't do any good."

"Thanks, Doc. I appreciate that. And Elliot does too."

The pager went off a second time, and Ian made a beeline for the circular desk at the center of the floor that served as the nurses' station and grabbed a phone.

CHAPTER 35

Follow-up

FOR ONCE THE nurse had dialed the wrong number. Since Ian was no longer in a hurry to reach the emergency department, he decided to check on Elliot while the regular staff were off so that no one need know he was poking his nose into another doctor's case. Lifting the chart from the trolley, he strolled slowly down the hall toward the room. He didn't need to look up the number because he could hear the heart-wrenching moans that came from that direction.

According to the medical history on the chart, Elliot had been a heavy smoker all his life having started smoking when cigarettes were given freely to the men going overseas. They had little idea of how deadly they were then, and besides, a lot of the men wouldn't be coming back so it didn't matter that they were developing a habit that would kill them twenty or thirty years down the road.

Rapping lightly on the door, Ian entered and felt his self-control being tested as he stared at the wasted lanky man with half his face eaten away with cancer. The original tumor had metastasized and spread to his face. "How are you doing, Elliot?" he asked.

"Not too good, Doc. I ain't afraid of dying, but I can't take much more of this pain."

"Did the nurse give you your shot of morphine tonight?"

"Right on the dot. Marigold is an angel of mercy. Most of the other ladies can't stand nursing me. Can't say that I blame them. Wouldn't want to have a mirror to see what I look like. So most days Marigold switches with the girl who is supposed to take care of me. They are mighty grateful. I hear snatches of their conversations down the hall. So I don't want to complain. But it gets mighty bad sometimes."

"I'm not your doctor so I don't have the right to change your medication, Elliot. But I'll look into it and see if I can talk to Dr. Stalgard. He's a reasonable man."

"Thank you, Doctor. I really appreciate that."

"I see here that you are due for another injection in half an hour. I think I will stick around and give it to you myself." Ian walked slowly toward the nursing station still reading the chart. Most nights Elliot's pain medication didn't seem to work. Then the odd night he seemed to be all right. Ian was intrigued as to why the dosage was adequate some nights and not on others. He didn't want to even think about why there was a discrepancy. But he could make sure that night the old man got the right dosage.

Ian ambled up to the horseshoe-shaped desk that served as the nurses' station and asked the lone occupant, "Hi! Who is the head nurse on tonight?"

A carrottopped girl who looked more like a high school student than a nurse turned and smiled at Ian. "Hi! I'm Gena. You want Marigold."

"And where can I find Marigold?" Ian couldn't drag his eyes away from the too young-looking nurse. He resisted the urge to ask her if she was old enough to be left alone on the floor.

"Oh, she's down with Mrs. MaGillicutti. Marigold is a gem. She takes all the terminals so we don't have to."

"Terminals?" It sounded like bus depots to Ian.

"You know," Gena whispered, "the patients who are dying. Some of them are really gruesome and the smell!"

"So you really appreciate Marigold taking them on?"

"You bet. I would have had to transfer off this floor if it wasn't for her."

"Too hard to deal with?"

"You want to believe it. When I decided to become a nurse, I had no idea how hard it would be. It's bad enough having to change their diapers and wipe bums. But smelling flesh rotting away was just not what I had envisioned for myself."

"Join the club. I think there are few people in the medical profession that realize exactly how unglamorous the job can be. No Dr. Kildare or Marcus Welby around here."

"Huh? Dr. Kildare? Is he on staff here?" Gena asked with a puzzled look on her face since she was too young to remember the popular medical show.

It wasn't as if Ian was old enough either, except his mother loved all the medical shows including *MASH* and watched them over and over again on the rerun channel. Ian couldn't remember a night when he didn't do homework to the theme song of one of those programs echoing up the stairs in the old farmhouse.

"Never mind." Ian walked into the medication room and flipped to the page where the current day's drugs were entered.

Within a few minutes, a tall, thin woman with lank straight hair cut in a short unflattering bob and dressed in an old-fashioned white uniform and cap walked into the cubicle where the drugs were prepared. "And who are you?" she demanded of Ian.

"Dr. Ian McLintock. You must be the angel of mercy, Marigold."

"Yes. I don't recognize you as one of the regular doctors."

"A friend of Elliot's asked me to check on him. He appears to be having unbearable pain despite the morphine."

"Well, I can't help that. I don't order the medication, I only administer it." Pale washed out gray eyes glinted with hatred at Ian.

"I understand your problem, and I'm not here to criticize. I know that Elliot is not my patient, but I promised that I would make sure he got his medication tonight."

"Exactly what are you hinting at, Doctor?"

"Nothing. I didn't mean anything other than that I am going to administer his morphine tonight under your supervision."

"Well. I've never heard of the like. His doctor trusts me."

"I trust you as well. But I am just following through on my promise. After Elliot gets his injection, I intend on sitting with him for a while so that I can report back to his regular doctor. If the man needs more medication, we need to report that. I have heard glowing reports from your staff about how good you are with the more difficult patients. So I hope you will continue doing the excellent job you have in the past. We both want what is best for the patient, so I know you won't mind watching while I give Elliot his injection." Ian knew he was laying it on a little thick, but he didn't want to alienate the only nurse who seemed not to mind caring for the dying.

"Well, if you insist. But he isn't supposed to get another injection for ten minutes."

"I'm sure that we can bend the rules tonight. I stopped in, and the man is in agony."

"Some patients exaggerate."

"Maybe, but for tonight let's give him the benefit of the doubt." Ian selected the vial and withdrew the maximum dosage allowed. There was no wastage to sign for so Marigold stood and watched and then followed Ian down to Elliot's room.

"Thank the lord," muttered the man as he saw them nearing his bed. Injecting the morphine into the IV line, it took only seconds before the poor man's taut body relaxed, and he began to doze off.

Glancing over his shoulder, Ian saw the look of hatred on Marigold's face. Maybe that was why she could stand to nurse them. The other women would never think of questioning her motives since they were only too happy to let her take over the most difficult cases.

"I'll be sitting here for a while." Ian motioned to the Cadillac chair he was pulling up alongside the bed. "It will give you a short break from this patient."

If Ian thought Marigold was going to thank him, he was in for a big disappointment as she stomped out of the room, and he heard her footsteps echoing in the empty corridor as she made her way back to the nursing station.

Even after an hour, Elliot was resting peacefully. Ian didn't want to think about the suspicions hovering around in the back of his brain. But there had been previous cases where patients did not receive enough pain medication for one reason or another. Sometimes, the older nurses got confused with the milliliters on the syringe. But it wasn't his job to speculate. Just let the regular doctor know that there was a problem and hope he wasn't one of these guys who got overly sensitive when a colleague took it upon himself to look in on his patient.

CHAPTER 36

Whose Fingerprints

FOR ONCE IAN had managed to get out of the hospital on time and was trudging as fast as his tired feet would take him home, to beer and the hockey game. As he came up the flight of stairs, he heard the sound of his phone ringing.

Before he could unlock the door, there was a click as the answering machine picked up, and Ian listened to sound of the boring announcement he'd recorded when he first bought the device some three years ago. He really had to change that message! It was so dorky that he cringed until he heard the person phoning begin to talk.

"Hey, Doc! It's Harold. There's something that I need to tell you about the fingerprints on that carafe."

Racing across the room, he picked up the phone and said, "Harold! Just got in the door. What's this about the fingerprints?"

"I know it's late, Doc, but do you want to come over and I'll explain it to you? Got a case of beer and the set is tuned in for the big game."

Although Ian had hoped to sprawl on his bed and catnap during commercials, he knew how lonely Harold was cooped up in his apartment, hobbling around on crutches. Hell, he needed some social interaction that didn't involve sick people too. "Love to come over, Harold. It will give us a chance to plot some strategy."

After a fast shower and a change into old jeans that his mother threatened to take scissors to every time he went home, Ian ran down the steps two at a time, finding that the prospect of spending an evening not talking about medicine had given him a boost of energy. With Harold's apartment a stone's throw away, he made it to his door in less than ten minutes and found his knock intercepted by Harold standing with one arm firmly supported by the crutch.

"Come on in, Doc! I ordered pizza as soon as you hung up. Hope you like everything on it."

"Yeah. Didn't realize I was hungry until you mentioned food." Following Harold over to two stuffed chesterfield chairs that looked like they had been resurrected from his grandparent's attic, Ian slouched into a comfortable position until he realized Harold was going to try and get a beer for each of them by hobbling on the crutches across the floor.

"Hey! Sit, Harold. It's easier for me to get them." Two strides to the refrigerator and Ian beat Harold to the beer.

"Didn't invite you over to wait on me, Doc!"

"It's Ian. I would like to forget what I do for a living even if it's just for one night."

"Gotcha, Doc . . . Ian."

The TV was blaring out commercials that led up to the beginning of the game. Harold hit the mute button and said, "Might as well tell you what I found out while we're waiting for the game to get underway."

"Yeah. Sounds like you managed to identify the person who handled the coffee urn."

"That's what's so strange. Uncle Charlie used those tickets you gave me to bribe this guy, Dr. Mosey of the forensic staff to run the fingerprints through the database. It's a good thing he said yes 'cause I had no idea how complicated it could get."

"It's too bad your uncle won't get to see the games. But I could always put the touch on the guys the next time I see them."

"Hey, that'd be great. But wait till I tell you about those fingerprint databases. I thought there was only one search engine, the AFIS, which stands for automated fingerprint identification system. But there's more. One is for criminals, and then there's another for civilians." Harold went on enthusiastically oblivious to Ian's glazed look.

"So it took a while, but you found a match?" Ian finally interrupted Harold.

"Yeah. But it took a heck of a long time. If I had been trying alone, we would have never found them."

"So who left their prints on the coffee urn?" Ian waited impatiently for the answer.

"They belong to this widow of the head honcho at a pharmaceutical company. She was fingerprinted by their security firm because her husband died and left everything to her. Otherwise, we wouldn't have ever found a match. And for some reason, someone decided to investigate her background because she emigrated from Germany after the war."

"That's downright weird. So what's the name of the person, Harold?"

Getting up and hobbling over to the table, Harold came back with the printout.

"What do ya think, Doc?" He opened it to an official-looking document that appeared to be a duplicate or printout of a computer-generated file.

"Holy shit. Rebecca Cornwell. Guess I shouldn't be surprised because one of the other women on the Hospital Auxiliary told me she had been helping out the day Samantha disappeared."

"Samantha disappeared? Doc, you gotta tell me what happened. I ain't gonna spill the beans to no one." Harold looked like he was dying of curiosity.

"Okay. But no one else can ever find out I told you." Ian gave Harold a rundown of the events of the night he found Samantha in the morgue.

"It's a good thing this Samantha wasn't claustrophobic, or she coulda had a heart attack waking up in a closed-in space like that with no light."

"Yeah. She was lucky." Somehow that seemed to be a contradiction, to be found alive in a cold slab in the morgue was anything but fortunate.

"So what do we do now, Doc?"

"Nothing until I can find out why this Rebecca Cornwell would want to harm the Samantha." Ian wasn't about to tell Harold about his theory that the Dean of Medicine was the intended victim and not Samantha. That really would have been too much information.

"So I guess we might as well watch the game." As the puck was dropped, the teams skirmished to get control. Into the second half of the game, it was a foregone conclusion who would win. The local team had gone from being aggressive to acting like whipped puppies.

Finally, Harold hit the mute button and looked at Ian. "Let's figure out what we're going to do next, Doc. We know who's gonna win this game already."

"Much as I hate to admit it, you're right. Son of a bitch. I had ten bucks riding on that game."

"That's all? My uncle is gonna spit nails. He owes me fifty. Said it was a sure thing and was lording it over me all night, saying he was gonna buy the guys at the tavern a beer on me. Just shows ya it ain't over until it's over."

"I have another idea, Harold, but it is probably too late to do anything about it."

"What's that, Doc?"

Ian felt a little irritated that Harold had reverted back to calling him doctor but didn't want to offend his host. "I should have tried to get fingerprints from the morgue the night we found Samantha."

"Listen, Doc. You might think it's too late to get any prints, but I can tell you from when I worked those summers in the hospital that most of the night staff don't clean anything. They do a little while the boss is roaming around and then find an empty stretcher to lie down on for the rest of their shift. If you can get me into the morgue, I'll bet we could find a couple of partial prints."

"Let me work on it, Harold. They've beefed up security ever since we found Samantha. Getting into the morgue unescorted is almost as hard as breaking into Fort Knox."

All of a sudden, the home team scored with just minutes left in the game. Harold put the sound on and swore as the game was suddenly tied by a second goal and was forced into overtime.

Glancing at his watch, Ian groaned to himself as he wondered if he could escape before they broke the tie. Looking at Harold, who was on the edge of his seat swearing a blue streak, Ian knew it would be unthinkable not to stay to the end. Fighting sleep, he thought about how he would sneak somebody on crutches into the morgue without raising suspicions.

CHAPTER 37

Who Cleans?

THINKING ABOUT WHAT happened really depressed him. A glance at the clock reminded Ian that he had to move if he was going to make it in for the graveyard shift in the ER.

There was something comforting about being in familiar surroundings that made the tension of the unknown bearable. And tonight was no exception as Ian wandered through the halls linking the cubicles, some glassed in and some only with curtains separating the beds. Finally, he made his way to the employee entrance and was startled to see Samantha with her husband, Larry.

Larry gave his wife a quick kiss and retreated like he was escaping a firing squad. "Hi, Samantha!" Ian decided to waylay her before she got a chance to go to her locker.

"Dr. McLintock! You're on tonight!" Samantha turned to see that Larry had already fled. "My husband doesn't like being late for work so he dropped me off half an hour early. He would have had me here at eleven if I had let him."

"I'm glad you're early, Samantha, because I wanted to talk to you."

The pink bloom disappeared from the cleaner's cheeks as she turned an ashen color. The terror in her eyes showed just how close to the surface her trauma still lurked. "Did you find out something about that night, Dr. McLintock?"

"No. Sorry, Samantha. But I am working on it. And I need your help. Let's go to the lounge, where we can talk in private."

As Samantha sat opposite him, Ian was relieved to see her cheeks had regained some color and she had relaxed again. "You know I'll help in any way I can."

"What I need to know is which cleaner does the morgue."

The word morgue made Samantha start in fright. But she regained control and said, "I don't know, but I can call up my friend Sarah. She would be able to tell me."

"And I need to know what his routine is. Like what kind of cleaning he does. The order he does it in. You know. Like your job."

After glancing at her watch, Samantha said, "Sarah may still be up. She's a real night owl. Let me try and get her on the phone."

"Good. I have a patient waiting so I'll leave you to it. Just page me if you get any information." Ian had lied about the patient but didn't want to stop Samantha from phoning.

He wandered out to the nurses' station and noted gratefully that the board was clear. With any luck, they might have a quiet night. He knew that he had a visit to make and said to the charge nurse, "Shirley, I'm going down to the all-night doughnut shop. Do you want a coffee or something to eat?"

Laughter made the rolls of the big woman's stomach jiggle. "No! Do I look like I need a doughnut?" After that statement, Shirley sat herself down onto a swivel chair, removed her shoes, put her feet up on the desk, and began perusing an old *National Geographic*.

"Be careful you don't get too comfortable," teased Ian as he trotted out the sliding doors into the dark dirty street, where a neon beacon of a light in the shape of a doughnut flashed at the end of the block.

It took less time than expected since Ian and the clerk were the only humans in the shop. Balancing a box of doughnuts and a tray of coffees with creamers and sugars filling the empty holes, he made it back to the hospital in record time, descending to the bowels of the building and down the long darkened corridors to the dispatch office. Sitting there were Jake and Roger arguing animatedly over last night's game.

"Well, look who is slumming again," grinned Jake as he spied the coffee and doughnuts.

"What brings you down to our neck of the woods?" asked Roger as he reached his long bony arm out and grabbed two doughnuts. "These are for us, aren't they?"

"Yeah. Just a little thank you for your help the other night."

"So Harold and you got together. How is the lad doing? Is he still in a cast?" Jake picked a huge doughnut and shoved the whole thing into his mouth, gulping a mouth full of coffee to wash it down. Then he snatched a coconut-covered chocolate delight, and it followed the fate of the first doughnut.

"Yeah. Harold's still hobbling around, but he's been a big help."

"You never did tell us what it was all about, Doc. How about filling us in on the details?"

"Sorry, guys. Like I told you the other night, it's strictly confidential. If I so much as whisper about it, I could not only lose any chance for my residency next year, but they would fire my ass so fast that my head would spin."

"Come on, Doc. You gotta be exaggerating a little."

"Nope. They would probably make sure no other hospital in the greater United States of America hired me either. So it's still hush, hush."

"We heard that some patient got put in the morgue when they were still alive," said Roger smugly, watching for Ian's reaction.

"Don't be ridiculous. Of course, that never happened." Ian laughed, hoping that he was giving a convincing performance.

"Well, we also heard that you saw a ghost down by the morgue," added Jake.

"Who started that rumor?" Ian felt the red flush rise up his face and knew this time he wasn't going to get away with bluffing.

"One of the porters heard two interns talking in the conference room. So it's true, isn't it, Doc?" Jake pointed his bony finger at Ian and nodded his head knowingly.

"They got it wrong. I went to a stag party, then got stuck doing a double shift. So I was hung over and hallucinating at the time."

"We've been working in this hospital too long to not know the truth when we hear it, eh, Roger?" This time Jake pointed his skeletal hand in Roger's direction.

"Yeah, Doc. We know all about that pathologist Histane, who got the shit scared out of him so bad that he won't show up in the morgue at night without his specially trained technician at his side. So we know you have seen this thing that walks the halls outside the morgue."

"I saw something, and yes, everyone has been gossiping about it. But I would really appreciate it if our conversation stayed in this room. As far as I'm concerned, there is no ghost, and it was the result of extreme fatigue. And Harold is doing a little research for me to prove that this specter doesn't exist."

"Specter? Whatcha mean, Doc?" asked Jake.

"It's another name for somebody that haunts live people dummy," sneered Roger with an air of superiority.

"Good luck, Doc. There are a lot of people who've seen it." Jake shook his head knowingly.

The pager started its annoying ping, ping, ping. This time Ian was relieved to have an excuse to leave. "Thanks again, fellows. Guess I have to go back to work."

"Come back any time, Doc. Especially if you have coffee." Roger laughed as he stuffed another doughnut into his mouth.

Down the corridor, Ian looked at the number and guessed that Samantha had paged him. Even in the basement of the hospital, you could still hear the siren, and Ian hadn't heard any ambulances arriving.

CHAPTER 38

Cleaner Isn't Mr. Clean

"*D*R. MCLINTOCK!" SAMANTHA waddled toward him as he approached to entrance to the ER.
"You got a hold of your friend?"
"Yeah, and did she give me an earful?"
After listening to the dean rant on about the documentation someone went to all the trouble to accumulate and send him, Ian was sure he had a pretty good idea what Samantha had found out. But he let her tell him.
". . . and he doesn't have to do much inside the morgue itself because the technicians wash down the metal stretchers and floors every day. So he probably hasn't wiped down the lockers where they keep the bodies for at least a month."
The thought of the amount of bacteria and pathogens building up on the stainless steel drawers was enough to make Ian gag. But at least they would be able to get some fingerprints off them if they could figure out a way to get past the security guards.
"Thanks, Samantha. You've been a big help."
The woman glowed at being praised, and a cherry red tinge crept from her throat into her cheeks. "You don't have to thank me, Dr. McLintock. After all, you are trying to find out what happened to me."
"And this may bring us one step closer to the truth." Although he said it, Ian really wasn't sure it would help at all. There would be the prints of all those people who normally worked in the pathology labs to eliminate before they could be certain they had a suspect. Their only hope was that someone from outside the hospital had been involved and that he had been fingerprinted somewhere along the line. It really was a long shot. But he was not about to tell Samantha that.

CHAPTER 39

Blackmail or Whatever Works

RACING ALONGSIDE A gurney with a patient to the X-ray department, Ian wondered how he could get into the morgue.

"Watch it, Doc!" yelled the porter as they wheeled the stretcher around the corner and almost collided with another coming out of an examination room.

"Earth to, Ian," yelled Marla as she held the IV pole to stop it from toppling over as they screeched to a halt.

"Sorry, Marla. I stayed up to see the hockey game instead of hitting the sack like I should have. And I'm trying to solve a problem."

"Don't apologize to me. If we had run into that other stretcher, we could have had two patients on the floor."

"I'm awake now, believe me!" He had no idea how consumed he had become by the problem of getting Harold into the morgue. "At least the X-ray technician is ready for us so we won't have to sit around waiting for our patient."

The look Marla gave Ian told him that she didn't really think there had been any point to the mad dash they had made from the ER to the X-ray department. In fact, Ian would have laid odds that the CAT scan would confirm that their patient was brain-dead. The machines keeping his organs alive were just a formality until they could consult with his wife and ask if she would consider donating the poor fellow's organs.

It had been a freak accident with the man being in the wrong place at the wrong time. The blow to his head had knocked out all real life and left just the brain stem functioning. As they watched the team transfer the man onto the stretcher bed that moved the patient's head into the tunnel of the CAT scan machine, Ian wondered about the woman he would have to face in the next half hour.

No matter how many times he did it, it never got any easier. And the staff doctor on that night was notorious for passing the buck, as if he was loathe to face the emotional outburst that followed the revelation that the person was a vegetable. For all intents and purposes, a dead man with no hope of recovery.

Sitting next to Marla, Ian felt the warmth of her body and enjoyed her intoxicating fragrance that he was hard-pressed to identify. "It's a bitch, isn't it?"

"Maybe we're wrong this time, Ian."

"I hope you're right, Marla. This is one time I really want to be wrong."

"What's the problem you've been trying to figure out? Is it a patient you are trying to diagnose?"

"Nope. Do you remember Harold, the student who worked in portering for three summers in a row while going to college?"

"There were a lot of students working during the summer. If he's the one I remember, he worked straight nights."

"Yeah! I think Harold did say he chose that shift so he could earn a few more bucks with the shift premium."

"So what's this problem got to do with Harold? He's the one that attended the police academy, wasn't he? He should be a full-fledged cop by now."

"Yeah. And he got knocked off his motorcycle by someone who ran a red light."

"Is he all right?" The horror on Marla's face told Ian that she thought he was in the hospital.

"Yeah. It happened several weeks ago. His leg is in a cast. I decided to get him to help me with the problem of Samantha."

"Oh! How could he help?"

"I haven't had a chance to talk to you, but I discovered that Samantha Rutledge probably wasn't the intended victim."

"You've been holding out on me, Dr. Ian McLintock. Fill me in on the details."

While they waited for the results of the CAT scan, Ian brought Marla up-to-date on everything he had discovered.

"So do you have any ideas how I can sneak Harold into the morgue to dust the locker for prints?"

"Actually, I do. One of the security guards on nights owes me a favor."

"How's that? What did you do for him, Marla?"

"That's none of your business. But I know if I ask, he will open the morgue and stand guard while you and Harold 'dust for prints' as you so aptly described it. You know, we sound like a page out of an old detective novel, an Erle Stanley Gardner story."

"You arrange the time, and I'll let Harold know when to show up with his equipment."

The doors of the examination room swung open as the technicians rolled their patient out. From the bleak look on the radiologists face, Ian knew that he had a grim task ahead of him, facing the man's relatives.

"Sorry, guys, but he's toast," muttered the radiologist before he turned down the hall and wandered back toward his office.

"What a bummer," commented the tiny blonde technician as she removed the lead apron. "What a dirty rotten shame."

The return trip was a slow solemn procession since there was no longer any hurry. As long as the respirator continued to provide oxygen to the vital organs, that was all that mattered. *Son of a bitch,* Ian muttered to himself. This just wasn't his day. Too many things had gone wrong and now this.

CHAPTER 40

Advice Needed

FOR ONCE THE department was calm and the staff unnaturally quiet as they waited for the transplant team to claim the man still on the respirator. Ian glanced over and saw from the look on Marla's face that the whole incident had brought back bad memories from the night of her father's death.

"Coffee and doughnuts with me at the shop at the end of the street if you can stand the cheerful company." Ian gently nudged Marla's shoulder in a platonic gesture that covered what he really felt like doing.

"Did some nice little old lady die and leave you her estate all of a sudden?" Marla blushed as she realized what she had said and how inappropriate it was given the circumstances.

"Nope. Just thought that we had better seize the day. That guy we pronounced was my age. It really hits home just how fleeting life can be. And I get the feeling that you're calling me a scrooge. I treat once in a while!" Feigning hurt, Ian put on his saddest look.

"Don't try that with me, Dr. McLintock. I know you scraped through medical school on scholarships and bursaries. It's my treat if you will listen and give me some advice."

"You want my advice? What's up?"

"Let's wait until we get to the coffee shop. I don't want anyone listening in on our conversation. And I swear the walls have ears around here."

"Know exactly what you mean, Marla." They headed to a secluded booth at the back of the doughnut shop, even though there were only two other customers sitting over coffees in the place.

Sliding into the seat opposite Ian, Marla glanced up in surprise as the gum-chewing bleached blonde in a too tight top and miniskirt more suited to soliciting on the streets than waitressing stood over them, pencil poised over a pad. "Whatcha want tonight, kids?"

Ian glanced at Marla who said, "Two coffees and one super deluxe cream puff with dark chocolate and extra whip cream."

"An whatchyou having?" Blondie stared at Ian and gave what she probably thought was a seductive wiggle of her derriere wrapped in a skintight skirt that left nothing to the imagination.

"I'll have two coffees and another super deluxe cream puff."

"Two heart attacks and four javas," screamed the girl to the open window that separated the kitchen from the counter as Blondie wiggled her way back to the TV set on the counter that she watched between customers.

Marla put her head down and tried to stifle the giggles. "Whatcha want?" she imitated the waitress.

Shaking his head in disbelief, Ian asked, "Is she new here or have I just never seen her before?"

"Gloria found a sugar daddy and gave notice. Guess word got out that this is a good place to find a husband and is attracting high-class help."

"You have a real gift for irony, Marla, but don't try stand-up comedy just yet. You probably need to keep your job at the hospital for a while longer."

"Which brings us to the reason I wanted to talk to you. There's a nursing management position coming up in the ER, and a friend of mine is pushing me to apply for it. Can you be brutally honest, Ian? I don't want to get myself in over my head, especially after what happened to our last manager."

"Brutally honest? Well, I think that you would make an excellent manager, Marla, and have wondered why you haven't tried for some of the better jobs before now. The staff like and trust you, and you are the fairest person I've ever met. Go for it! And good luck."

She had hoped that he would encourage her, but Marla found herself blushing at the praise Ian heaped on her. "I guess that's a yes then?" She smiled and tried to regain control.

"You are beautiful when you get flustered."

"Stop. You are really embarrassing me."

"I didn't mean to, and besides, you did ask me to be brutally honest."

"But I didn't expect you to lay it on that thick."

The sight of their waitress brought an abrupt halt to their conversation. "The cream puffs are fresh tonight. We had a real run on them so you're in luck." Blondie banged the four cups of coffee down and two oversized desserts and then the little piece of paper with their bill on it.

Waiting until she was out of earshot, they began giggling. "This is fun. We should do this more often," Ian grinned.

"You might be able to, but I would be a blimp before three months were out."

"I don't believe it. You never stop running all the time you're at work."

"But I still can't eat desserts with this much fat and stay slim. I have a good metabolism, but there's such a thing as pushing a good thing too far." Marla sighed and then took a tiny bite out of the cream puff.

They were finished eating and onto their second cup of coffee when the wail of an incoming ambulance at the hospital echoed down the street to the doughnut shop. There was nothing to do but cut short their break.

CHAPTER 41

The Burglary

TWO HOURS LATER, Ian ripped off the blood-soaked surgical scrubs and headed to the showers. There was nothing but the echo of his footsteps in the change room. Grateful for time alone, he stood in the cubicle and let the water pound down full force, still feeling as if he could fall asleep under the torrent punishing his body. With a towel around him, he staggered into the lounge, put his feet up and head back, and nodded off.

Chasing down the darkened corridor, Ian pursued the strangely clad intern whose stethoscope banged wildly against his chest. He would catch him this time and prove that he was not a ghost. The young man rounded the corner, disappearing out of sight. But Ian pursued him and slid around the same bend only to skid to a terrified halt. Staring him in the face were skeletal remains, desiccated skin clinging to the bones and skull. An arm composed only of ulna, and radius pointed at Ian, while ghastly eyes still in the orbits of the skull looked accusingly at him. Ian searched frantically for help and saw the fire alarm, which he reached over to pull. That would bring help running, and he would have proof.

The ding, ding, ding of the bell kept ringing nonstop as Ian struggled to open his eyes. He had been dreaming again, and it was his damn pager. Sheepishly admitting to himself that he was actually grateful to have been woken from such a dreadful nightmare, Ian stared at the number. At least it was an outside phone. A cold breeze made him look down to find that the towel had slipped off him while he was sleeping, and he was now sitting stark naked.

Winding the towel around his waist, Ian was two steps away from the phone when Giselle, a female intern, walked in. "Hope you're comfy,

Ian?" She stared at his body, unaware that she had just missed getting the full Monty.

"There wasn't anyone in here, and I just closed my eyes for a minute." Why the hell was he trying to explain his lack of clothes?

"Never mind. I only came in to get a case file from the locker." She walked swiftly over to the row of cabinets that looked like they were rejects from an old high school. Once Giselle had the folder, she left just as quickly as she had entered the room, leaving behind the scent of some exotic perfume that had a remarkable effect on Ian. If it didn't have pheromones in it, it sure had something fairly powerful to arouse him so swiftly.

Dialing the unfamiliar number on his pager, Ian wondered who had called. After just two rings, the phone was picked up, and a female said in a breathless voice, "It's on for tonight!"

Unable to recognize the voice, Ian stood holding the phone at a distance, racking his brain. It had to be a prank call! "Who the hell is this and what's on for tonight?" he bellowed into the receiver.

"Ian! It's Marla!"

"Oh! Sorry. You woke me up, and I'm not quite with it yet. So give me the details."

"Why were you sleeping? It's only 2:30 in the afternoon!"

"I just can't seem to get caught up. So I catnap whenever I get a chance. Back to tonight, who is going to let us into the morgue?"

"Roger is the security guard that I told you about who owes me a favor. And Samantha is also working the midnight shift tonight, so she has agreed to help us. Do you want to contact Harold?"

"Sure. Where are we going to meet?"

"Tell Harold to show up at the entrance of the ER. Samantha said she would be waiting for him with a wheelchair so no one will question what he's doing in the hospital. She figured that if she wheeled Harold down to the path lab, it would speed things up."

"The path lab?"

"Yeah. Roger figures that if we meet outside the lab, it would draw less attention than if we have some of us standing outside the morgue."

"And what time are we meeting, Marla?"

"At midnight. Most people avoid the morgue at that time of night because of the ghost that is supposed to haunt the corridors down there."

"You've thought of everything."

"So you'll call Harold and make sure he shows up tonight?"

"You can count on me." *Damn,* he thought! He had really been looking forward to going home and hitting the sack early tonight. Now he had a midnight rendezvous in the morgue. Hell. He was doomed to have sleep deprivation until he hung out his shingle.

The door of the lounge swung open, and Frank Woo looked at Ian, still standing naked except for the towel. "Heard you had a couple real rough ones today?"

"Nothing I couldn't handle."

"So what are you doing?" Frank stared at Ian. It was a little unusual to be standing around with just a towel wrapped around your waist in the middle of the afternoon.

"I had a shower and dropped off to sleep before I could get dressed."

"Go home, Ian. I'll cover until Louis shows up."

"Really! Thanks, Frank." Ian strode quickly into the change room and was dressed and on his way out the door when he suddenly stopped. He had to call Harold before he left. Once inside the apartment, he knew that everything would leave his head, and he would be sound asleep before he knew it.

Dialing Harold's number, he hoped that he wouldn't have to leave a message.

"Hi!" Harold picked up on the second ring.

"Harold! Ian here. We're on for midnight tonight. Show up at the ER entrance, and a cleaner by the name of Samantha will meet you with a wheelchair."

"Great news, Doc. I was starting to get shack happy again!"

"And don't forget to bring your fingerprinting kit."

"You know me, Doc. Prepared for every situation. See you at the witching hour."

"Thanks, Harold."

"No problem, Doc. Hate to admit it, but I am really looking forward to examining the scene of the crime."

"Glad one of us is happy about this midnight rendezvous, Harold, 'cause I would rather sleep."

CHAPTER 42

Who's Not Dead?

*B*EFORE IAN REACHED the exit, he remembered a patient file still sitting on the reception desk. Confidentiality was strictly enforced, and Ian didn't want another "interview" with the dean. A glance through the glass partition revealed enough medical personnel in the trauma room that Ian would have only been in the way. He breathed a sigh of relief and sat down at the receptionist's part of the U-shaped nursing station.

Picking up the chart of the patient Ian had admitted earlier that day, he was deep into paperwork necessitated by the health care coverage when the phone rang. Looking around for Joshua or one of the nurses, it became apparent that they were otherwise occupied. Reluctantly, Ian picked up the receiver. "St. Cinnabar Hospital. How may I help you?"

"Hello. I'm looking for my grandson."

"What is his name and when did he come into emergency?"

"No! No! He's not a patient. He's a doctor." The woman sounded old and dotty on the other end of the line.

"If you tell me his name, I will pass a message on to him."

"Dr. Paul Cormorant. I'm his grandmother from Manhattan. We just arrived in town, and I want to take him out to dinner."

"I thought you died," blurted Ian.

"That's not funny, young man. Who are you? I'm going to report your impertinence to the head of the hospital."

"Sorry, ma'am! I didn't mean to be rude. Perhaps it's his other grandmother who died."

"Not as far as I know. Yvonne was quite well the last time I saw her. Now stop playing games and put Paul on the phone immediately!" This woman sounded like she was used to getting her own way.

"My apologies, Mrs. Cormorant. I must have your grandson mixed up with another intern."

"It's not Mrs. Cormorant. That's Yvonne. I'm Mrs. Lucinda Velvoline of the Boston Velvolines. Now put my grandson on immediately."

If the surname Velvoline was supposed to impress Ian, it didn't. He had never heard of the family before. "Please give me a number where you can be reached, Mrs. Velvoline, and I will have Paul call you as soon as he comes in. I promise!"

"Very well then." The woman rattled off a local number.

Both grandmothers were alive, so whose funeral did Paul attend? Ian tried to finish the chart he had been working on, but the memory of those twenty-four hours he had worked so Paul could goof off infuriated him. And to think Paul had used the funeral of his grandmother as an excuse! Ian looked at the rotation roster and saw that Paul was on the floor that afternoon.

He had to give Paul his grandmother's message anyways, so he paged him. Twenty minutes later, Paul phoned the receptionist desk. "Paul Cormorant."

"Hi, Paul. Ian here. I need to talk to you."

"I'm really busy here. Can't this wait?"

"No, you weasel! I had a very interesting conversation with your grandmother, the one whose funeral you had attended."

There was a long silence at the other end. Then Paul said, "It was my other grandmother."

"Not according to the dear woman I was talking to. She said that both of them were alive and well. So where did you go for the three days of compassionate leave?"

"Shut up, Ian. Someone might hear you! I'll meet you in the doctors' lounge in a few minutes. We can work this out, can't we?"

"It depends. Be there in exactly five minutes, Paul, or I'm going to the dean." Ian hung up and resisted the temptation to do a victory dance since the medical team who had been working on the MVA were leaving the trauma room. Not only did they have the downcast look of having lost a patient, but they might also ask him what he was so happy about. And Ian knew he had to keep Paul's secret so that he could use it for all it was worth.

Facing Ian in the lounge, Paul tried to convince him that he had a legitimate reason for taking time off. Although Ian had a reputation as a "pushover" among his fellow interns, Paul could see his arguments were completely useless. Ian suppressed his desire to yell and rant at Paul for using him, keeping a low and persuasive tone instead to convince Paul of his ruthless need for revenge and determination to carry through with his threats. Once Ian knew that he had Paul sufficiently intimidated that he could ask his fellow intern to do almost anything rather than get ratted out to the dean, Ian made tracks for the exit before another ambulance could pull into the bay.

CHAPTER 43

Midnight Madness

THE NIGHT WAS dark and dreary with a slow, steady rain that obscured the city lights. Larry was impatient to drop off Samantha at the hospital. She dreaded facing the interior of the morgue but couldn't help being excited by the prospect of being included in the search for evidence. Samantha had barely closed the car door when her husband pulled out of the circular drive, headed for the factory. Sometimes, Samantha wondered what the men did before their shift got underway. But she knew better than to question her husband who had been ill-tempered ever since he found out that he had to take her with him when he was on midnights.

There, standing on crutches next to the sliding doors was the young man Marla had described for her. "You must be Harold, the police officer," she commented.

"Yes, ma'am. And you must be Samantha."

"Give me a minute to get rid of my things, and I'll go find a wheelchair for you."

"Don't rush, ma'am. I know I'm early. It's just that I'm awfully bored stuck in my apartment with this leg." Harold pointed to the plaster cast.

Samantha waddled off to the change room, where it took several minutes to get the combination lock to open. While she was trying to get it open, Samantha thought about how different her husband, Larry, was from that nice young cop. Though she did think Larry was the best thing since sliced bread when she first met him, Larry had changed a lot since they tied the knot. But that young Harold would never turn out like her husband, self-centered and boorish. Samantha was sure of it.

Pushing the wheelchair she found in the corridor outside the reception area of the ER, Samantha went to collect Harold. She was going to suggest that they would go to the small coffee room where all the vending machines were until it was time to go meet Marla and Ian.

CHAPTER 44

Revelations

*H*AROLD EXPECTED TO be twiddling his thumbs for a while because Samantha had ambled away from him as if hurry wasn't in her vocabulary. He was grateful that Samantha hadn't returned yet when he noticed a gorgeous dark-haired nurse with oriental-looking eyes walking down the corridor toward him.

There was something familiar about the woman, but Harold couldn't remember where he had seen her before. And he wondered if this luscious lady would consider going out on a date with him. It was too bad that he wasn't in uniform since it tended to impress the female population and enhance his chances for a date.

Sauntering up to him with a sensual sway to her hips, the nurse said, "You must be Harold, Ian's friend."

Damn. Harold knew then that he had two chances with the beautiful woman standing in front of him would go on a date, fat and slim. "Yes, ma'am, I'm Harold. And you must be Marla."

"Wasn't there a woman in a cleaner's uniform here to meet you?"

"Yes, ma'am, Samantha met me at the door. She's just gone to get a wheelchair so we can move a bit faster."

"I might as well wait for her too. I thought I recognized you from the last summer you worked in the hospital. You probably don't remember me because we were seldom on the same shift. But the patients all commented on how polite and considerate you were."

"Now that you mention it, I do recall seeing you at least once. They had me doing permanent midnights so I'm surprised anyone saw me all the time I worked here. You were here the day they brought that fireman in. Terrible thing that was."

Marla didn't want to tell him that it was her father so she just said, "Yes, awful."

"One of the regular guys had a wedding, so I did the 8:00 to 4:00. The fire was in the high school I attended so I took a personal interest."

"You went to Hawthorn High School?" Marla shook her long dark hair, trying to get rid of the image of her father's severely burned body.

"Yeah. We never had anything happen like that when I went there. But I heard from the cops on duty that night that the fireman went in after some kid who was supposed to be still in the building. It turned out that the stupid bugger had skipped out and didn't tell anyone."

"Oh!" Marla wanted to change the subject but was so distraught at the memory of her father that she couldn't think of anything to say.

"Yeah. Turned out it was Dr. Whales's son Carson. His teachers were glad when Dr. Whales saw the handwriting on the wall and sent Carson off to a private school somewhere. Everyone suspected that Carson not only skipped out on class but was the kid who threw the Molotov cocktail in through the window and started the blaze."

Gulping back a mixture of rage and tears, Marla silently prayed for Samantha to return so that she would be able to change the topic of conversation. Standing and waiting, she couldn't trust herself to say anything for fear that she would break down and cry. Marla never knew who her father had gone back into the burning building to rescue until tonight. And it was more than she could bear. *Hurry up, Samantha,* Marla prayed.

Unaware of the effect he was having on Marla, Harold continued, "My dad said that if that kid had his ass whipped when he started stealing from the corner store, he would never have gotten into so much trouble. But you know what it's like being a doctor's kid. They get everything given to them. And then when his parents divorced, I think they both tried to buy him off.

"The only thing that saved that kid from ending up in juvey was the old man's money. He made one hell of a big donation to the fireman's ball and the policemen's association right after that fireman died. And all of a sudden, the investigation got bogged down and ground to a halt. I still say that Carson did it. And got off scot-free too."

The sight of Samantha pushing the wheelchair down the hall saved Marla from any more of Harold's views. Grateful to the cleaner for deflecting his attention, Marla tried breathing deeply and humming to herself the way she had learnt to do in the yoga classes. Despite her efforts, she could feel the tears welling up in her eyes. She never knew the bastard had a son or that he was responsible for her father's death.

"Guess everyone is nervous," commented Samantha, taking Marla's solemn look as a sign that she was not looking forward to their expedition. Marla hung back as Samantha pushed Harold with his crutches perched sideways on the chair. By the time they arrived at the rendezvous point, she felt like she was less likely to break down.

CHAPTER 45

Gotcha

*R*OGER HAD BEEN pacing the corridor outside the path lab, stopping to stare at his reflection in the window and admiring the uniform. He had tried to join the police force and was bitterly disappointed when he hadn't made the cut. But the security guard uniform got him enough looks from the women that he had rationalized that it was better than no uniform.

At first, he had tried to weasel out of opening the morgue for Marla. Roger was not in the habit of doing favors, especially ones that could cost him his job. But Marla was different. She had helped him when he had nowhere else to turn. And he knew that he could trust Marla to keep her mouth shut. It was the other three people involved who worried Roger. He had no way of knowing whether this Dr. McLintock, Harold, and Samantha wouldn't go blabbing about it to their friends. One word and his job would be done for.

"Hi! How long have you been waiting?" Marla watched Roger as he paced up and down the corridor. She knew he really hated using his position as a security guard to let them into an area they were told to guard.

"Not long."

"We're all here except for Dr. McLintock then?"

"He was supposed to be here right at midnight," Marla said as she glanced at her watch pinned upside down on her uniform.

"He'll be here," said Harold.

"Why don't I let the three of you in the morgue and let this Dr. McLintock in when he shows up?" Roger really didn't want to stand around in the corridor with a group of people any longer than he had to.

"Good idea. That'll give me a chance to get started," Harold said as he opened the tackle box on his lap.

The doors swung open, and Samantha pushed Harold into the morgue followed by Marla. The cold and creepy silence made her shiver involuntarily.

"You okay with this, Samantha?" Marla put her hand on Samantha's arm.

"It's scary, but I'll be okay."

"Which slab were you laid out on?" asked Harold.

Samantha studied the row of stainless steel drawers and shook her head. "I'm really not sure. I thought that Marla and Dr. McLintock would be able to tell you."

Marla paced the room, trying to remember. "It was the last one on the far wall," she said, walking over to it. The night she walked in and saw Ian standing over a woman stretched out fully clothed in a cold box was something she would never forget.

"Let's get started then." Harold hobbled over and put his tackle box on a stainless steel table that he wheeled close to the drawer. "I'll concentrate on this one, but if we have time, I will dust the two lockers on either side just in case."

"Sounds good to me. How can we help you, Harold?" asked Marla.

"Samantha can help support me, and you can hand me the celluloid tape when I ask for them."

At first they seemed to be working at cross-purposes until Harold got a system going. Then they found the work proceeded quickly and were ready to leave by 12:30.

"The doctor still hasn't shown up," commented Harold as he packed away the marked envelopes and gear.

"We didn't need him anyways," said Marla.

"Can I lock up now?" demanded Roger as they left the morgue.

"Yep. And thanks for your help." Marla gave Roger what she hoped was a seductive smile as they went their separate ways.

Samantha had suggested that she would wheel Harold to another exit to avoid drawing attention toward them. Marla was headed to the nearest phone. She wanted to know what happened to Ian.

CHAPTER 46

Sleep Deprivation

*T*HE CONSTANT RINGING just wouldn't stop. Finally, he rolled over and grabbed the phone.

"Ian? Are you okay?"

"Marla. What time is it?"

"Past midnight?"

"Shit. Sorry. My alarm didn't go off."

"Don't worry about it, Ian. We pulled it off without you. Harold got his prints and will give you a call as soon as he gets a match or anything that looks suspicious."

"He'll need samples of the people who work in the morgue every day."

"I beat you to it. Had quite a day wining and dining the morgue staff. One of the ladies in the cafeteria saw me stuffing glasses into my purse. I'm sure she thinks I'm refurbishing my kitchen with hospital dishes."

"You really have been busy! Good thing somebody's on the ball."

"Go back to sleep, Ian. You sound like a drunk. We can discuss this later at that special restaurant you promised to take me to."

"Good idea. Sorry, I missed all the fun."

"Good night, Ian."

He didn't need any more encouragement and laid his head down.

The suffocating rectangular hole where he lay had sides too slippery to climb and too high to vault. A faceless form in a long trench coat stood above him, shovel full of dirt, poised to begin burying him alive. He tried to scream at the man, tried to move, wave, and shout that he was alive, but he was paralyzed. Not one finger would uncurl from the terrified fist that remained motionless despite every attempt to move it.

Suddenly, something began vibrating on the ground beside him, and he hoped that the man who had begun to fling the piles of earth down onto him would hear it and stop.

Jumping upright with a gasp, Ian knew it was another nightmare, and it was his alarm going off amongst the bedsheets that jolted him out of the ghastly dream. Already 7:30, Ian raced to the shower and slid into the rumpled trousers that he had dropped on the floor. Not sure that he had time to make the weekly conference in the auditorium; he raced out the door and down the street. When he glanced at his watch again, it was as if his eyes were playing tricks as he realized that not only would he be on time, but he also had more than half an hour to spare.

Slowing down to a trudge, Ian forced himself to focus on what they had found out since the night he discovered Samantha, in an effort to forget the nightmare that still replayed in his mind.

Deliberately reviewing everything he had discovered to date, Ian wondered if Harold would come up with anything from the dusting of the morgue lockers or if their efforts to find out who put Samantha in the morgue was doomed to failure.

The break-in of the dean's office did not eliminate him as a possible victim. With the fingerprints of Rebecca Cornwell on the carafe, Ian wondered what the woman was doing in the boondocks of Slatington after having lived most of her life among the elite society of New York.

Before he finished running through the list, he was standing in front of St. Cinnabar.

CHAPTER 47

Facing the Dean Again

*F*OR SOME STRANGE reason, Ian felt as if he was looking at the entrance to St. Cinnabar Hospital for the first time. Burnished yellow light made the facade of the old building seems like something out of the old west. The stone front and strange construction made the building appear as if the architect had tried to copy the entrance to Versailles and failed. Whatever the builder's intentions, the hospital looked bizarre, like a transplanted castle from some spooky European country like Transylvania.

Hunkering down against an unusually cold blast of wind swirling around the entrance, Ian hurried up the steps. He was standing by his locker and almost changed when his pager began vibrating.

Ian swore under his breath as he wondered who the hell wanted him that early in the morning. A number that he did not recognize had come up on the display. Sullenly stomping to the phone on the wall, Ian dialed the extension.

"Dean Chesterton Whales's office," chirped the high-pitched cheery voice of Brandi, the secretary. "How may I help you?"

Stop being so damned cheerful this hour of the morning, Ian wanted to say. Instead, he asked, "Did someone from your office page me?"

"And who am I speaking to?"

"Dr. McLintock."

"Oh yes, Dr. McLintock. The dean would like to see you as soon as possible."

"Did he say what for?" Icy fingers gripped his guts as he wondered if the dean had discovered that Harold and Marla had broken into the morgue last night. But there was no way he could have found out. *Get a grip*, Ian told himself. *It's your guilty conscience that is going to give you away.*

"No. But the dean did say it was very important. Shall I tell him that you are on your way?"

"Yes." Hell and damnation, what did the old man want to see him about now? Ian wished that he had never found Samantha or gotten involved in their amateurish investigation. He knew better than that. To succeed, you needed to keep a real low profile in the hospital and mind your p's and q's. He had broken every rule for success and was sure that he not only wouldn't get the residency that he wanted but might even be asked to leave the hospital.

His feet felt like they were lead as he walked the long corridor to the dean's office and hesitated for a few minutes before knocking. Brandi opened her door and said, "You don't have to knock before entering my office."

Dumb, Ian told himself. Of course, he knew enough to walk into the secretary's office. Maybe it was wishful thinking on his part, hoping that somehow there wouldn't be anyone there.

"Have a seat, Dr. McLintock. The dean will be with you in a minute."

Ian had just rested his buttocks on the hard chair when the oak door crashed open, and the huge man stood staring at Ian with a stern look in his eyes. "Come in, young man."

Ian trudged in and stood waiting.

"Have a seat." The dean waved to the leather swivel chair opposite his side of the desk.

Ian wanted to deny the knowledge of everything immediately but knew that rule number one was to shut up and always listen. There were several questions that could land him in hot water, and he wasn't sure which one the dean was about to ask him.

"Do you know why I called you to my office?" demanded the dean.

"No, sir, but I'm sure you will tell me."

"Don't get smart with me. You have ruffled quite a few feathers, and they were upset enough to come to me."

At that point, Ian was really puzzled, having given more than several individuals reason to be upset if they found out what he had been up to. But he considered confessing that he wasn't sure what the dean was talking about would be the best route to take.

"I have no idea whom I have upset. And I would appreciate it if you would enlighten me as to what I am supposed to have done." Feeling a little more secure and self-righteous, Ian stared back at the huge man facing him.

"Did you look in on a patient by the name of Elliot Steelman?"

"Oh! Dr. Conway is a friend of Elliot's and was worried about him. He said that Elliot was in extreme pain and the morphine they were giving him wasn't helping. Dr. Conway asked me to look in on his friend. So I did. I know that I should have talked to Elliot's doctor first. But the man was moaning so loud that you could hear it coming down the hall. I found his nurse, Marigold, and asked her if I could give Elliot his next morphine injection. Then I stayed with him to see whether the drug was working."

"And was it?" The bushy eyebrows were raised in question as he stared at Ian.

"Yes. Elliot fell asleep and seemed to be relatively pain-free. I reviewed his chart and found that some nights his medication controlled his pain and other nights it didn't. I was going to talk to his physician, but I guess the nurse, Marigold, got to him first."

"She felt that you had overstepped your bounds and had made some insinuations about her care of the patient."

"That is the furthest from the truth. The nursing staff all like Marigold because she is willing to take on the care of the dying. And in Elliot's case, he is a fright to look at with his face ravaged with cancer. So I told her that the staff all praised her. And I was just looking in on Elliot because I had promised a friend of his. She must have misconstrued my intentions."

"Ahem." The dean cleared his throat and stared at Ian before continuing. "Perhaps I had better clear one thing up."

"What's that?"

"This is confidential, not even on the patient's chart. But the poor man's face isn't ravaged by cancer. When he found out that he was dying, he tried to kill himself. A family member tried to stop him, but he still blew away part of his face."

"Oh!" Ian was too stunned to say anything else.

"So you see, we have to be careful because the poor man may be trying to speed up the process by claiming to have more pain than he does. There is a thin line between pain control and the point at which too much morphine can become lethal."

"You believe that Elliot might have been trying to use me?"

"Perhaps, perhaps not. But I will talk to his physician and explain that you had the best intentions and was not trying to step on his toes, so to speak."

"Thank you, Dean."

"And you had the patient's welfare at heart."

"Of course."

"Perhaps I will look into the pain management of some of these terminal cases. You probably don't know this, but my father died of cancer. It is brutal at the end. I always thought they could have done more to make his last hours less painful. But as a family member, I wasn't allowed a say. So you can be sure that I will follow up on this patient, Elliot."

"Thank you, Dean. I really appreciate that." Ian rose and leaned over to shake the man's hand.

"Just one other question, Dr. McLintock."

"What's that, Dean?"

"Any more progress on who put that poor woman, Samantha, wasn't it, in the morgue?"

"No, unfortunately. I have pulled in some favors to try and get to the bottom of it, but I'm not a trained detective and seem to be fumbling around in the dark."

"You will tell me if you find out anything?"

"Of course, Dean, you will be the first to know." Ian had his fingers crossed behind his back. The dean would be the last person he would tell unless he could hand over concrete evidence to the police.

"Drop in anytime you need to. My door is always open."

"Thank you!" Ian left the dean's office with what he hoped was a relaxed stride until he was out of sight. Then he felt his body wilt with relief.

CHAPTER 48

Tickets for Prints

*N*OW THAT THE grilling by the Dean of Medicine was over with, Ian remembered that he had promised Harold another pair of tickets to bribe the forensic technician to look up some more fingerprints, assuming that not all of them belonged to the people working in the morgue or on the hospital staff.

He walked to the nearest pay phone and called home. The Hornets had a short break between games, and Ian knew that one of the guys from his high school basketball team who had made the big league, Spiderlegs, would be home visiting his parents. Ian chuckled to himself as he thought about the coach saying that his teammate ran the length of the basketball court as if he had six legs instead of two. One of his teammates had yelled out, "Hey, Spiderlegs," and the nickname stuck. Ian had trouble remembering the guy's real name now.

Ian's dad loved to go over and talk to Spiderlegs whenever he got a break from being on the road and came home to visit his parents. It wasn't the first time Ian had used their friendship to get a couple of free passes to a game, and he wondered if the well would go dry just as he needed that one last pair of tickets.

The ringing stopped, and his father said, "Hi!"

"Dad, it's Ian."

"You aren't broke again, are you?"

"Naw. Need a favor and Spiderlegs should be visiting his parents."

"Yeah. Saw them dining out at the Superior Hotel Lounge. Must be nice to be earning that kind of money."

"So what were you doing there, Dad?"

"It's for sure your mother and I weren't out painting the town red. They needed a delivery from the hardware store, and I was showing Joe how to install this fancy new marble counter in their bar when I spotted Spiderlegs and his parents."

"What kind of mood was Spiderlegs in?"

"Ian, you don't want tickets again, do you? It's getting embarrassing. I might have pulled Spiderlegs from that well when he was a kid, but I think this is pushing gratitude a tad far."

"I wouldn't ask if I didn't need them, Dad. Besides, I can always give him free health care as soon as I'm finished."

"What are you doing with those tickets anyways? Scalping them to pay your way?" Ian's father had always been touchy about his inability to contribute more to his son's education, and it came through in the timbre of his voice. "It better not be for anything illegal, Ian!"

"Dad, just trust me. I'll explain when it's over."

"What if Spiderlegs says no this time?"

"He won't. That's why you don't want to ask."

"UPS again?"

"Yeah, Dad. The sooner the better."

CHAPTER 49

Detectives R Us

*H*AROLD WAS AWASH in celluloid tapes and all the glasses that Marla had brought over to him.

After seven hours of working at lifting fingerprints and then labeling them with the names provided by Marla, then peering through a microscope to match them up with those taken off the cold box, Harold had a crick in his neck and swore that he would never try for a job as a CSI, no matter how much his mother nagged him to change careers.

The accident had been a fluke. And besides that he had been watching videos on evasive techniques that stunt riders learned for motorcycle scenes. He was sure that he could avoid a repeat of what happened to him.

Staring out the window at the scarlet sunset, the phone rang. It took him more than ten rings to hobble over and grab the receiver from the cradle before the answering machine could pick up.

"Hi! I'm here!" Too many hours alone made him desperate for company, and he didn't want the person to hang up.

"Hey, Harold, how's the fingerprinting business going?"

"Hi, Ian. Damn slow. Want to come over, Doc? I could use some company."

"Yeah! I've got something for you in case we need to use your friend Dr. Mosey again."

When Harold told his uncle he needed to do another search, the sarge turned beet red and said, "No! Absolutely positively not." If Charlie hadn't been so browbeaten by his sister over the accident, Harold was sure his uncle would have refused to help him one more time. But Harold needed Dr. Mosey to help search for several prints that he couldn't match up to the hospital staff.

It took another Sunday dinner and the Lakers game tickets before Charlie caved in. And that was only because the detective in charge of the office was away at a crime prevention conference that was being held in Michigan.

That Wednesday night, the sergeant brought in a couple of boxes of doughnuts and coffee for everyone just as the basketball game got underway. He had already approached Dr. Mosey, who was beginning to wonder if there wasn't more than just a learning experience involved in all these fingerprint searches. But the Lakers tickets helped him turn a blind eye to the reason behind Harold's sudden interest in forensic science.

With everyone occupied in the staff lunchroom, Harold followed Dr. Mosey through the double doors to the forensic lab, and they set to work searching for a match for the fingerprints Harold had.

Dr. Mosey played the game of mentor and let Harold log on to the computer and feed the information in. It was faster this time because Harold knew what he was doing. They got a match fairly quickly, and Harold could hardly contain his joy, especially when the name of a PI flashed on the screen.

A PI named Reggie Johnson had been in the morgue and left evidence that he was involved in putting Samantha Rutledge in the locker. The big question was why? Despite Harold's impulse to log off and go tell Ian, he fed in a couple more sets of prints until he was sure Dr. Mosey didn't suspect that Harold had found out what he was looking for.

Finally, they joined the others in the lunchroom for the rest of the game. Much as he wanted to take off, it would have looked strange for him to cut out before they knew who had won, especially since they had a pool on the outcome of the match. When he did finally return home, it was too late to do anything else. And the late night in the morgue had left him exhausted, so he hit the sack after setting his alarm.

CHAPTER 50

Marigold

*B*Y THE MIDAFTERNOON of the next day, Harold dragged himself out of bed and began running through the yellow pages of the telephone directory. It wasn't long before he found the name Reggie Johnson and the ridiculous name for his investigation company—Detectives R Us. Unable to believe his eyes, Harold wondered if it was a joke or a front for some other business. And what would a PI be doing hiding a body in a morgue at St. Cinnabar?

The city registry and city directories at the library did not add much to what Harold already knew about Reggie Johnson. It was time to stake out the office of the idiot that named his business Detectives R Us.

But the cast had prevented Harold from driving, and he wasn't about to show up at the hospital and get it cut off until he knew for sure that he wouldn't need to do another search on the police computers. If his uncle ever found out that he had been hobbling around on crutches for an extra two weeks for the sympathy that he got, Harold would never hear the end of it. Even his mother's Sunday meals wouldn't save him from his uncle's wrath.

He couldn't wait to see the doc's face when he heard the news. And he needed someone to drive him to the building on the east side where Reggie had his office.

When Harold got around to calling Ian, it was 3:00 in the afternoon, and there was no answer. Harold was fairly sure that Ian would be too busy to return an outside call.

Too keyed up to just sit and wait, Harold decided to go and visit some old friends at the hospital while looking for Ian. The trip by taxi was as fast as two blocks in a vehicle could go, and the cabbie gave Harold a dirty look as he handed over the measly fare.

"Yaw coulda walked this far!"

"On crutches?"

"Why, when I was a kid, I walked twenty miles to school every day. Even after I broke my ankle, I still made it."

"Ya, ya, ya," muttered Harold under his breath as he hobbled to the hospital entrance.

There were no ambulances waiting at the door, and there was only the security guard at the triage desk. "What's going on?"

"Oh, they're having a meeting since it's quiet for a change."

"Is Dr. McLintock in the meeting too?"

"Naw. He had something to do up on the floor. Seems that he looked in on another doctor's patient, and now there's a hell to pay. Can't see why it should be any different than the other patients who play guinea pig to the baby docs who are learning the trade."

"Where is this patient he was checking up on?"

"Don't know for sure. But rumor has it that it's an old veteran by the name of Elliot Steelman. Just a minute, young fella, and I'll look up the room number fer ya. Don't expect ya wanta wander too many miles with a leg in a cast. Here it is. Room 6-705."

"Thanks!" Harold made his way to the bank of elevators and thanked his lucky stars that he had worked summers in the hospital. Otherwise, he would have been lost in the twisting and turning of the hospital corridors that were the result of each new addition that was added on to the old building.

The nurses' station was empty, except for a very young-looking nurse with carrot-red hair and a cute turned-up nose. Staring at her, Harold forgot why he was there. He wondered if she had a boyfriend or was married. But she looked almost too young to be a real nurse. More like a student or a very recent graduate.

Gena sensed that someone was staring at her and turned toward Harold. A glance at his crutches and she came over to him. "Can I help you? I know you don't belong to this floor, but a lot of patients get lost."

"Uh." Harold found himself tongue-tied as he stared into the eyes of the most beautiful girl he had encountered in a long time. Realizing he was acting like a dork, he said, "I'm not a patient. I'm looking for Dr. McLintock, and the security guard in emergency said he thought that he had come up here to see a patient named Elliot Steelman."

"Oh! I hope not. Marigold was furious that he had interfered the other night. I tried to stop her, but she said she was going to report him to the dean. Dr. McLintock is barred from seeing Elliot again, the poor dear."

Harold wasn't sure whether carrottop meant Dr. McLintock or the patient. "What did Dr. McLintock do to get Marigold so upset?"

"She takes care of all the terminally ill patients. But Dr. McLintock said he wanted to give Elliot his morphine injection the other night. I know he didn't mean anything by it, but Marigold took offense."

"Can I talk to Elliot? I'm not a doctor, and I can't see why Marigold would object to me seeing him."

"You really don't want to see him, Mr . . . . ?"

"Harold. What's your name?"

"Gena O'Hallahan. Pleased to meet you, Harold. I just want to warn you that Elliot's face is eaten away with cancer, and the smell is dreadful even with the air fresheners."

"The poor man!"

"Yes, and that's him moaning and groaning down the hall. He carries on like that for hours even after he has his pain medication. Sometimes, I can hardly stand to listen to him."

"Well, I'm going to go see Elliot. I'm a cop and have seen some dreadful things. At least this guy is alive."

"Okay, but if I come in, you better leave fast because I don't want to get Marigold angry again. If she stops taking care of Elliot, we will all have to take a turn, and I don't think I can stomach it."

"That gruesome?" Harold felt a flutter as his stomach flipped over, and he wondered if he would get through this without being sick. Nothing would be more embarrassing than having to run out of a patient's room to go and barf.

Gena walked with him up to the doorway and called in, "Elliot, you have a visitor if you're up to it?"

"Sure, send the poor sod in. Maybe it will take my mind off myself." A glance into the room where almost no light penetrated made Elliot appear as only a fuzzy profile from that distance.

But Harold found that as he got closer the gaping maw that was the left side of Elliot's head upset him profoundly. "Hi. You don't know me, but I'm a friend of Dr. McLintock. My name is Harold or Harry if you prefer."

Despite the hole that enlarged his mouth, Elliot was able to speak. "You're a brave lad, Harry. Most people see me and flee back out the door. I take it you have a reason for coming to see me?"

The sound of Elliot's voice coming through in distinct understandable words surprised Harold, who expected to find that the nasty-looking gap caused the poor man to slur his speech at least.

"I was looking for Dr. McLintock but figured that since I had got this far, I might as well find out why he's in such trouble."

"For making sure I got my morphine the other night?"

"Guess so. Gena said that Marigold complained to the dean that Dr. McLintock was interfering with another doctor's patient."

"She's a strange one."

"Marigold?"

"Yeah. She takes on all of us terminal cases because the other nurses don't want to, and then they are so grateful that they turn a blind eye. I hate to say this, but the only night I felt I could stand the pain was the night Dr. McLintock came and gave me my injection."

Harold whistled low. "That sounds like someone is stealing drugs."

"I know what it sounds like, young man, and I would appreciate it if you wouldn't repeat it."

"Tell me everything you know about this nurse, Marigold."

"She doesn't talk much, but I hear the gossip at the desk. They think they are far enough away that I can't hear. But I survived the war because I could hear the enemy's footsteps in the dead of night. Woke up and saved my unit one night when we were out on reconnaissance."

"So what do the other nurses say about Marigold?"

"She came to this hospital about six months ago. Marigold had been working in Australia and then in New Zealand and then in England. Only stayed about eight months in each country. One of the nurses said she thought Marigold had a secret that she was running away from. But the others told her to be quiet. As long as Marigold was willing to take the worst patients, they didn't care what she was hiding."

"That's interesting. Marigold comes into your room quite often?"

"Of course!" Elliot gave Harold a look that said "how dumb are you." "She is my nurse!"

"The glass of water there, have you touched it since she brought it in?"

"No. Why are you asking such dang fool questions?"

Removing his handkerchief from his pocket, Harold carefully picked up the glass by the rim and hobbled over to the sink, where he poured out the water. "I'll get Gena to bring in another glass for you."

"You're taking my water glass? What for?"

"You're better off not knowing. May I come back and see you again, Elliot?"

"If I'm still here, you're more than welcome. I don't get a lot of visitors." Elliot gave a chuckle as the irony of the statement struck him funny.

"Thanks, Elliot. And keep listening. I want to know as much about Marigold as you can find out."

"That's easy, young man, 'cause I ain't going anywhere."

After hobbling back to the nurses' station, Harold was relieved to find that Gena was still alone. "Would you get a bag for me?"

"You're stealing a water glass?"

"I'll return it so technically I'm not stealing, just borrowing. And Elliot needs a new glass of water."

"Who are you, Harold?"

"If you go out with me, I'll tell you." Harold tried to make light of his invitation as if he was just joking.

"Okay. When?"

Harold was too stunned to say anything at first. Then he mumbled, "When are you free?"

"How about this afternoon? There's a good matinee at the Tivoli Theatre that starts right after I finish my shift."

"What time is that?" Harold glanced down at his watch.

"In half an hour. But I can't leave immediately because I have to give my report. Why don't you stick around and we can stop at my place on the way to the movies?"

"Sure. Where shall I sit and wait?"

Gena led Harold to a stool just on the other side of the glass partition that hid him from view. But he saw that the windows acted like two-way mirrors, and he watched as another tall lanky nurse in an old-fashioned nurse's uniform walked into the medication room. "Who's that?" Harold whispered.

"Marigold. Don't worry, she can't see you here. Besides, I'm going to tell her that you are my brother who's come to pick me up. She would never object to having someone from my family come in and wait for me." Gena had an innocent look on her face that would have fooled the most suspicious person.

Harold wondered if he was the first person Gena had sit here and wait for her to get off duty. But he really didn't care at that moment. She was going on a date with him, and he had totally forgotten why he had come to the hospital that day.

"Stay here until I come and get you," ordered Gena. She turned and walked briskly down the hall while Harold watched Marigold prepare the medications for the night through the glass. The woman seemed to be very meticulous and did nothing out of the ordinary. Then she rolled the small medication trolley out of the room and down the hall where she disappeared from sight.

Preparing for a boring wait, Harold sat and thought about what had brought him to St. Cinnabar. Suddenly, he remembered and felt stupid. He was looking for Ian. Too bad. He had a date with Gena, and his information could wait.

Staring out the double set of windows that worked almost like a horizontal periscope, Harold wondered if Gena used this spot to sit and rest while making sure she wasn't caught goofing off on the job. No one could possibly sneak up on a person sitting where Harold was.

With no one in sight, Harold started at the sound of a creak, as if a door was being opened somewhere. Then he saw it. The fire door that should have been locked on the stairwell side opened a crack as a young man with matted hair, scruffy beard, and filthy jeans slid into the corridor, a ring of keys in his hands.

Harold figured the man was about his age, although it was hard to tell with the layer of dirt that seemed to cover him. It had to be a junky who'd managed to steal some passkeys to the hospital. Sure enough the guy checked to make sure no one was at the nurses' station and then walked into the medicine room.

What happened next shocked Harold and made him sure that this guy was not only familiar with the hospital and nurses routine, but also the medications locked in the small cabinet. The guy brought several small brown glass vials out of his pocket that looked exactly like the ones stocked in the cabinet.

Harold was sure that if he could test the contents of the vials being used by Marigold, they would contain nothing more than sterile water. And the druggie was taking vials of morphine that were supposed to be used on patients like Elliot.

No wonder the poor guy was still in agony after Marigold gave him his injection!

It was a relief to know that the nurse was completely innocent and that this lowlife who appeared to know the hospital like the back of his hand was stealing the drugs intended for pain-racked cancer patients. Harold wished he had his fingerprinting kit with him. But all he could do was sit and wait for Gena to finish her shift. He would have to sneak back in and hope that the cleaning staff didn't pick that night to spit and polish the med room.

Finally, Gena sauntered up to the alcove where Harold was sitting and said, "I'm ready to go!" She looked even more gorgeous with the smile of freedom that comes at the end of the day.

"When we stop at your place for you to change, I need to make a call. Would that be okay?"

"Of course." Gena walked slowly alongside Harold as he used his crutches to slow their exit from the hospital, hoping that he might see Ian on their way out. No such luck! He would have to call him from Gena's apartment.

Even though Gena slowed her walk to match Harold's slow hobble down the sidewalk, they seemed to fly down the street. Much to Harold's surprise, when they reached his apartment building, Gena turned to walk up to the entrance. Harold asked, "You live here?"

"Yeah. Why?"

"'cause I live here too!"

"Small world, isn't it?" grinned Gena.

"Listen, Gena, since we're in the same building, why don't I go up to my apartment to make the call. And then I'll swing back down to get you."

"Sure. But you could use my phone."

"It's kinda private. I will tell you about it later. But right now I have to keep it a secret." Harold hoped Gena wouldn't take offense.

"Hey. It's none of my business. Just show up in the next fifteen minutes, or I'll think you are trying to weasel out of our date."

"Oh no! I really want to go out with you!" Suddenly realizing what he sounded like, Harold blushed.

"Go make your call!" Gena stopped at an apartment on the first floor and inserted her key.

Harold made a note of the number and hobbled on to the elevator.

He could hardly contain himself as he grabbed the phone and dialed Ian's pager. It took almost ten minutes, and Harold was about to give up when Ian answered his phone.

"Hi, Doc. Got some good news for you."

"You sound out of breath. Where are you? The receptionist said that you were looking for me and went up to Elliot's room. But Elliot said you had left a while ago—with that sexy young nurse Gena."

"How did he know? Listen, Doc. Gena is waiting for me downstairs. We're going on a date, but I need to tell you something. Can I drop around tonight?"

"Not even an act of God can stop me from getting some sleep tonight. Whatever it is can wait until morning."

"But, Doc, I know whom one set of prints belong to."

"Who?"

"Some small-time private eye by the name of Reggie Johnson. Calls his agency Detectives R Us. Do you think he graduated from high school?"

"Probably not. Do you know where to find this guy?"

"Yep. Only I need someone to drive me over to his building. But there's something else that I found out while I was waiting for Gena to get off duty."

"And this can't wait?"

"There's some druggie with a set of passkeys to the hospital who is replacing the vials of morphine with ones that look the same. This guy looks like he really knows what he is doing."

"And why do you want to see me tonight?"

"I need to get this guy's fingerprints off the drug cabinet before they get obliterated."

Giving a long tired sigh, Ian said, "Okay. But don't stay out too late on this date."

"Don't worry, Doc. We're going to an afternoon matinee."

"And you are going to drop this woman off at her apartment to come and see me? What line are you going to feed her so she isn't offended?"

"My grandmother is seriously ill, and I have to go visit her."

"I think I've heard that line before."

"See you about seven, Doc."

"Have fun, Harold."

When Frank Woo showed up early for his shift in the ER, Ian could hardly believe his eyes. It didn't require much arm-twisting to get Frank to cover for him, so Ian left early and headed home to bed. Only this time he made sure the alarm was set for seven that night and not the next morning. He knew that the druggie Harold saw could point them in an entirely new direction.

It seemed like Ian had only put his head down when the annoying ring of the alarm clock woke him. It was dark out, so Ian knew that he hadn't slept twelve hours like the last time. Then he heard a loud banging on his door.

"Give me a minute, Harold," he yelled out as he stumbled around, found the light switch, and slipped into his jeans. Opening the door, he saw Harold standing there with his famous tackle box. "Come on in. I've got to finish dressing."

Harold was propped up against the side of the chesterfield when Ian returned fully clothed. "Got any ideas how we can get in there without getting caught?"

"Yeah. I've been thinking about it since you told me. I think Elliot will help us out if I explain the situation."

"You gonna call a cardiac arrest and get everyone in his room?"

"Yeah! You must have been thinking the same thing, Harold."

"The idea did occur to me, but I wasn't sure whether there was a law against call a false cardiac arrest or whether you would go for it."

"It will work, but I may have to face the Dean of Medicine again."

"Why?"

"I've been ordered to stay away from Elliot because Marigold complained that I was interfering with another doctor's patient."

"So you shouldn't be there?"

"But I have some friends who owe me a favor and will be more than willing to show up if I ask them."

Ian picked up his phone and dialed a number while Harold waited. Their side of the conversation let Harold know that Paul Cormorant, the intern Ian was talking to, had no choice but to help. That Ian had found out something that could get the guy kicked out of medicine. Even though the guy was upset about the blatant use of blackmail, he agreed to run interference.

There was a smirk of spiteful pleasure on Ian's face as he hung up the phone and said, "When we get there, Harold, we wait for the call for a cardiac arrest. I stand guard, and you dust and lift prints as fast as you can. Understood?"

"Sounds good to me, Doc."

CHAPTER 51

Blackmail Works

*P*AUL CORMORANT WAS waiting by the elevator when Harold and Ian got off. "If I get in trouble over this, you're going down with me, Ian!" The surly look on his face made the intern look infantile.

"Elliot knows the drill. He will back you up if half the hospital comes running."

"What about this Marigold? How do I explain my presence in his room?"

"You were walking down the corridor when you heard him moaning. When you walked in and checked on him, he didn't have a pulse. Come on, Paul. You didn't have any trouble lying about your grandmother."

"You are going to hold that over my head forever, Ian?"

"Only when I need something. Now go call a cardiac arrest and keep everyone busy as long as you can. But try to hold off on the paddles. I don't think Elliot would appreciate getting zapped when he doesn't need to be."

"You are a real . . ."

But Ian had already left and didn't hear what Paul called him.

CHAPTER 52

Casing the Joint

"*THAT WAS FUN* last night," commented Harold from the backseat of his car.

"Glad you enjoyed it 'cause I almost lost it when that nurse showed up."

"But Gena likes me, and when I showed her my badge, she was totally impressed. We're on again for tonight."

"How did your Uncle Charlie take it when you asked to do another fingerprint search?"

"He said he would only ask Dr. Mosey if hell freezes over. Someone told Uncle Charlie that Dr. Mosey is gay. And now Dr. Mosey had this idea that Uncle Charlie is making a play for him by using me, if you get my drift."

"That must make the sergeant really nervous, having the department head of CSI romantically interested in him. So how are you going to find a match to your prints?"

"I'm thinking about it, Doc. Might have to make a little visit to the station late at night and try running the search without Dr. Mosey."

"Don't you have to have a password?"

"Hey, Doc, this Dr. Mosey let me see everything. I know the password. I just got to pick my time real careful so I don't get caught. First big homicide, they'll all be out in the field, and I walk in, do my search, and walk out before they come back with their evidence."

"So how are you gonna know when?"

"I've got some friends monitoring the police band. They'll call me on my cell phone as soon as something comes up."

As they motored through the city toward the address that Harold had found in the city directory, it became obvious that Reggie Johnson of Detectives R Us had not built up a lucrative clientele.

By the time they passed seedy-looking tenement buildings and pulled up in front of a high-rise building that looked like it was ripe for the wrecker's ball, Ian looked at Harold in the backseat and asked, "You sure you want to go through with this?"

"No turning back now, Doc. Besides, even the lowlife that lives around here wouldn't pick on a cripple."

"I'm not sure about that, Harold." They both watched as two kids with tattooed arms and hunting knives hanging from their belts swaggered by. Rake thin with nose and lip rings, they were dressed alike, except the one had green hair and the other purple.

"Shouldn't they be in school?" asked Harold.

"Probably. But if you were their teacher, would you send the truant officer out to retrieve them?"

They both laughed, releasing the tension. "You wait here, Doc. I'll go up and see if I can hire this dude to find the hit-and-run driver who did this to me."

"Good angle. If you're not back in half an hour, I'll come looking for you or call the cops."

"Whatever." Harold maneuvered himself out the back door and pitched himself upright onto the crutches. In a few minutes, he had hobbled across the litter-strewn street, past a grungy-looking homeless man who looked as though he should be in a retirement home and not lounging on the hard cement of the roughest section of the city. He muttered something to Harold as he hobbled by. The shake of his head told Ian that Harold must have told the man he didn't have any change on him.

Inside the filthy entrance that had remnants of a more prosperous past as a posh office building, Harold surveyed the elevators and hoped they worked. The board with the names listed on a panel had its glass shattered, and the razor sharp fragments stuck out around the edge. The name of the detective agency was still legible despite missing letters. Harold headed over and pushed the buttons and prayed. There was no way he wanted to make it up six flights of stairs on crutches. The ding and opening doors were music to his ears, despite the smell of urine and a sticky puddle in the corner of the lift.

Hopping off at the sixth floor, he saw that the cleanliness of the building had not improved with elevation. Making his way past piles of litter, there appeared to be no signs of life despite the list in the lobby. Trying the door of the office with Detectives R Us, Harold found it locked. He pulled out a lock pick and thanked his lucky stars that his uncle had befriended an old ex-con who had been sent up for burglary.

Crusty Smelton had no family and did odd jobs for food. It was during the last year Harold was in high school that he got Crusty to teach him his trade. With time hanging heavy on his hands with his leg in a cast, Harold had brushed up on his lock-picking skills.

One glance and he knew that the cheap dead bolt would be a cinch as he worked away in plain view, secure that no one was around to see what he was doing. And even if there was someone, they probably wouldn't care.

Once inside, Harold went to the only filing cabinet and found that most of the drawers were empty. The phone was disconnected, and the office appeared to no longer be in use. "Where did you go, Mr. Johnson?"

He knew the man was still in town because his fingerprints were on the morgue locker. But he no longer ran his business from this less than stellar establishment. It would have been too easy to just walk in and hire the guy.

Back in the lobby, Harold looked at the list of other occupants and made a quick list. He could always give them a call from home and try to locate Reggie that way.

"You didn't take very long," commented Ian as he opened the back door for Harold.

"The guy has up and moved out of the best prime real estate in the city."

"Oh yeah. Just where I'd like to set up my practice when I am finished my residency."

"The rent should be real cheap. Not too many customers vying for the office space down here, Doc."

"Ha! Ha! Guess we'll have to try and run down Mr. Johnson another way."

"Yep. But I haven't given up yet, Doc. You just drive me home, and I'll get started chasing this guy down."

"Back to the police headquarters and their data banks?"

"Maybe. And just maybe I won't need them this time."

"You're the detective, Harold. I've run out of ideas."

"One thing we need is a picture of this guy. Too bad I didn't think of that when I was looking up the fingerprints."

"Yeah, it would help to know what Reggie looks like because he may still be lurking around the hospital dressed as an orderly or a cleaner."

"I've got an idea, Doc." Harold flipped open his cell phone and talked to his uncle.

With just his side of the conversation to go on, Ian knew they were about to change directions.

"Instead of taking me home, drive me over to the police station. Uncle Charlie said that if I want to use the computer again, I'd better do it now 'cause the chief is expected back from Detroit this evening. And they just had a triple homicide on the north side near the bay. Boy, I am glad I brought the tackle box along for the ride. Now we don't have circle back to my place and pick it up."

"So what made your uncle change his mind and decide to help you one last time?"

"He's really curious and wants to know what is happening. I figured if I let him think about it, he would come around."

Harold slid out of the backseat, maneuvered himself upright on the crutches, and hobbled off toward the entrance of the police station. Pausing, he turned and said, "Just drop the keys in my mailbox. Uncle Charlie will drive me home. And I'll call you about getting a photo over to you."

Ian watched Harold disappear through the door before driving off. He had forgotten what freedom a set of wheels gave you. After parking the car around the corner, he jogged back to Harold's apartment, dropping the keys in the mailbox. He really didn't have much hope that this Reggie Johnson was going to be easy to find or that he would tell them why Samantha Rutledge had ended up on a slab in the morgue. But it sure stopped life from getting too boring.

CHAPTER 53

If It Walks and Talks Like a Duck . . .

*H*OBBLING PAST A bunch of misfits sitting on the hard narrow benches lining the wall made of stark gray concrete blocks, Harold tried to block out the stench of fear-induced body odor. The foul smell of sweat mingled with farts gave the station a real atmosphere that it could have done without.

At the end of the hall, Harold saw his uncle waving him on toward the partitioned area where the forensic office door was.

"Got a head start on you, my boy," he whispered when Harold reached him.

"What did you get?"

Waving some pictures under Harold's nose, his uncle beamed. "Didn't even have to use one of those dang computers. We have a file with all the local PI's pictures in it. Some jerk without enough to do had spent some time compiling it a while ago. Almost forgot all about it until you called. Then I remembered it got stashed away in the back room 'cause nobody thought we'd ever have a use for it."

Harold studied the picture his uncle had handed him. "With mousy brown hair and washed-out gray eyes, this guy looks like he could blend into any crowd if he wasn't so tall."

"Yep. That's what makes somebody a good investigator. If he doesn't look the part, no one ever suspects what he's up to."

"I need about ten copies of this picture, Uncle Charlie. The doctor is gonna keep an eye out around the hospital. He figures this Reggie may be impersonating an orderly or cleaner to have gotten into the morgue without anyone seeing him."

"So when are you gonna tell me what this is all about, Harold? Here I am putting my career on the line to help you and you won't tell me what's going on."

"Sorry, Uncle Charlie. The doctor had to sign a nondisclosure clause so the hospital wouldn't get sued."

After giving a low whistle, the sergeant shook his head and left Harold, standing with the picture in his hand. It was while Harold was busy photocopying the picture that he overheard a couple of the beat cops talking about the triple homicide on what they lovingly referred to as "rich bitch" row.

"That should keep the geeks out there crawling around on their hands and knees filling their little plastic baggies until the wee hours of the morning."

With the lab empty, Harold punched in the password and was finished with his search in less than half an hour. He could hardly believe whom the prints belonged to. But it sure explained his familiarity with the hospital and how he managed to get passkeys to everything.

Harold hated to wait until morning but figured the doctor probably needed sleep. And it was too late to go looking for either Reggie Johnson or this kid who was stealing drugs from the hospital medicine rooms. So he hobbled over to his uncle's desk to wait for a ride.

CHAPTER 54

Sleepwalking

"*YOU DIDN'T TELL* me about the ghost of St. Cinnabar," Ian accused the old black orderly as if he had deliberately lied to him.

Mo flashed his broad pearly white smile that creased his coffee-colored skin into a mass of wrinkles that showed his true age. "Ian, there's lots of spirits haunting this old hospital. It was built on top of an old Civil War hospital. Some nights down in the tunnels, you can still hear those young soldiers screaming as they had their shattered limbs sawed off without any anesthetic. They died in agony, and now they walk the tunnels in search of their missing legs."

Ian stared at Mo to make sure the old orderly wasn't pulling his leg. "So how come I've only seen one ghost?"

"Izzy was the only dead man who had a message for you, Ian. It takes a lot of energy to break through into the land of the living. And then the idiot who sees you doesn't always believe their eyes. Too scared to admit to themselves, let alone anyone else, that they've seen a dead person. So they pretend it didn't happen."

An awful ringing interrupted the conversation as Ian turned to answer his phone. But the receiver crashed to the floor, and he sat bolt upright in bed, opening his eyes. Ian knew that he had either been hallucinating or Mo's ghost had come to him in a dream. But it was so real that he felt his body quaking with fear. This had to stop. He was going to face another long day with next to no sleep.

The morning was a blur as Ian rushed to deal with an inordinately large number of casualties for that time of day. By noon, there was no one left in the triage area so he walked over to the nurses' station. "June, I've got to see someone up on the floor. So don't look for me in the lounge, just page me."

The nurse barely glanced at Ian from the mound of patient records she was dealing with and grunted, "Sure. Whatever."

Ian stopped at a terminal and checked to see if Lester Conway had a roommate. With a sigh of relief, he saw that Lester's roommate had been transferred to another room that morning. With any luck, Lester would be having a nap after eating lunch and wouldn't notice Ian.

As Ian tiptoed into Lester Conway's hospital room, he was delighted to hear the loud snoring. And Ian didn't have to pull the curtains around the bed next to Dr. Conway since they were already drawn. Taking off his shoes and putting them on the chair beside the bed, Ian lay down and closed his eyes.

It was a loud bang of the door closing that woke him. Ian glanced at his watch and was surprised to see that he had only been asleep for half an hour. It was too late to let them know he was in the room. And Lester seemed quite upset at his visitor.

"Helena, I don't know what you think you are up to, but I can tell you right now that I would never tell a complete stranger anything about you."

"Rebecca Cornwell isn't a complete stranger, and you know that, Lester!" The rage in the woman's voice was unsettling, even though Ian wasn't the target of her wrath.

"What do you mean, Helena? The poor woman has just lost her husband after thirty some years of marriage and decided to sell her home in New York and moved to Slatington. So what ulterior motives could Rebecca have?"

"That poor woman, as you so kindly put it, is Izzy's sister."

There was a stunned silence. Finally, Lester Conway asked, "Are you sure of that, Helena? You never met Izzy's sister. She arrived from Europe just months before his death. And before that, she was in a concentration camp."

"Izzy brought me back to his place one night, and I saw her picture on his nightstand. She still looks like him even now."

"Are you sure that you haven't made a mistake?"

"What do you think, Lester! It's too much of a coincidence that Rebecca left her rich friends and high society in New York to move to our tiny city of Slatington. You have to ask yourself what's she doing here?"

Helena's tone of voice made Ian cringe on the other side of the curtain. There was no mistaking the fact that she had just called Dr. Conway a dolt because he fell for Rebecca's poor widow routine.

"Even if you are right, Helena, that doesn't mean that Rebecca is here for any other reason than she wanted to escape the memory of her dead husband."

"Grow up, Lester. That's like saying that Chester became the Dean of Medicine to help educate young doctors or that he didn't deliberately make sure Izzy wasn't around to get the surgical residency that he wanted."

"You have your secrets too, Helena," Dr. Conway reminded her.

"And just what do you know?"

"Enough to ruin your position in this city. So you had better rethink your attitude. I'm the only person who doesn't have anything to lose here."

"You forget that Chester wanted to marry me. And he would have if his father hadn't found out about me. So I know about the paper you stole from Izzy. You can act as self-righteous as you want, but you knew that Chester and Leon were up to no good. You could have warned Izzy if you wanted to. But you caved in when Chester threatened to expose you for the thief you were."

"But I went to the professor and told him that Izzy had written the paper and that someone had stolen it. So Izzy wasn't penalized."

"But you forgot to tell the professor that you were the one who took it."

"Helena! This happened over forty years ago. Can't we let sleeping dogs lie?"

"I would be more than happy to forget everything, but Rebecca knows something, and she has been dogging Chester's footsteps around this hospital until he looks like he's about to have a nervous breakdown. And if he crumbles under the pressure, remember we could go down with him too."

"So what are you suggesting, Helena? That we try and get rid of Rebecca?"

"You are such a dolt. No! You're a widower, and she has no idea who you are. So marry her."

"You have to be joking!"

"If you are lucky, she may turn you down."

"Get out of here, Helena. I've had enough of you and your wild ideas. Until someone proves otherwise, I will assume that Rebecca is here as a volunteer and nothing else."

"Have it your way, Lester. But don't forget that I warned you."

Ian was dying to know what Helena was hiding but felt that he had to lie there and hope that Dr. Conway either fell back to sleep or decided to go for a walk. He really didn't want him to know that Ian had overheard their entire conversation. Just to be on the safe side, Ian turned off the sound on his pager so that he wouldn't give himself away. Time seemed to drag as he heard the long sighs from Lester in the bed next to him.

Suddenly, the door swung open again with such force that it slammed against the wall with a bang. "Chester! What are you doing here?"

"That's what I want to know about Helena. What was that bitch talking to you about, Lester?"

"Geez. I'm a sick man. Can't you two leave me alone?"

"Save it for the interns you're tutoring. This is your old classmate you're talking to. And, by the way, I want to know who that woman Rebecca Cornwell is."

"Not you too, Lester."

"You mean Helena was asking about her too."

"No. Helena thinks that Rebecca Cornwell is Izzy's sister. She has some wild idea that Rebecca is here to find out about Izzy's death."

"Is that what Helena said?"

"Yes. But I know how Helena's mind works. When your father hired that private detective and discovered that she worked for the British army under the name of Gretchen Filistein, he didn't exactly make her feel welcome the next time you brought her home."

"Helena didn't want anyone to know that she was Jewish nor that she had escaped from a concentration camp."

"But your father found out, didn't he?"

"Yes. And Helena found out about what we did to Izzy. So we have had a stalemate on our hands as long as Helena and I have something on each other."

"How convenient. Is that how she got to sit in on the board meetings?" sneered Lester.

"How did you know about that?"

"You forget, Chester, I have had nothing but time on my hands and many of the women on the Women's Hospital Auxiliary are lonely widows who love nothing better than to confide in me. If I were you, I would watch my back. Helena could sink your ship mighty fast if she ever let it be know what you and Leon did to Rebecca's brother."

"But she won't, Lester. Helena is smart enough to know that I can destroy her position in this community with a word in the right ear. So why don't we leave things as they are? Nobody need to be the wiser." Chester had lost all the bluster he had when he first came into the room. There was a tremor of fear in his voice that was unmistakable.

"Remember the saying 'the good die young,' Chester. You could add to that adage 'and those convicted of murder.'"

"But it was an accident, Lester. We never meant for Izzy to die."

"You'd have one hell of a time trying to prove it. All I did was steal a paper, and I've finished my career."

"Don't get self-righteous with me, you incompetent old windbag. If it hadn't been for Izzy, you would never have made it through medical school."

"Don't I know it. Not a day goes by that I don't regret not helping him."

"Just keep your mouth shut."

"Or what, Chester. You know, I've always wanted to go to Hawaii, but it's always been a little too rich for my blood."

"Blackmail? Here! It's worth the money to see the back of you, Lester!" There was the sound of paper rattling.

"Sounds good to me, Chester. And don't worry about Rebecca. I haven't told her anything. If she suspects what happened to her brother, that's all it is, just suspicion."

There was the sound of feet stomping out of the room.

"Hallelujah," breathed Lester, "I'm going on an extended vacation."

Just then there was a timid knock at the door. "Dr. Lester Conway?"

"Yes, dear. How can I help you?"

"I've come to take you down for a test."

"Oh. I'd forgotten all about the scan. Can't see what good it will do."

"Do you need any help getting into the chair?"

"No, darling. You just push, and we'll be on our way."

Ian sighed with relief as he heard the whisper of wheels fading down the corridor. His pager had been going off and would have alerted them to his presence if he hadn't turned off the sound. Not unexpectedly he heard himself being paged overhead, "Dr. McLintock, Dr. Ian McLintock."

After checking to make sure that Dr. Conway and the porter had disappeared down the elevator, Ian walked briskly down the empty hallway to the nearest phone. If his presence was really needed, he could use the tunnels. But first, he dialed the emergency department.

"ER, Joshua speaking. How may I help you?"

Stunned at Joshua's ultraprofessional telephone manner, Ian stood speechless for a moment. Then he said, "It's Ian. Do you know why they are paging me?"

"Nothing serious, Doc. The staff doctor just went in to take a look at this druggie who looks like he overdosed. So take your time."

"Uh, thanks, Joshua. It may take me a few minutes to get there. Will you cover for me if they ask?"

"Sure, Doc, no problem."

CHAPTER 55

Asking Marla

*T*HE GILT-EDGED ENVELOPE dropped through the mail slot as Ian was standing with nothing but a towel around his waist. It was nearly noon, and he was relishing the fact that Paul was covering his shift. There were swallows nesting in the eaves of the old house next door, and the amber light that filtered through the buildings gave everything the look of burnished gold.

Stooping down, he picked up what looked like an invitation. There had to be a mistake since only alumni, board members, and the incredibly wealthy patrons of the hospital were expected to attend the fifty-year medical alumni reunion. The hospital was a rumor mill with everyone guessing who would attend from the who's who of Slatington's elite society.

But the envelope was addressed to him. Inside the gilded invitation asked for Ian's presence and escort at the function. It didn't make sense except that the dean might feel some need to thank Ian for keeping the fiasco with Samantha quiet. That had to be it.

Ian had mixed feelings over the invitation because he wanted to go but had to find a date. And there was only one person he wanted to attend the function with him—Marla.

Despite being off work, Ian made a quick trip to the emergency department and got a dark look from Paul, who appeared to be swamped with a family suffering from food poisoning. "You here to help?" Paul yelled across the kids leaning over buckets.

"Nope. You look like you are handling the situation. I need to talk to Marla. Do you know where she is?"

Paul scowled and pointed to a curtained cubical at the far end of the department.

Before Ian reached the bed hidden by drawn curtains, Marla pushed her head through the opening and asked, "What are you doing her on your day off?"

"I need to talk to you if you have a minute."

"Give me five, and I'll meet you in the lounge."

Once he reached the silence of the room, Ian almost reached for his cup and some coffee. But the smell of burnt brew stopped him before he poured it. With nothing to do but wait and wonder what Marla's answer would be, Ian paced the room and cracked his knuckles. It was worse than being sent to the principal's office when he was a kid. He rehearsed in his head what he would say. But nothing he could think of seemed good enough. *Just spit it out,* he told himself.

Finally, the door creaked open, and Marla walked in. "What's so important that it couldn't wait?"

"Um. I got invited to the alumni party."

"That's wonderful, Ian. You will be able to rub elbows with some of the most influential doctors in this country. It may lead to an opening in one of the better hospitals."

"Yeah. But I need a date. You wouldn't consider, um, going to it with me?"

"I would be honored, Ian."

"You would? Of course. Um. Then I will pick you up at your place on Friday night?"

"Why don't you come over that afternoon and change at my apartment. Then you wouldn't have to pay for a limo. We could just walk across the street into the hospital auditorium."

"I can afford the limo."

"This is me you're talking to. I know you have gotten this far on scholarships and your father's support. Why waste money when we can get ready together and just make our entrance by walking over to the hospital? Unless you're trying to impress someone."

"No! So what time would you like me to show up?"

"Let's make an afternoon of it. Just relax and then change, unless you don't want to."

Want to? Ian couldn't believe his luck. "Sounds great to me. So about three? Will that be early enough?"

"I'll see you then. They probably won't serve the meal until later in the evening so I will prepare a light meal for us. Are you going to rent a tuxedo?"

"Still have the one my parents bought me for my sister's wedding. Hope it still fits."

An overhead page for Marla interrupted their conversation. "Got to go, Ian. But I am really excited about the gala. It should be fun!"

CHAPTER 56

Moonstruck

*T*HE WEEK WAS over before Ian realized. Vans from the city's finest interior design studio, set building, catering firm, and various other personnel had competed with the normal truck and delivery traffic at the unloading docks. There were murmurs of approval from several quarters at the lavishness of the affair being prepared. Others grumbled that the money would have been better spent redoing one of the dilapidated wings of the hospital.

With the construction of backdrops and decorations being put up over several days, workmen coming and going with loads of wood, Ian found himself wondering what the place would look like the night of the dance.

By three thirty on Friday, Ian was headed out of the hospital, arms full of dry cleaning, to the tiny cottage that faced St. Cinnabar. It was the first time Ian had ever set foot in Marla's house. It had been in her family for generations, and although she had mentioned selling it after her father died, she reconsidered. Not that there wasn't a long line of real estate agents anxious to put it on the market.

Before he could knock, Marla had opened the door. "Come in. Here, let me take that from you." Marla had the suit of clothes hung on a hook before Ian could protest. He had showered at the end of his shift but still felt like the smell of the hospital lingered on his clothing and hair.

"Sit down. Make yourself comfortable." Marla had put an old Frank Sinatra tape on, and while Ian sank into a comfortable chesterfield, she went into the kitchen. In a few minutes, she returned with a tray of drinks and sandwiches.

"Hope you like ham, tuna, and egg salad sandwiches?"

"Anything is great. I had no idea how hungry I was until I smelled the food." Ian found that he had wolfed down half the crustless sandwiches before he realized that Marla was in a dressing gown.

"Did I interrupt something?" he asked.

"No." She blushed and sat next to Ian. "I just thought I might as well be comfortable."

The filmy chenille drooped showing ample cleavage as Marla sat next to Ian and sipped her wine.

Her pink nipples strained against the thin material, and Ian found himself staring at Marla's chest. With effort, he forced his gaze up to her face and saw that her eyes were laughing at him. Gently she ran her silky fingertips across his lips and then leaned closer so that her scent made him only too aware of how close she was.

"Kiss me!"

Ian bent forward and ran his fingertips over her breasts as their lips touched in a silken caress. Suddenly, Marla was in his arms, her mouth hungrily searching his with her tongue. The overwhelming passion left Ian breathless.

Taking his hand, Marla led him to the bedroom. "Are you sure?" Ian whispered.

"Yes! For once don't be a gentleman, Ian." With those words, Marla let her robe drop to the floor and pulled Ian's hands to the rose buds that had been straining at the fabric just moments earlier. As he caressed her, Marla moaned, arched her back, and pulled him to her.

CHAPTER 57

The Dean Is Missing

*A*LUMNI FROM EVERY year paraded into the auditorium, dressed in their finest. Their wives and trophy wives dressed in gowns that would have put a good dent in most people's mortgages.

As they paused at the beginning of the reception line, Ian gazed at Marla, who radiated youthful elegance, outshining every other woman in the auditorium as her spectacular gown accentuated her perfect silhouette. The fuchsia color reflected off pale skin that covered an elegant bone structure worthy of a model.

"What are you thinking, Ian?" Marla's smile revealed her perfect white teeth as she beamed with joy.

"How lucky I am that you said yes."

The hint of pink began at Marla's cleavage and spread quickly up to her cheeks. She gave Ian a light tap on the shoulder, "Stop teasing. You're embarrassing me!"

"That wasn't my intention, but you look gorgeous in pink."

"Oh, look, Ian. Isn't that Rebecca Cornwell with Dr. Conway?"

"Damned if it isn't. The old guy really looks good once he has clothes on."

"Most people look terrible in hospital gowns. I am so glad he asked Mrs. Cornwell to come to the ball. She is a very attractive woman. Those volunteer smocks certainly don't do anything for one's figure. Who would have guessed a woman of her age would look that good in a Christian Dior creation?"

"Is that what it is?"

"Guess dress designers and haute couture aren't your specialty, Ian?"

"No. Medicine doesn't leave much time for other things. Guess we'd better move on, or the reception line will still be here when they serve the meal."

Ian steered Marla to the first of the board members standing on a slightly elevated platform with their wives at their side. Each one mumbled a meaningless greeting and swiftly passed on to the next couple.

As they searched for their table, Marla asked, "Why do they still do it?"

"Do what?" Ian thought the whole affair was anachronistic with its elaborate etiquette and the extent to which the committee had strived to recreate a ballroom scene out of a period movie.

"The reception line? What did you think I was referring to?"

"The whole thing is like a scene plucked out of some Southern cotillion, so why should they eliminate the chance for the mucky-mucks to show how important they are by standing in a row and shaking everyone's hand."

Even though they made fun of the event, Ian couldn't help feeling awestruck by the jewels on the women and the collection of gowns that must have put the world of haute couture into overdrive.

As the band played a waltz, many couples rose and showed that ballroom dancing still existed in all its elegance. "Shall we try out the floor?" Ian held Marla's hand, and they moved through the tables until they reached the swirling couples.

The idea of waltzing was so daunting that Ian had even signed up for dance lessons the week preceding the reunion, not that he didn't know how to dance.

Despite his humble origins, Ian's mother had the foresight to make him take dance lessons much to his chagrin. Now he wanted to hug her for making him do what every other boy in the town considered sissified activity. It only took a couple of lessons before Ian knew that he hadn't forgotten how to do the foxtrot, waltz, and the various other dances he would need for a night like this.

The evening meal was to precede the series of speeches, and the couples found their tables as the emcee picked up the microphone. A coterie of waiters and waitresses brought out the food to make the servings as simultaneous as possible. "This is so good," murmured Marla as she began the entree.

"Only the best for our alumni."

"How did you get an invitation, Ian? I don't see any of the other interns here?"

"Beats me. Guess the dean feels obligated to me in some way." Ian had confided in Marla about his suspicions and that he went to warn Dr. Chesterton Whales that he was the intended victim instead of Samantha.

"Well, at least the old goat shows someone some gratitude."

"You too?" Ian looked at Marla in surprise.

"You really don't have a clue about people, do you, Ian? You must be the only person on staff at this hospital that doesn't loathe the man."

"That's because I have no reason to. But I don't understand why you dislike him." Ian studied Marla's face as she grimaced and seemed about to clam up.

"Women tend to stick together, Ian. You hurt one of us and we all tend to turn on you, especially if you're a man."

"Oh. His first secretary that he fired?"

"Yeah, plus several other things that are probably best forgotten for the moment."

The soothing waltz music, low amber lighting, and genial ambience of the night had lulled Ian into a feeling of well-being until he looked over at the long table full of food. Standing next to it was a very tall man with a pencil-thin mustache and neatly trimmed goatee. He wore a short tailored white coat and trousers that identified him as one of the waiters hired by the catering team for the evening.

There was something familiar about the man that Ian couldn't quite place. No matter how he tried, Ian couldn't figure out where he had seen the man before and had decided to put it out of his mind when he realized it was the man's height that had jogged his memory.

The waiter resembled the picture Harold had given Ian of the PI Reggie Johnson. The mustache and goatee had changed his appearance, but the man's height had given him away despite the attempt at a disguise.

"Would you excuse me while I freshen up?" Ian whispered to Marla.

"My, aren't we formal tonight!" she bubbled with amusement until she saw Ian's face. "What's going on, Ian?"

"Tell you when I get back. I just need to take a closer look at someone." Taking a long way around to the exit brought him almost face-to-face with the man who had the demeanor of a maitre d' of an elegant restaurant. Ian knew he wasn't mistaken. He hurried out into the corridor and flipped open his cell phone.

After several unsuccessful attempts, he realized the hospital had a system in place that blocked all cell phones. Sighing with disgust, he trudged down the long hallway out into the warm night where he had better success.

"Harold. Can you get down to the hospital immediately?"

"Who is this?" demanded a sleepy voice.

"It's Ian. Sorry! Did I wake you up?"

"Yeah, man! Fell asleep on the couch watching TV. So what's going on, Doc?"

"You know that picture you showed me of Reggie Johnson?"

"Yeah!"

"Well, I think he got a job serving tables tonight at the reunion gala."

"You gotta be kidding, Doc. After all our efforts to find this joker and here he is working right under our noses. I'll be there."

"There's just one thing, Harold."

"What's that?"

"Can you try and dress up? If you're going to tail this guy, we don't want you sticking out like a sore thumb."

"Sure, Doc. Good thing I haven't got around to returning that tuxedo I rented for my cousin's wedding. Just give me a few minutes."

"I'll wait for you under the south-wing portico. You know where that is?"

"Yeah, Doc. I worked four summers in that hospital. There isn't any part of it that I don't know. See you in a jiffy."

Ian flipped close his phone and slipped it into his pocket. He hated standing outside while Marla sat alone. But he didn't want to miss Harold when he showed up. He just hoped that Reggie didn't suspect anything. If the man had even an inkling that they were trying to find him, he would be out of there in a flash.

Time seemed to stand still as Ian waited in the dark and listened to the sound of scurrying in the forested plot of land next door that had been left in its natural state. A screech in the woods nearby made Ian jump. Then he heard the flapping of wings and realized it was just an owl swooping down on some unsuspecting prey. Finally, he saw the low amber beams of Harold's old jalopy crawling up the street. Ian wondered why Harold was driving so slowly.

"Sorry to take so long, Doc. But I forgot to fill up with gas. Almost ran out before I got here."

"Well, let's hope Reggie doesn't hop in his car and take off."

"It's okay, Doc. I phoned Uncle Charlie. He's going to bring over a container full of gas and fill my tank. So lead the way and show me this guy."

Once inside the banquet hall, Ian was startled to see that the waiter had left his station. He glanced over the crowd on the dance floor and wondered if they were too late. Then he saw the man as he brought another platter full of food out to the long table.

"That's him," Ian whispered to Harold. "What do you think? Is it Reggie?"

"It's got to be him, Doc, unless he's got a twin. So what do you want me to do?"

"Come back over to our table, and we'll pretend you're a member of our party. Then you can mingle and see if you can keep an eye on Reggie. Find out what name he's using for this job."

"Good idea, Doc."

When they reached the table, Marla was almost at the exit, and she turned to give Ian a wave. "Must be going to powder her nose," commented Harold.

"Can't blame her. I left her sitting by herself for about twenty minutes. And most of these old geezers wouldn't give her the time of day because she isn't one of them." Ian looked at the head table and realized that the dean had left his place. Not that it was unusual with all that wine flowing for an elderly man to need to excuse himself.

Harold and Ian relaxed over the bottle of wine and discussed strategy. As the time dragged on, Ian wondered what was taking Marla so long. Then Dr. Reginald Hammersmith motioned for Ian to come up to the head table. "Guess you're on your own, Harold. I'm being summoned."

Ian walked up to where Dr. Hammersmith sat. "Would you go check on the dean for me? He's our first speaker, and he has been gone for fifteen minutes. Hope he hasn't decided to have a heart attack."

"Or got locked in the men's washroom?" Ian chuckled and tried to smile. But the icy cold fingers clutched at his chest, and he found it hard to breathe. Whoever had tried to kill the dean earlier might have decided that tonight would make an even bigger splash if he succeeded.

Walking out of the hall, Ian broke into a run as soon as none of the guests could see him. He tried the nearest toilets and found them empty. Then he raced down a flight of stairs to the office next to the main entrance. He stopped dead in his tracks as he saw the outer door of the dean's office was open.

Realizing that he would look like a fool if he raced in and found the dean sitting calmly at his desk, Ian walked toward the open door only to be rammed by Rebecca Cornwell. She had knocked the wind out of Ian as she raced past him toward the elevators.

He couldn't believe what he saw at first, and then, as he struggled to get his breath, Ian realized that Mrs. Cornwell's gown had been splattered with blood. The elevators closed behind the woman, and Ian watched as the lift went to the top floor. His first impulse was to race after the woman, but he had to check the dean's office first. What the hell would Rebecca Cornwell want on the top floor of the hospital?

A dim amber light shone from the inner office as Ian walked in. Lying on his back, a dagger sticking out of his obese abdomen, the Dean of Medicine lay spread-eagled on the plush sand-colored carpet, now stained with large rust-colored patch of congealing blood. At first, Ian thought the man was dead, but he soon felt a fluttering pulse in the man's neck. He felt the warm breath barely coming from the gaping mouth that had a ruby red trickle running from it.

Calmly dialing emergency, Ian recognized Louis's voice. "Whatca want?" he asked.

"Louis, it's Ian here. Someone's stabbed the dean in his office. Get down here as fast as you can. He's still alive but just barely."

"Holy shit. You're serious!"

"Just get here as fast as you can and have the staff alert the OR. He's going to need surgery fast if he's going to make it."

Once he knew help was on its way, Ian bent over and watched the painful rising and falling of the dean's chest despite the knife handle that protruded from his rotund belly. Ian couldn't help thinking about the irony of the situation. Most people die from being that overweight, but the dean's girth was probably what had saved him.

There was nothing he could do until help arrived, and it seemed to be taking an eternity. *Just don't go into cardiac arrest,* Ian thought. There was no way he wanted to attempt resuscitation with the knife still sticking in the dean. God only knew how close to a vital organ the blade was. A wrong move and a major artery could be sliced. As it was, the dean had not bled out copious amounts, which meant that whoever tried to kill him had missed the heart and any other vital organs.

"What the hell?" demanded Louis Parker as he and Steve Tragalar rolled the stretcher into the office.

"He's alive. I've got to go after the person who did this. I think she may have headed for the rooftop of the hospital." Ian didn't bother with the elevator, taking the stairs two at a time, grateful that he was still in good enough shape to do it.

CHAPTER 58

Rebecca

A VIOLENT WIND was banging the door to the roof against the jam, making the whole frame shudder with each impact. Solid black night and thick swirling mist acted like a wall, stopping Ian from seeing even two inches in front of his face. Even as his eyes adjusted to the gloom, it was only when a pale full moon peeked from behind thunderous clouds that Ian could see the faint streetlight that barely penetrated the shadows up to the tenth floor.

Mrs. Cornwell had to be out there, perhaps feeling her way slowly to the edge of the roof. Despite the urgent need to stop the woman, Ian had no choice but to grope his way slowly through the darkness.

He reached for his watch to see how much time had passed and realized that he had left it on the dresser, determined not to be ruled by a clock tonight. His only hope lay with the possible struggle going on within the woman.

Usually, suicides did not have the courage to jump immediately. Peering through the pea-soup-thick fog, Ian tried to make out the woman's silhouette against the wall. But even the edge surrounding the flat roof was impossible to see through the mist that had risen from the water lying on the warm roof.

Stumbling forward, Ian bumped into the ledge that ran around the edge of the roof. A ghostly shape that he recognized as the cooling unit rose up like a huge chimney. Inching around the perimeter, Ian stopped and listened for any sound that was different than the barely audible traffic from the street below.

All noises were so muffled by the fog that Ian was about to give up when he finally heard the faint sound of someone weeping. He stood still, trying to discern which direction the sound was coming from. Deciding it was hopeless, Ian groped forward, praying that he would find her before Mrs. Cornwell got enough courage to jump.

He felt her presence like warmth in the night before her tiny dark silhouette became visible. The muffled choking sobs crossed the space between them as he inched forward, hopeful that she was still too absorbed by her grief to realize that he was approaching her.

"Don't come any closer, or I'll jump," she sobbed.

Hell, now what? He had no training in suicide prevention. The only trump card Ian had was the knowledge that Mrs. Cornwell hadn't succeeded in killing the dean.

CHAPTER 59

Last-ditch Effort

"MRS. CORNWELL?" IAN hoped he had the right tone in his voice.

"Go away." The despair in the woman's voice was gut-wrenching. Ian had never thought that you could feel another's despair so intently. But he could and didn't know what to do.

"The dean isn't dead."

"You're lying to me!"

"Why would I lie?"

"You know what I'm going to do, and you can't stop me."

Ian took a step toward Mrs. Cornwell and immediately regretted it as she stepped up onto the ledge.

"At least tell me why you hate Dr. Whales so much? Don't you owe everyone an explanation before you kill yourself?" He had no idea if that was what you were supposed to say to a potential suicide. Maybe he should have pretended that she was just upset and not planning on taking her own life.

"He killed my brother." The racking sobs shook the woman's body so hard that Ian was terrified that she would fall.

"Who was your brother? I know that you have a good reason for being upset, but I am totally in the dark." *And it ain't just this pitch-black night either,* thought Ian.

"Izzy was in the same class as Dr. Chester Whales. He and another intern killed him."

"You mean that your brother was the Intern Isaac Steinman who died a couple of nights before he graduated?" Suddenly, Ian felt a cold pass through him, enough to make him shiver.

"Yes. They hated him because he was smarter than them. So they put Izzy on a slab in the morgue."

It all fit in. Izzy was the ghost that haunted the corridor outside the morgue. If Ian hadn't seen the apparition himself, he wouldn't have believed it possible. But now that he had this woman talking, maybe, just maybe, he could stall her until someone more qualified than him in suicide prevention arrived.

"What is your first name? I just know you as Mrs. Cornwell."

"Rebecca."

"My name is Ian. May I call you Rebecca?"

"Yes. What does it matter now?"

"Rebecca, how did you find out what had happened to Izzy?"

There was a long pause as Rebecca seemed to be mulling over whether she wanted to tell Ian. Then, with a deep sigh, she began, "After Sam died, I had to go through all his possessions. There were papers he had kept locked away. I always respected his right to privacy. At least, after I hired Reggie Johnson and found out that Sam had nothing to hide." Rebecca moaned as if just talking was too much effort.

"Who is this Reggie Johnson and why did you hire him?" *Keep her talking*, Ian told himself. *The longer I keep her going, the better chance of getting her to change her mind.*

"Shortly after Sam and I were married, he kept staying late at work every night. I felt that he only married me because he felt sorry for me. That he was having an affair on the side. So I hired a PI. I didn't want to pay very much because I was using the money Sam gave me every day for pocket money. It was a lot even by today's standards, but I didn't want to make any huge withdrawals from my bank account. Guess I was ashamed of hiring Reggie Johnson and not trusting Sam. But I had to know. And Reggie was the cheapest private eye I could hire."

"So this man, Reggie Johnson, started following your husband?"

"Yes. The name of the agency should have told me how low class the man was. 'Detectives R Us' was painted in bold letters on the door of this tiny one-room office that looked like it hadn't been cleaned in years. But, as I said, he asked for the least amount of money."

"And what did he find out for you?" Ian watched nervously as Rebecca leaned over the ledge and looked down. *For Christ's sake, don't give up now,* he muttered to himself.

"Reggie took money from me for two months and then finally admitted that Sam was just working late at the company every night.

He was doing research and needed to keep on top of everything that was happening in the lab. Once they made a breakthrough, Sam started coming home early again, and I felt so ashamed of what I had done that I never pried again. So when I found that he kept several of the desk drawers in his office at home locked, I never worried about it. He had to be careful that another company didn't steal their ideas."

"So what changed?"

"Sam died."

"And you were forced to look in the locked drawers?"

"Yes," Rebecca's voice trailed off in a sob.

"What did you find, Rebecca?"

"A letter." The words caught in a torrent of tears as she shook with grief.

"Who was the letter from?"

Several minutes went by as Ian wondered if he had lost the hold he had on the woman. He couldn't see her features except when the thunderous clouds parted briefly to let the pale yellow moonlight penetrate the pitch-black night. Then it seemed that the unbearable grief had aged Rebecca's face since the last time Ian saw her in the auditorium. Ian repeated the question. "Who sent Sam a letter?"

Finally, with a heaving breath, she answered, "Dr. Leon Finegard."

"Who is this Dr. Leon Finegard?"

"He was in the same medical class as my brother Izzy and Chester."

This was going nowhere. Ian knew that Chester was the Dean of Medicine and Izzy was probably Isaac Steinman, the medical student who was found dead two days before graduation.

"So he was a classmate of Chester Whales," Ian repeated. He was running out of stalling tactics and was hoping Louis or Paul would come up to help him soon.

"Yes. Leon and Chester grew up together. Their fathers were both famous surgeons."

"So Izzy was a friend of theirs?"

The laugh snorted out of the fragile woman's nose in distain. "Hardly. They picked on Izzy because he stood first in the class. Chester was afraid that Izzy would get the appointment at the hospital. So the two of them made life hell for Izzy."

"Didn't Izzy go to the authorities?"

"He felt that it wasn't that bad, at least not in comparison with what had happened to our family in Austria. Everyone was sent to the concentration camp where they died. I was the only one who survived."

"Oh!" Stunned, Ian just looked at the poor woman at a loss for words. Anything he could come up with would sound condescending.

"You asked about the letter." Rebecca sensed the impact her revelation had on Ian.

"Yes. What was in the letter?"

"It was a suicide note from Dr. Leon Finegard."

"Why would he send a suicide note to your husband, Sam?"

"It wasn't addressed to Sam." Rebecca choked back a sob and continued in a barely audible voice, "My husband must have opened it by mistake and knew what effect it would have on me. That's why he hid it all those years."

"He wanted to spare you the pain of knowing what really happened."

"Why didn't Sam destroy the letter then?" cried Rebecca.

Ian wondered the same thing. Rebecca's husband must have died suddenly, leaving behind things he would have gotten rid of had he known his life would end soon. It wouldn't be the first time someone was killed leaving behind secrets that should have been destroyed. He had to keep Rebecca talking and said, "Dr. Finegard must have regretted what happened to your brother."

"That bastard Leon Finegard set up practice. He put his part in my brother's death behind him as the lucrative practice brought him everything money could buy. It was only when he found out that he was dying of cancer that he decided he could not live with the guilt any longer." Hysterical laughter rang through the mist-filled air, adding to the already frenzied expression on Rebecca's face. Her carefully coiffed and sprayed hair, which was now standing on end, gave her the appearance of a madwoman, someone who had escaped from an asylum.

Rebecca repeated the words again as if needing convince herself, "To make peace with what had happened. Why couldn't he have left me alone? He never thought about how the truth would affect me."

"People who are dying are not always rational. As you said, he probably wanted to atone for what he did and thought that by telling you the truth, he would be forgiven."

"Forgiven! No. He wanted to pass his hell on to me. How did he ever find me after all those years?"

"What was in the letter, Mrs. Cornwell?" She was looking over the side into the black abyss below. If he could just keep her talking until someone with more experience than him arrived, perhaps they could stop her.

"In the letter?" Her voice seemed distant for a moment as if she had already left the land of the living. Then Rebecca sighed and said, "He confessed his part. Chester slipped Izzy a drug, and once my brother was unconscious, they put him on a gurney and covered him with a shroud so no one would suspect that they were delivering a live person to the morgue."

"But Izzy woke up in the dark prison of the morgue drawer?"

"Leon swore that they never intended to harm Izzy. That it was just a prank. But when they returned to take him out of the drawer, his fingers were a bloody mass from clawing at the metal. And Izzy was dead."

"He was scared to death," Ian murmured half to himself. "It is now standard practice in medical school to explain that extreme fear can kill. But Chester and Leon wouldn't have known that back then." It wasn't justification for what they did, but Ian had to keep Rebecca talking.

"That's what Leon had said in his letter, as if it excused what they did! He confessed his part in Izzy's death. He said that it would be the last thing he did before ending his pain with an overdose of morphine," Rebecca wailed into the white-shrouded night. "The bastard told me he killed my brother and then made sure I couldn't revenge his death."

"But you knew that Chester was still alive somewhere and you decided to track him down?"

"I had Reggie Johnson track down Chester Whales. And then I planned to make him pay for what he did to my brother." Words failed her as she began weeping uncontrollably.

"So you stabbed him?" Ian wondered if the emotion was helping or hurting his efforts to talk the woman down as another gust of wind almost pushed her over the edge. "Rebecca?"

There was no answer, and Ian despaired as he watched her swaying with each breeze. Finally, she stopped crying and said, "No!"

"But I saw you running away from his office. You are covered in his blood!" It was cruel to taunt her, but he had to keep her talking.

"It wasn't me. Someone beat me to it. They stole my reason for living. With Chester Whales dead, I have no reason to go on."

"But he isn't dead. At least he wasn't when I left him in the care of the other two interns."

"It won't work. I know you are lying to get me to come down."

"I have no reason to lie to you, Mrs. Cornwell. They were rushing him to the operating room when I left." Stumped for something to say, Ian racked his brain and then said, "So Chester and Leon moved Isaac's body so that no one would suspect what really happened."

"The bastards only thought about what effect Izzy's death would have on their careers if anyone found out. With nothing to explain why Izzy had died of a heart attack, the police didn't try to explore the state of Izzy's hands. In Leon's letter, he said that they suspected something had happened but did not want to investigate any further because they had no suspects and only rumors about the harassment Leon and Chester had put Izzy through. Without any evidence, the police weren't about to pursue the sons of two prominent physicians."

"And you never knew how your brother died until you found the letter in your husband's desk drawer?"

"No! I wished I had never found it. It was terrible enough to lose my family to those Nazi swine. But I couldn't bear the thought that poor Isaac had been scared to death. The hope of our family had died on a slab in the morgue." The wrenching sobs shook Rebecca so hard that Ian had no choice but to take a few steps closer.

The poor woman was in such a state that she seemed oblivious to Ian's approach. He watched in terror, sure that Rebecca would lose her balance and accidentally fall over the ledge separating her from instant death, her body shook with such violent emotion.

A weak light coming from the direction of the door made Ian want to turn around. But he was afraid to take his eyes off Rebecca. Finally, someone had come to help. "Hello! We're over here," he yelled.

"Go away! I will jump," shouted Mrs. Cornwell.

"Wait. You have to give him a chance." Ian kept his back to the doctor approaching them. He kept eye contact with Mrs. Cornwell and hoped to hell the guy was experienced at dealing with potential suicides. Then he noticed the startled look on the Rebecca's face, as if she knew the doctor.

Unwilling to take his eyes off her, Ian said, "Can you talk to Mrs. Cornwell please? I don't seem to be doing too well."

The doctor didn't say anything, and Ian could sense his movement toward Mrs. Cornwell until he was about two feet away from her. Not willing to chance even the slightest movement, Ian kept his eyes on Mrs. Cornwell, even though he wanted to see who had joined them on the roof, especially since his presence was having such a bizarre effect on the woman.

Rebecca looked terrified and overjoyed at the same time. Such a weird combination of emotions piqued Ian's curiosity, and he was about to turn and look at the other doctor when Rebecca stepped out from the ledge, arms extended as if to embrace whoever had come to rescue her. The words, "Izzy, you've come back," echoed through the mist.

Ian turned, and the image dissipated into thin air just as Mrs. Cornwell fainted into a heap onto the pebble and tar surface.

Ian muttered to himself, "What the tarnation was that?" But the brief glimpse of the apparition was enough for him to recognize the intern he had followed into the morgue the night he had found Samantha Rutledge.

Mrs. Cornwell's pulse was weak but steady. Only minutes later, Ian glanced up as the door to the rooftop was flung open, and the banging of heavy footsteps rang out across the roof. Several men wheeling a gurney came running, as the rooftop was lit up with floodlights.

"You did it, Ian," said Dr. Hammersmith.

"Help me lift her up." Ian wasn't going to try and explain what happened. He really didn't want to be relegated to the confines of a psychiatric ward. And he wondered exactly what this woman would say when asked about why she changed her mind.

CHAPTER 60

Dead Men Don't Tell

EVEN WITH FIVE strong men, maneuvering a loaded stretcher down two flights of stairs proved to be a daunting task. Once they reached the elevators, Ian breathed a sigh of relief.

"What made you go up to the roof?" asked Louis Parker.

"I saw her run toward the elevator when she left the dean's office."

"She stabbed Dean Whales?" Dr. Hammersmith gave Rebecca a strange look as he ran alongside the stretcher toward the emergency department, looking like an overstuffed penguin in his black tails and protruding stomach covered in an ultra-white shirt.

"It appears that she did." Ian knew it looked bad for the woman but had a niggling doubt in the back of his mind.

"Shit! Why would she do that?" Louis Parker shook his head in amazement.

"We should wait until the police ask her." Ian knew the woman deserved to have a lawyer present before they tried and convicted her on the way to the ER.

"I think I had better go and try to salvage the rest of the evening," Dr. Hammersmith broke away and walked briskly toward the auditorium.

"What do you think he's going to tell them?" Louis looked enviously after the older doctor's disappearing back as if he wanted to follow him and find out how he was going to deal with what would be the biggest news in the hospital's history.

"Why don't you go and find Marla and tell her that I'm going to be busy for the next hour or so." Ian really didn't want Louis around when Mrs. Cornwell came to and decided to use his curiosity to get rid of him.

"Really?"

"Maybe you could keep her company if she wants to stay for the rest of the evening."

"Sure. Be glad to." Louis left as they rolled the stretcher into the glassed cubicle.

Ian knew that once Marla found out what happened, she would want to leave. But this would give him a chance to revive Mrs. Cornwell and advise her to call a lawyer.

As expected, the detectives who had been waiting by the entrance came toward the room. Holding up his hand in a stop sign, Ian said, "Not yet, fellows. She's still unconscious, and until she comes around, there will be no point in having you in the room."

The older detective with a ruddy complexion and fifty pounds, too many on his stocky frame, shrugged good-naturedly. The thin detective with small beady eyes and a pallor that made him look like a walking cadaver looked angry and said, "We want to talk to her as soon as she's awake."

After sliding the glass partition shut, Ian pulled the curtains around the bed and felt Mrs. Cornwell's pulse. "Hi, how are you?" He knew that she had regained consciousness but was wily enough to keep her eyes shut until the police had left.

"Miserable. I should have jumped."

"No, you shouldn't have. We need to talk before the cops out there discover that you are awake." Picking up the phone on the bedside table, Ian handed it to the woman. "You need to call your lawyer now."

Meekly taking the instrument from him, Mrs. Cornwell dialed a number and waited. Ian was about to leave when she motioned for him to stay. "Jacob? Sorry to wake you at this time of night, but I'm in trouble."

There was a long pause as the man on the other end of the line spoke at length.

"No, I haven't said anything, and I will wait until you arrive. I'm at St. Cinnabar Hospital. All I can tell you is they think I stabbed the Dean of Medicine. But I didn't."

If he hadn't already heard Rebecca tell him that she didn't do it while standing on the hospital roof, Ian wouldn't have believed it. But the woman was so distraught that Ian knew Rebecca was telling the truth. The problem was, who did try and kill the dean and why?

Once Mrs. Cornwell was finished, Ian picked up the phone and dialed the main desk. "Can you tell me how Dr. Whales is doing?"

Joshua was on duty, and Ian stood with the phone growing out of his ear for several minutes, listening to the ward clerk fill him in on the latest gossip going around the emergency department.

When he finally hung up the phone, Rebecca demanded, "Well? Is he dead? Am I to be charged with his murder?"

Her dark eyes were filled with anger. Ian wondered if her rage had helped the woman go round the point of no return, whether Rebecca Cornwell would no longer want to hurl herself from the rooftop of some building. He sincerely hoped so as he told her, "He is in the operating room, and they think he will pull through."

"So he hasn't escaped revenge!" Triumph put a bloom of color in her cheeks.

Ian wondered what she meant, if Rebecca was still bent on killing the man. "If you didn't stab the dean, then who did?"

"I don't know. He left the head table after Dr. Conway went to the men's room, and I decided to confront him with the letter, to tell him that I knew he killed my brother, Izzy. But I thought the dean had also gone to the washroom.

When Dr. Conway came out and asked what I was doing, I just told him that I needed to speak to the dean before he gave his speech and was waiting for him to leave the toilet. Dr. Conway said the dean wasn't in there, so I went looking for him."

"And you went to his office?"

"Yes. But someone had beaten me to it. There was a dagger protruding from his abdomen, and I thought he was dead."

"How did you get blood all over you if you didn't stab him?"

"I was so furious that he had already been murdered that I hit him with my fists. Then, realizing that I couldn't kill him, I decided to end it all. And you know the rest."

"You pounded Dr. Whales with your fists because you thought he was dead?" Ian felt like there was an echo in the room, and he was it. There was no way to be certain, but if the dean appeared to be dead before Rebecca began striking him, the blows could have started his heart beating again by unintentionally performing external cardiac massage. He knew better than to reveal the irony to the woman whose sole purpose in life had been to even the score for her brother's murder.

A loud knock on the closed partition interrupted any further discussion. A tall stately gentleman dressed in a very expensive tailored suit strode past the two detectives. His gray-haired head held high, the man marched with a rigid military bearing that announced to the world that he was used to getting his own way.

Looking at Ian with piercing black eyes, he nodded his beaked nose and then extended his hand and said, "Jacob Mordicaie of Mordicaie, Steinwiez, and Phillips."

"Dr. Ian McLintock, Rebecca's physician at the moment." It was really hard to compete with a three-name law firm, but Ian was not about to let his position in the hospital be denigrated.

The detectives were so close that when Jacob Mordicaie backed up a bit; seeing that Rebecca's eyes were still closed, he stepped on the thin one's foot. Without apologizing, he said, "We need some privacy here, gentlemen."

With a huff, the two policemen turned and left. Ian noticed that Rebecca opened her eyes again as soon as they were alone with her.

"Jacob, you made excellent time!"

"My dear, Rebecca. How are you? Your chauffeur called just after you did and offered to pick me up. He is anxiously awaiting news of you in the limousine."

"Dear, Reggie, how thoughtful of him. Would you excuse us, Dr. McLintock?"

Ian was startled to hear the first name of Rebecca's chauffeur. He wondered if there was any connection to Reggie of Detectives R Us?

"Of course, Mrs. Cornwell. I will look in on you later." Ian left. There was nothing more he could do.

CHAPTER 61

Loose Ends

*M*OST OF THE staff suffered from the endless boredom that the dull daily routine in the hospital produced. Relief came from the occasional incident that set the whole place abuzz with rumor. The stabbing of the Dean of Medicine made for intense speculation as groups of cleaners, porters, nursing staff, and doctors huddled and exchanged the latest tidbits of information. As soon as he approached, Ian discovered the buzz of gossip stopped and multiple pairs of eyes stared at him as he walked by.

He spotted Marla at the triage desk trying to soothe Greta, who had pulled the short straw and was stuck doing the most detested duty of the ER. Eager for someone to talk to, Ian knew better than to disturb them. He waited around the bend of the corridor until Marla walked away from a still disgruntled Greta.

"Have you heard how the dean is doing?" he asked as she turned corner.

Marla apparently hadn't see Ian and jumped. "Hell and damnation, don't say hi or anything!"

"I'm sorry. I didn't mean to startle you."

Marla's normally pink complexion was a waxy white, giving her the air of having been under an extreme strain. "He's alive but hasn't woken up yet. Someone has been spreading the rumor that Rebecca Cornwell told the police that she didn't stab him." Marla stared at Ian with a scarcely disguised look of suspicion as if she thought he was hiding something.

"That's what she told me. But until the dean regains consciousness, there is little proof of her innocence." Ian wondered why Marla was acting so peculiar. "Do you have any idea who tried to kill him?" Ian asked.

"Why would I know anything more than you?" Marla blushed.

"It's just that you are acting guilty, as if you're hiding something."

"You're the one who found him with a knife stuck in his stomach."

"I can't believe we're having this conversation, Marla. Why would I want to kill the dean?"

Without warning, Marla started weeping. Ian grabbed her arm and steered her into an empty linen closet. "What aren't you telling me?"

After a few more sobs, Marla took a deep breath and said, "I hit him over the head with a paperweight."

"You did what? Why on earth would you hit the Dean of Medicine on the head? And what were you doing in his office?"

"He came over to our table while you were out, waiting for Harold to arrive. He asked me to meet him in his office. Said that he had something to discuss with me."

"The Dean of Medicine asked you to leave the biggest party in the history of the hospital to come and talk to him in his office? Why?"

"You sound like you don't believe me." Marla started crying again.

"Just tell me what happened."

"When I showed up, he said he wanted to discuss my application for the job of manager of the ER." Breaking down in tears, Marla's body shook so hard with emotion that Ian gathered her in his arms and handed her a handkerchief.

After a few minutes, Marla pushed her way out of his embrace and said, "He tried to force me to have sex with him."

"So he would endorse your application? That's harassment. You obviously said no. Then what happened?"

"He had me bent over his desk and his hand up my dress. I grabbed the first thing I could reach and hit him with it. He fell to the floor. I was sure that I had killed him. Then everyone said that you found him and he had been stabbed, so I thought you had followed me and saw what happened and . . ." Out of breath and crimson with shame, Marla stopped blurting out the details.

"No, I didn't know what he did, or maybe I would have tried to kill the horny old goat."

With a long sigh, Marla said, "What a relief. I was so worried that it was you that I didn't know what to do."

"So all the rumors about him are true!" Ian was livid with rage.

"He didn't succeed in raping me, Ian!"

"But he tried!"

"Someone else stabbed him. Who do you think did it, Ian?"

"Beats me. Everyone has an alibi so far." Although Marla was now in control, Ian drew her into his arms once more and described what happened on the roof of the hospital, including the ghost who saved Rebecca.

"How weird. You've seen the ghost twice now. And both times he helped you save someone."

"Yeah. But there's no way I could ever tell the police. They'd have me locked up as a lunatic. But I know Rebecca didn't stab the dean. That was why she was on the roof. Someone beat her to it, and she no longer had any reason for living."

"So everyone still thinks she tried to kill the dean? What's she going to do?"

"Rebecca called her lawyer when we took her down to the ER and was advised against making any statement. But I think the police are keeping an open mind. The only evidence against Mrs. Cornwell is her intense hatred of the man and the fact that she found him with the dagger sticking in his gut."

"Is that why they've posted a guard on the dean's room?"

"The police must believe Rebecca Cornwell is telling the truth, and the murderer may try and finish the job."

"Since Rebecca is on the psych ward and under lock and key, they don't have to worry about her."

"Exactly. I'm not sure what evidence they have for another suspect in the case, but they would look really stupid if they let someone else walk in and finish the man off."

"Who do you think it is, Ian?" Marla asked again, her eyes riveted on Ian's face, waiting for him to say something.

"What makes you think I would know?"

"You've got that look on your face, Ian. You know something that you haven't told me."

After a long pause, Ian said, "And I don't think I should either."

"Don't do this to me. You know I can keep a secret. What happened the day you went to warn the dean? I know you didn't see him because you came back right away and looked like you had run into a very embarrassing situation."

"Whatever gave you that idea?"

"You blush when something embarrasses you, and you were so upset that your face stayed red for almost an hour after you returned from the dean's office."

"He was banging his secretary," Ian blurted out, and then his face flushed red.

"What? You mean they were doing the down and dirty right in the dean's office? I guess that shouldn't surprise me after what he tried to do to me."

"It was only later that I discovered that the outer door was supposed to be locked, but this woman came rushing out and almost knocked me over. I was about to rap on the dean's door when I heard . . . er, uh."

"I get the picture. Who was the woman who almost knocked you down?"

"You remember when I met you in the cafeteria and asked you to point out the Dean of Medicine's wife among the Women's Hospital Auxiliary group that were having a meeting?"

"You mean his wife walked in on that?"

"No! I thought maybe the woman was the dean's wife and asked you to point her out to me. But she wasn't the woman who came racing out of the office that day."

"Who was she then?" Marla's curiosity had made her cheeks flush pink and her eyes bright.

"Hate to disappoint you, but I didn't find out."

"But you have a suspicion and you're not going to tell me?"

"Whoa, Marla. What I think and what I know are two different things. We should leave it up to the police to find the killer."

"Ian, if you don't tell me, I am liable to kill you!"

"Stop it." Ian knew Marla was joking, but he could tell that she was like a terrier that had gotten hold of a rat and wasn't about to let go.

"You owe me, Ian McLintock. So spill your guts."

"You have to swear to keep this a secret. It's based entirely upon unfounded gossip so it could be a pack of lies for all I know."

"Just tell me!"

"Sally said that the dean had tried to force the secretary before Brandi to have sex with him. When she refused, he hired Brandi and then let the other one go."

"I knew that!"

"Well, Sally said that the dean wouldn't give the old secretary a recommendation, and she couldn't get another job. That she was desperate. So it could have been her that came in to ask him to reconsider, and she stumbled on the dean and his current secretary. That would be enough to make her want to murder him, especially since he had fired her for refusing to do what Brandi was in the process of doing."

"So are you going to tell the police this?"

"I'm going to let them find out on their own. If I know, it can't be that hard for them to discover if they track down everyone who had an ax to grind with Dr. Chesterton Whales."

"What if they don't go looking for someone else and just assume that Rebecca is the killer?"

"She has one of the best lawyers money can buy. And she also knows a detective by the name of Reggie Johnson, who can ferret out the real killer."

"Aren't you being a little heartless?"

"I have spent way too much time as it is, on Samantha Rutledge and Rebecca Cornwell. You forget that I'm a doctor, not a private eye. From now on I'm leaving the detective work up to the police. That's what we pay tax dollars for."

"You haven't convinced me, Ian McLintock!" Marla glanced at her watch. "My break was over ten minutes ago. Do I look like I've been crying?"

"No. You look beautiful." Ian bent down and kissed Marla.

"Stop that. People will think we were in this closet for the wrong reason."

Ian grabbed a handful of linen and gave it to Marla. "Now they won't suspect a thing, especially if I wait a few minutes before leaving." Ian watched as Marla slid out the partially opened door and leaned up against the wall. *Who hated the man enough to stab him?* The dark quiet of the closet was broken by the pager in Ian's pocket vibrating. Grateful that he had reset the alarm so that it couldn't be heard a mile away, Ian ducked out into the corridor and was relieved to see that there was no one in sight.

The number on his pager was from outside the hospital so he knew it wasn't an emergency. Clicking the delete button, the number disappeared, and Ian trotted off toward the ER. He had only a month left of his rotation in emergency medicine, and it couldn't end too soon as far as he was concerned. Most of the mayhem that landed people in the ER could be avoided if everyone just slowed down and exercised some common sense. But it was too much to hope that human nature could be altered and with it the needless death and destruction that landed them in the trauma room. Within sight of the entrance, Ian recognized one of the detectives who had interviewed everyone at the alumni dance.

CHAPTER 62

Interrogated

"**D**R. IAN MCLINTOCK?" barked the hulking overweight detective.

"Yes?"

"Detectives Watsitou and Feldman." The heavy-jowled pudgy officer of the law appeared to be referring to himself as Watsitou since he motioned with his head toward his partner when he said Feldman.

"You seemed to have escaped us when we questioned everyone at the dance. If Mrs. DuCarthenson hadn't mentioned that you were there at the reunion, we would have overlooked you altogether." Dark eyes scowled at Ian as if he had deliberately left the dance to evade them.

Some people have really big mouths, thought Ian. "I presume that Mrs. DuCarthenson told you that I stopped Mrs. Cornwell from jumping off the roof of the hospital." Why did Helena have to bring his name up anyways? There were certain things Ian would prefer to ignore and was not a good enough liar to bluff his way past these guys if they decided to ask the right questions.

"You neglected to tell us that you were the one who found the dean with a knife sticking out of his chest," reproached the tall skinny detective named Feldman.

"That is easily explained. Dr. Hammersmith sent me to look for the dean because he hadn't come back and he was the first speaker of the night."

"So you think that clears you then?" The look that Watsitou gave as he looked up at Ian's six-foot-something frame was skeptical.

"No. But I had no reason to harm the dean."

"Rumor has it that you knew someone did have reason and you warned the dean to be careful. Who did you think had it in for Dr. Chesterton Whales and why?"

"It was pure conjecture on my part." Ian noticed several nurses who had stopped within earshot. "We better find somewhere private to talk."

"Why don't we go back to the scene of the crime, Dr. McLintock?" Detective Feldman steered Ian in the direction of the dean's office.

"Where I found the dean?"

"Yes. Will that bother you?" The look the detectives gave Ian would have made a guilty man sweat. But Ian knew he was innocent. He just didn't want to be the one to let slip that Marla had left earlier in the evening to talk to the dean in his office and what had transpired.

The long walk to the other end of the hospital took place in hostile silence as Ian tried to figure out what he could say so that he wouldn't appear to be holding back information.

As they crossed the yellow crime tape, the detective said, "For someone who hasn't anything to hide, Dr. McLintock, you have a mighty guilty look about you."

"You probably tell all the people you question the same thing. I don't imagine anyone likes being interrogated by the police during a murder investigation."

"Attempted murder. Dr. Whales is still alive, and if the guilty party were to confess, it would go a lot easier on them."

"Well, I didn't do it, and I certainly don't know who did. So I can't see how this will help you."

"There was an unidentified young man who joined you and your lady friend halfway through the evening. Who was that?"

"There were several people who joined us at our table. Could you be more precise, Detective?"

"Don't be coy with me, Dr. McLintock. Dr. Hammersmith noticed that you left the auditorium for some time. Then you returned accompanied by this young man who was not on the invitation list. Dr. Hammersmith mentioned that he took an exceptional interest in one of the servers who had brought in a plate of food."

The detective paused and waited for Ian to answer. When Ian kept silent, the detective finally said, "After Dr. Hammersmith sent you to find the dean, this same young man and the waiter disappeared. Don't tell me you have no idea who they were or why they suddenly left the hospital just as the dean was being stabbed."

"No, I don't know who you are talking about. If Dr. Hammersmith mentioned them, he must know who these men are."

"Do you know what obstruction of justice is, Dr. McLintock?"

Ian was livid to think the man was trying to intimidate him after all he had tried to do to protect the Dean of Medicine. "Yes, I certainly do. And I have spent way too much time trying to find out who put Samantha in the morgue." *Ooops, he really shouldn't have said that.*

"Who is this Samantha and why was she put in the morgue?"

"You are going to have to talk to the hospital lawyer about that one. We had to sign a confidentiality clause. Given the circumstances, Richard Lucresfeld would probably tell you what happened. It may not have anything to do with the dean's stabbing, but at the time I thought that the dean was the intended victim and not Samantha. I went to warn him." *Shut your mouth,* Ian told himself.

"Are you trying to tell me that you knew the dean was in danger weeks before this happened?"

"I didn't know anything for sure. But I warned him just in case my hunch was right."

"And what was the basis of this hunch?"

"You will have to talk to Tricky . . . eh, Richard Lucresfeld, the hospital lawyer. And that's all I'm going to say. Now if you don't mind, I have patients to see." Almost as if on cue, Ian's pager went off, and he looked for the nearest phone.

"You haven't heard the last of me, Dr. McLintock," sneered Detective Watsitou.

Ian had a patient waiting in the ER for him. It wasn't an emergency, just an old friend of Mo's to whom Ian had been giving free medical treatment. But he pretended that it was an emergency and took off in a rush toward the nearest stairwell, only too aware of the detectives' stare that was boring holes in his back.

CHAPTER 63

Chasing a Rat

MANDY WASHINGTON STARED at Ian with old eyes that looked out from remarkably wrinkle-free skin, considering the woman had to be close to a hundred years old. Once Ian had gained Mo's confidence, he found himself treating several other patients of Afro-American descent who could have attended one of the few free clinics. But Mo had sung Ian's praises and armed with his assurance that Ian was not only a good doctor but willing to help those falling through the cracks of the medical system for lack of money and private coverage, Ian found himself being paged on the odd occasion when a friend of Mo's, desperate for help, would show up at the ER. The staff turned a blind eye, and Ian relished the ability to really help people who had nowhere else to turn.

"When do you hang out your shingle, Doc?" asked Mandy as Ian listened to her lungs.

"Not for a couple of years if I get a residency here."

"Good!" exhaled Mandy.

"Why good?" Ian asked in surprise.

"'Cause that means I can still see you. Once you get a highfalutin practice, you won't want any old black woman showing up on your doorstep."

"You will always be welcome on my doorstep, Mandy. I owe that much to Mo."

"He said you ain't got no airs. Shore miss him badly."

"So do I, Mandy. So do I." Ian went to the medical room and searched for the samples left by the pharmaceutical representative and found enough pills for a month. Returning to the bedside, he held

Mandy's hand and slipped the packet into her palm. "This should keep you going for a while."

Suddenly, Ian found himself in a bear hug that only the old who have worked a lifetime doing manual labor can give. "God bless you, boy! Mo really hit the jackpot when he found you."

Embarrassed over the praise, Ian closed the curtain around the bed and said, "Take your time dressing, Mandy, and remember, you can see me any time you want, even after I'm a highfalutin doctor."

Walking toward Marla, Ian asked, "Anything else for me?"

"Nope. It's quiet on the front. You off somewhere?"

"Unfinished business. Just page me if you get busy. Paul should be in shortly since he's covering for me again." Ian gave a wicked laugh.

"He regrets what he did to you," said Marla.

"And he will continue to for as long as I can hold his grandmother's funeral over his head."

The exit was close to the examining stall, so Ian slipped out before anyone else could ask him for help. With all the nightmares, Ian still had avoided using the tunnels. But the maze running under the hospital cut the distance he had to travel in half. And Ian wanted to try and see the dean since he heard that Dr. Whales had regained consciousness.

Unlocking the door at the bottom of the unused stairwell, the hinges groaning from lack of use, Ian slid into the cramped dark tunnel. These small spaces were beginning to bother him. Claustrophobia had never been a problem for Ian, but the low fungus-covered beams that prevented the ceiling from collapsing into the space below seem to be even lower than usual as he ducked his six-foot-plus frame under the passageway.

Ian was halfway to the other side of the hospital when he turned a bend and glimpsed sight of another man in a porter's uniform. He was so stunned to see another person there that at first Ian thought he was looking at poor old Mo's ghost, except the man was white, alive, and moving quickly through the passage as if he was acquainted with the subterranean corridors. "Hey! Stop!" Ian yelled.

The man sprinted now, as fast as the twisting dark tunnels allowed anyone, using just the narrow beam of a flashlight. Around the corner was a fork, and Ian knew that if the man took the wrong junction, he would end up at a dead end. Running as fast as the crouched position allowed him to go, Ian saw the man hesitate at the junction and paused to see which way he would go. The porter, if that was what the man was, took the wrong branch.

Ian slowed to a quick trot and pulled out his cell phone, hoping that the signal would penetrate the building above. After several tries, he got a weak voice.

"Harold here. Is that you, Ian? Your batteries must almost be dead."

"Yeah, it's me. Listen, Harold, I'm following this guy in the tunnels below St. Cinnabar. He's headed to a dead end. Can you come and help me?"

"I can barely hear you, Ian. Did you say you're in the tunnels under St. Cinnabar?"

"Yeah. That's why the signal from my cell phone is so weak. Do you remember the stairwell next to the old weigh station from when you worked here during the summer?"

"Sure do, Doc. There's a locked door that no one ever tried to open."

"The door should be open unless a security guard came around and found it unlocked. Get here as soon as you can and come down the stairs. Turn right and follow the passage until you get to the fork and take the right branch."

"Gottcha, Doc."

"Oh, and bring some rope or a pair of handcuffs. I'm hoping I can catch this idiot. But we look evenly matched so I'm going to try and stall him until you get here."

"I'm on my way." The connection ended, and Ian slowed down. He knew the branch ran about a quarter of a mile, and the guy would slow down once he thought Ian wasn't chasing him anymore. Ian just hoped the man didn't find out too quickly that he had no escape route. The fact that he picked the dead end let Ian know he wasn't familiar with the network of tunnels under the hospital.

Slowly but surely each step bringing him closer to the man, Ian listened in case the guy decided to backtrack. But all he could hear was the scurrying of rats in the pitch-black corners, where his torch didn't penetrate. The drip, drip, dripping of water that came from somewhere up above gave the fungus enough moisture to breed its black nauseous slime on the cold filthy stone walls. Time seemed to stand still as Ian wondered who he was tracking in this dark hellhole and whether he was a match for him.

Picking his way even more slowly, he listened for footsteps or breathing while trying to move as quietly as possible through the rubble under foot. *Hurry up, Harold,* he thought. Even if he managed to beat the guy he was tracking, Ian knew he would feel a whole lot better if he had another person at his side.

Suddenly, a crouched form sprang at him. Years of basketball training had sharpened Ian's reflexes, and he sidestepped the man, kicking him as hard as he could in the shins as he missed and stumbled onto the gravelly dirt floor.

Unsure of how much damage he had inflicted, Ian lunged onto the man's back and pulled one arm back until the guy screamed in pain. "Get off you, lummox!" moaned the guy who was built like a wrestler and was almost as tall as Ian.

"Who are you and what are you doing prowling the basement of St. Cinnabar?"

"What's it to you? And I could ask you the same question."

Ian gave the arm another twist. The guy gave a loud yell but did not answer the question. Lifting his flashlight up and peering down at him, even with only a side view, Ian knew who the man was.

"You don't need to tell me because I know," he muttered.

"The hell you do?"

"Reggie Johnson of Detectives R Us, you are a hard man to find. So do you want to start by telling me why you abandoned your office on the east side? The rent couldn't have been that expensive in the dive where you were."

"What are you, a cop or security guard?"

Suddenly, they both listened as the sound of footsteps echoed through the narrow passageway. "Harold, is that you?" Ian couldn't believe he had got there so fast.

"I'm coming, Doc." The black void was pierced by a blinding flash of light. "You caught yourself a big one, Doc. Well, if it isn't Reggie Johnson. What's he doing here?"

"That's what I just asked him, Harold. But he isn't answering any questions. Figure we should Mirandize him or something first, except we're not cops." *That was a really dumb thing to say,* Ian thought. The look Harold gave him said as much. But it was really dark, and with Harold's flashlight half blinding Reggie, Ian hoped the guy wouldn't recognize Harold once he was back on the job.

"Huh! You guys could be charged with kidnapping and that's what I'm going to do as soon as I get free." Reggie was wiggling so violently that Ian was having trouble keeping him pinned to the ground.

"Where's the rope I asked you for, Harold?"

"Right here, Doc. You think if we tied Reggie up and left him in the dark with the rats for a while, he might find his tongue?"

"Gee. Why didn't I think of that, Harold?"

"You can't do that! And there aren't any rats down here!" Almost on cue, a fat pink-eyed rodent scampered by them as if to take a closer look. "Get me outa here!" The yell that came out of Reggie startled Ian badly enough that he let go, and Reggie would have escaped if Harold hadn't grabbed him. Hanging on to the man who outweighed him, Harold would have lost the battle if Ian hadn't jumped into the skirmish. Finally, Harold managed to tie him up while Ian held Reggie in a full nelson.

Ian didn't want the sounds of the man yelling to carry up to the hospital above, so he shoved his OR cap into Reggie's mouth. The terror in the man's eyes made Ian feel squeamish. But they had to find out what the man was up to. And terror was a very good method of interrogating those unwilling to talk.

With Reggie still face down so he couldn't get a clear view of Harold, they made sure his wrists were tied tightly behind his back; Harold looped the rope around both of Reggie's ankles to allow the man enough slack to take small steps but not to run if he got out of their grip. Then he took out a long silk scarf that appeared to belong to a woman and blindfolded the man. "Where to?" asked Harold.

"Back at the bend, there's an old storage closet where we can leave him until he has decided to let us know who hired him and who stabbed Dr. Chester Whales."

Muffled screams that emerged as grunts came from Reggie. It took their combined effort to force Reggie the short distance to the storage room. Just as they were a few steps from the door, Harold started. "Someone's coming, Doc!" he whispered.

Reggie heard them too and resisted their attempts to move him further. The sound of footsteps approaching grew louder. In desperation, they pushed Reggie to the ground and dragged him the few feet into the storage room and then closed the door.

Voices could be heard echoing down the tunnel. "The guy is hallucinating. There ain't anybody down here. And it gives me the willies coming through these old passageways."

"Whadya afraid of, Frank? Some overgrown rat gonna attack you?"

"It ain't natural. Haven't you heard rumors about a ghost haunting the hospital?"

"Don't believe in them. Hey! What's this door lead to?"

Harold and Ian had propped Reggie's body again the bottom half, and they were holding the door shut with their combined strength when the security guard gave a tremendous push. "It's probably boarded up on the other side. Let's go, Joe. There ain't anybody down here. That scream the doctor heard was probably some nutcase from the psyche ward. You know how sound travels in old building like these."

Ian gave a sigh of relief as they heard the footsteps retreating in the distance.

"Geez, Doc. That was a close one! I could see . . ." Remembering who was listening in, Harold did not finish his sentence.

Ian found a couple of old crates that he upended next to a pipe that ran just above the floor. After tying Reggie to the pipe, Ian motioned for Harold to follow him. Even with the material stuffed in Reggie's mouth, they could hear the grunts of terror. Then Ian realized that Reggie hadn't tried to alert the security guards when they were close enough to hear the muffled sounds coming from his mouth. Reggie didn't want to be found down there any more than they did!

Once they were out of earshot, Ian asked, "How did you get here so fast?"

Harold turned various shades of beet red and muttered, "Was visiting Gena."

"The nurse from the seventh floor?"

"Yeah," Harold said. "We'd better not leave him too long, Doc. What if someone else shows up and finds him."

"I'm more worried about him having a heart attack from fear if one of those rats decides to have a closer look at him. Tell you what. We wait exactly eight minutes from now and then go back. In the dark, it will seem a lot longer to Reggie. He'll probably split a gut trying to tell us everything he knows."

Even with a flashlight and company, the time seemed to stand still, and Ian was relieved when they started back to where Reggie was sitting on the box.

But they were nowhere as thankful as Reggie who started talking the moment they took the cloth out of his mouth.

"You gotta understand, I couldn't make a living where I was, and I discovered that these rich mucky-mucks had secrets that could ruin them."

"Start from the beginning, Reggie. Who hired you first?" Ian ordered.

"Rebecca Cornwell did. She knew me from when she got me to tail her husband, Sam. When he died and she found out her brother had been murdered, she asked me to track down one of his classmates."

"Chester Whales."

"How did you know?"

"Just tell us what you found out?" barked Ian. They couldn't afford to sit and verbally spar with the idiot. Someone might just send some more security guards down if their voices carried up to the floor above.

"He wasn't hard to locate because the AMA lists all doctors. Then I approached him, and he thought this Helena DuCarthenson had hired me. Well, I saw an opportunity to make some more money so I let him believe that it was Helena who was paying me."

"And he asked you to steal something from Helena?" Ian was guessing.

"Yeah. How did you know?"

"Just tell us what you stole."

"It was some letters and several false papers she used to get out of Germany. The identity card had this woman's picture when she was about twelve. It proved that she was the daughter of this concentration camp commandant in Germany. She even kept the phony identification papers she used to pass herself off as a Jewish immigrant when she traveled to England. Then she changed identities again and moved to Slatington."

"Holy cow," said Harold. "Helena DuCarthenson is really the daughter of a Nazi war criminal?"

"That's what the papers proved. Once I had them, I knew they were too valuable to turn over to the dean."

"So you started blackmailing Helena," Ian added.

"A man's got to make a living."

"Meanwhile, Helena thinks Chester is behind the blackmailing?"

"Yeah. But I used what Rebecca told me to blackmail Chester too."

Stifling an impulse to shake his head over the detective's naive boasting, Ian continued, "So Helena and Chester were at each other's throats?"

"And both were paying me to keep tabs on the other." Reggie almost beamed as if he were telling someone that he won an Oscar. He even paused as if waiting for praise from his interrogators.

Since Ian had walked away and had his back to them, Harold asked the next question, "And they both were paying you money thinking it was the other person who was blackmailing them?"

"Yeah." Grinning from ear to ear, Reggie really didn't seem to appreciate the gravity of his crime.

After gaining control of his emotions, Ian returned and demanded, "Where are these papers now?"

"Hey! A guy's got to make a living."

"If he's still alive. You look like the kind of man who would keep things in a safety deposit box in a bank?" Ian started going through Reggie's pockets and found his keys. One small round key was marked with the city crest of Slatington. "Which bank is it in?"

"Why should I tell you?"

"Because you don't want us to walk away and forget you're here," Harold said.

"There's only one bank in Slatington," muttered Reggie.

"And you don't want to be put away for blackmailing the Dean of Medicine or accused of his murder. So when we leave here, we're going to that safety deposit box and you are going to give me everything in it. Understood?" It was not in Ian's nature to play the heavy, but the reaction he got from Reggie proved that he was giving a convincing performance.

The PI's face dripped with sweat, and he wriggled to loosen the ropes around his wrists. "Hell. What am I going to live on if I hand it over to you?"

"Try doing some real detective work? And don't kid yourself, Reggie. We can prove that you put Samantha Rutledge in the morgue, which is enough to hand you over to the cops for a long stay in prison. While we're on the subject, do you want to explain how that happened?" Ian glanced at Harold with a knowing look.

"Well, it definitely wasn't my idea."

"We already figured that Reggie. Just give us the facts," muttered Harold.

"The dean called me up and said he wanted to rendezvous in our usual meetin' place in the park. Ya' coulda blown me over with a feather when the dean told me he's tired of being blackmailed and wanted to scare Helena. Of course, I couldn't tell him that it was me who was blackmailing him."

There was a long pause as Ian and Harold waited for Reggie to continue. Scurrying rats in the walls which squeaked out to each other at various intervals were the only sound to break the dark silence of the tunnels. Finally, Ian said, "And what exactly was the dean going to do to teach Helena a lesson?"

"The dean said he was gonna slip that date rape drug into Helena's coffee during the board meeting and that would leave her dopey but awake. And that I could show up and walk her to the morgue because according to the great Dr. Whales, once she drank the drugged coffee, Helena would do anything I told her to. When I got her outside the morgue, I was to pull the fire alarm and, while everyone was outside, put her in a cold box."

"But Helena wasn't the person sitting there when you showed up?" added Ian.

Reggie stared in surprise at Ian and Harold. "How'd you know that?"

"I'm psychic, Reggie," Ian answered.

"No kidding. You should see a shrink. Guess it would make a great defense if I turned you in for kidnapping me."

At first, Ian thought Reggie was joking. Then realized the guy thought he meant psycho. More than a little irritated, especially since Harold looked like he was about to laugh out loud, Ian muttered, "Just cut the crap, Reggie, and tell us what happened."

"Okay, okay! Instead of Helena, there was this short, fat cleaning lady sitting in the boardroom. She wasn't moving, and she weren't about to walk to no morgue. She looked like she was dead. Hell, I didn't bargain for no murder. But I knew I couldn't just leave her there so I followed through with the plan except that I had to get a gurney, lift her onto it, and cover her with a sheet. Since she looked dead, there was no point in going back to get her off the slab like the dean asked me to."

"You didn't see that she was just in a deep sleep?" Ian was disgusted.

"How was I supposed to know? She didn't appear to be breathing, and I figured the dean had put too much drug in the coffee."

"You are damned lucky you are not looking at attempted murder charges, Reggie. If I hadn't stumbled upon Samantha, she would have died of hypothermia."

"It wasn't my idea. The dean hired me to do a job, and I did it. How was I to know it involved killing a woman and putting her body in the morgue?"

Harold had been unusually quiet as he listened to Ian and Reggie. Then he said, "Holy cow, Doc. No wonder the dean wanted you to stop looking for whoever put Samantha in the morgue."

"Yeah. That explains a lot of things, except who stabbed the dean."

"Well, I didn't because your friend Harold here was trying to chase me down. Had to skip out on the catering company and they were so mad that they wouldn't pay me."

"Ahhhh! Too bad," Ian mocked.

"So what are you going to do now?" asked Reggie.

"We're going to escort you to the bank, and you are going to get the contents of the safety deposit box and turn them over to me."

"Why should I?"

"Reggie, have you been listening? Samantha almost died, and we can prove you put her in the cold box in the morgue. So let's cut the crap and get going."

The long walk through the tunnel was accomplished in silence. Reggie didn't even try to escape Ian and Harold, who kept close to him all the way to the bank.

Once Ian had his hands on the contents of the security box, they let Reggie go. "Guess we couldn't turn him over to the police?" Harold said.

"Nope. They might have a few questions for us if we did."

"What now?" asked Harold.

"Seems like I need to talk to Helena DuCarthenson."

"Yeah. I wonder how badly she wanted her parentage kept a secret, whether it was important enough to kill the dean? Guess you're going to try and find out, Doc?"

"That's my next step, Harold. I'll give you a call if I need any more help."

They parted company as Ian hailed a taxi.

CHAPTER 64

Dr. Conway

*T*HE PARCEL REGGIE handed over to Ian at the bank fit into his lab pocket, but Ian did not want to leave it in his locker in the doctors' lounge. There were too many thieves who found the flimsy locks only too tempting. The cabdriver was making excellent time as Ian said, "I need to make a stop before returning to the hospital."

"Where to, Doc?" The pug-nosed little man who looked Irish but spoke with a deep Southern drawl was in no hurry. Ian gave him his address, and within minutes, he was bounding up the stairs to his apartment. With the package safely hidden away, Ian returned to the taxi, and they headed for St. Cinnabar.

"Don't get too many doctors traveling downtown Slatington this time of day," the cabbie said.

Ignoring the opening, Ian answered, "Nope. Most of the time we don't have the time to be traipsing halfway across the city."

"Must have been something important to go to the bank for?" The driver persisted in digging for information. But the ride was over as they pulled up to the main entrance of the hospital, and Ian paid the taxi driver.

"You have a good day, young fella," said the cabbie as he drove off shaking his head.

The emergency department had a lull, and Ian decided that he would take the opportunity to go and confront Dr. Lester Conway. Passing the nurses' station, Ian approached the room Dr. Conway had been in. There were two new patients in the room. Back at the station, Ian looked up the patient record and saw that Lester had been discharged and was staying at a boarding house in the city. It made sense that the man was well enough to attend an alumni reunion, he no longer needed to be in hospital. And even if he didn't find a retirement home that he wanted to move into, a boarding house served the same purpose. There was someone to prepare his meals and make sure he didn't backslide into a depression.

It was a long day with very few patients in the waiting room. By five o'clock, Ian was relieved to see the end of his shift. He decided that he couldn't wait and called a taxi to take him to the Sunny Side Home Away From Home, as the boarding house was called. The impressive old mansion was in good shape.

A matronly woman with long curly gray hair piled neatly on top of her head answered the doorbell. Her smile produced deep dimples in both cheeks as she looked Ian up and down as if sizing up a prize horse for sale. "How may I help you, dear?" she asked.

"I'm here to see Dr. Lester Conway if he's at home."

"Oh my, yes! He will be delighted to have a visitor. Come right this way." The plump woman led the way as she waddled to a room on the main floor. "The doctor had a heart attack and didn't want to have to climb stairs so I gave him my husband's old room. Excuse my manners. My name is Dolly Ridgeway. Who shall I tell Lester is here to see him?"

"Ian McLintock."

A rap on the door was answered by the shuffling of feet as Lester came to open the door. "To what do I owe the honor of a house call?"

"Just passing through the neighborhood and thought I would check up on you."

"Well, come on in, young fella. I think I can rustle up a drink for you." Lester closed the door on his landlady, and Ian waited until her footsteps could no longer be heard.

During the trip across the city to the boarding house, Ian had deliberated whether to tell Lester Conway that he had overheard not one but three private conversations the night he decided to have a nap in the empty bed next to the doctor. But there was nothing to be gained from it, and Ian decided that it would only upset the old man. So he figured he should just use his encounter with Reggie to reveal what he knew about Helena, Chester, and Rebecca.

"There's something I've found out that I want to discuss with you, Dr. Conway."

"This must be serious if you're calling me Dr. Conway again. Can't stand formalities. Call me Lester and sit down. Nothing can be that important that it can't wait for us to have a drink." Lester poured himself a stiff drink of bourbon.

Ian waved away the drink Dr. Conway was about to pour him. "Got to get up early tomorrow, and alcohol gives me insomnia." It was partly true. But Ian felt guilty enough having overheard what he did without drinking the man's liquor. Besides, once Lester heard what Ian had to say, he might ask him to leave.

"You look mighty solemn. I suppose it has to do with the stabbing of the Dean of Medicine. Should have known you'd get around to talking to me."

"This friend of mine who's a cop helped me to track down a sleazy PI by the name of Reggie Johnson. Don't suppose you've heard of him?"

"Can't rightly say so. But the name does sound familiar. Wasn't there a famous athlete with that name?"

"Yeah. But there's no relation. This is difficult to tell you, but the man was blackmailing the dean and Helena DuCarthenson. We think he may have confronted you too."

"Nope. Have nothing to hide."

"That's not exactly what I heard. But I don't care about that. I know you had an alibi for the time the dean was stabbed. What I want to know is who did it. And I think you might be able to help me find out."

"You know about Chester and Leon's part in Izzy's death then?" It was more of a statement than a question as Lester ran a gnarled hand over his thin wrinkled face.

"Let's say that this PI found out a lot more than any one of you would have wanted him to, and he was using it to blackmail Chester and Helena over Izzy's death. Would you care to fill in the details, Dr. Conway?"

There was a long silence that was broken by a sigh. "I overheard them talking about drugging Izzy and putting him on a slab in the morgue. It was one of those all night shifts, and they didn't know I was catching a few winks on a gurney behind the curtain in emergency. I was going to get up and warn Izzy, but I fell asleep. When I finally woke up, it was too late."

"They killed him?"

"Not deliberately. As far as I can figure, they put him in the drawer, and when Izzy woke up, he must have been scared to death. When Chester and his friend went back to let him out, he was dead. So they moved his body and let someone else find him. They declared his death as a heart attack. Despite suspicions, there was no investigation into the circumstances, especially since Chester's dad was a famous cardiac surgeon. I don't think Chester and Leon knew that you could scare someone to death."

"That was terrible."

"Worse than that. It was a damn shame. Izzy would have been a brilliant doctor, and because of Chester's jealousy, a valuable medical man died before his time."

"Do you have any idea who might have wanted to kill Chester? So far the police think Rebecca Cornwell did it, but I know that she couldn't have."

"Oh! Well, I'll be damned. I found out she was Izzy's sister and was hounding the dean. Figured it had to be her. If it wasn't her, then I can't help you, Dr. McLintock."

"You are sure that you have no idea whatsoever? Did Regina Whales leave the table and go after her husband?"

"Nope. She was dancing with Dr. Hammersmith. Hope Rebecca has a good lawyer because I think she did do it, no matter what you say. She had motive, means, and opportunity. Heard she was covered in Chester's blood when they took her out of jumping off the roof. Sorry, young man, but I can't help you."

"It's okay. I knew it was a long shot, but I figured I'd ask you anyways. So how are you getting along here in the boarding house?"

"Just fine. Dolly has been eyeing me up as a replacement for her dead husband. Gave me his old room because of my ticker, so she says. But I know when a woman is on the hunt for a man."

"Wouldn't hurt to have a good woman to care for you."

"That's what I was thinking. It was good of you to stop by, Dr. McLintock. Sorry I couldn't help you."

The man was obviously giving Ian a hint that he wanted him to go, so Ian rose and walked to the door. "Thanks for talking to me, Dr. Conway, and I hope things work out for you here." Ian found his way down to the main entrance where he asked Dolly to call a taxi for him. It seemed to have been a waste of his time, and all he succeeded in doing was upsetting the old doctor without discovering anything that would lead to the dean's assailant.

With Dr. Lester Conway off his list, Ian decided to confront the next person who had reason to kill the dean—Helena DuCarthenson. Sally had told him that there was a board meeting scheduled for that Wednesday morning to discuss the problem of Dean Chesterton Whales. With the dean in intensive care and the whole hospital gossiping about him, the board members decided they had to get together and do some damage control, or at least put up a unified front.

Sally had promised to page Ian as soon as the meeting started to break up so that he could "run" into Helena in the corridor. The last thing Ian wanted to do was confront Helena in front of the others. If it looked like his meeting with her was an accident, maybe she would talk to him.

There were three interns lounging about in the ER doctors' lounge when Ian felt his pager. "Paul."

"What?" snarled the other intern. He knew he was about to be asked to cover for Ian again and wasn't too happy about it.

"I have to be somewhere. Would you cover for me?"

"Do I have a choice?"

"Yes, of course." Ian smiled.

"Cover for you or get kicked out of the hospital."

"Yeah. See you in about half an hour."

As Ian walked out the door, he heard Louis ask Paul, "What's he got on you?"

"Just shut up!" yelled Paul as he, too, slammed out the other door.

Ian took the tunnel so that he wouldn't miss Helena. When he arrived at the hospital library, which was two doors down from the boardroom, he saw Sally rolling the food trolley toward him.

"They're coming out now," she whispered.

"You're an angel, Sally." She blushed furiously and wheeled the cart toward the cafeteria.

Ian walked into the library and took a book off the shelf. Standing so he could look down the hall, he waited as the board members filed out still talking to one another. But Helena was not among them. After waiting too long, Ian decided to go into the boardroom to see if she was still there. But the room was empty. Apparently, this was one meeting Helena did not attend.

CHAPTER 65

Helena's Secret

*T*HE TINY WOMAN who opened the door to Ian looked as if she should be in a nursing home; her face was so wizened that it reminded him of the apple-head dolls his mother used to make from dried-up mackintoshes. The wrinkled hands that held open the large ornate door were knotted with arthritis. "May I see Mrs. DuCarthenson?"

"Who is asking?" the woman asked in a guttural German accent.

"Dr. Ian McLintock."

Suddenly, Ian found himself pulled forcefully into the foyer. "They did send a doctor after all!" exclaimed the old housekeeper. "She won't eat, she won't sleep, and she won't stop weeping! I call and tell them to send doctor. They say doctor no make house call. Send woman to them. I tell them Mrs. DuCarthenson very important person. Not tell them she won't leave bed."

"Oh!" Before Ian could tell the housekeeper why he was there, he found himself being escorted up a long winding staircase that looked as if it had been built for a great cotillion ballroom. They entered an immense bedroom that would have held the average person's entire apartment.

The only evidence of another person in the room was a long narrow mound almost hidden by a huge downy cover. "They send doctor, Helena!" announced the housekeeper before she went to the large cathedral windows and drew back heavy curtains, letting bright light into the darkened room.

"Close those blinds!" ordered a muffled voice from beneath the covers.

"Doctor comes to see you!" repeated the old woman before she left the room.

Ian walked to the side of the bed, not sure what to do. He hadn't brought his black bag and was embarrassed that his real motive for coming was to ask Helena if she had stabbed the dean.

Curiosity overcame reticence, and Mrs. DuCarthenson pulled the covers down, just enough to peek at Ian. "You're not a doctor! You're just a bloody intern."

"You seem to be very depressed, Mrs. DuCarthenson," said Ian. "Perhaps I can help you."

"Nobody can help me!" Tears flowed from already red puffy eyes. But Helena did pull back the covers and sit up. "She's gone?"

"Your housekeeper left. Do you want me to get her?"

"No."

"What seems to be the problem? Are you running a fever? Do you have any aches, pains?" Without his black bag, Ian was hard-pressed to examine the woman.

"No, no, and no! I've always been healthy as a horse."

"You are upset over the stabbing of the dean?"

"Of course!" She hesitated and then asked, "Is he dead?"

"No, Dr. Whales came through the operation and is in the intensive care unit."

"Oh!" she sighed with relief.

It struck Ian as strange that Helena hadn't called anyone to find out whether the dean had pulled through or not. Even though she had reason to want him dead, most people in her situation would have put on a brave face, played the part of a concerned board member, and called to find out whether she was going to have to attend a funeral or not. It made Ian suspect that Helena tried to kill the dean. She had enough secrets that she would be at the top of the police department's investigation if they knew as much as Ian did.

Ian really didn't want to come right out and ask Mrs. DuCarthenson whether she was guilty or not. He decided that a circuitous route would be better. "Do you know who stabbed Dr. Whales?"

Pink flooded her cheeks as Helena responded with indignation, "Of course, not! Why on earth would I know who wanted Chester dead?"

"Where were you when he was stabbed?" So much for being delicate.

"Dancing with Dr. Hammersmith! I resent the implication, young man! Why on earth would I want to harm Dean Chesterton Whales?"

"Because he was blackmailing you."

"What? How did you . . . ?" Her face crumpled into a mass of emotions as tears streamed down her face once more.

"No one else knows." Ian was ashamed that he had upset Helena again. "You hired a detective by the name of Reggie Johnson, didn't you?"

"How did you know?"

"This private detective had the habit of approaching people he was hired to investigate and then using what he found out to blackmail them."

"It wasn't Chester then?"

"No. Reggie was hired first by Rebecca Cornwell. Then he tracked down the dean, and when Dr. Whales thought you had hired Reggie, he hired the detective to spy on you. And Mr. Johnson promptly offered his services to you. Am I correct?"

"Yes. How did you find that out?"

"Let's just say that I had a long heart-to-heart talk with the illustrious PI. He handed over something that belongs to you." Ian handed Helena a manila envelope. She immediately dumped the contents onto the bedspread and looked at the old passports.

"Reggie was behind all this? I was sure it was the dean. Then Rebecca moved into town, and I thought she was responsible."

"No one else knows about this, and Reggie understands that if he tries to use the information, he is going to jail for a long, long time."

"They discovered Rebecca standing over Chester. I thought the police had arrested her."

"She didn't stab him."

"How do you know that?"

"I was the one who stopped her from leaping off the roof of the hospital. She said someone else had got to him before her. When someone is about to commit suicide, they have no reason to lie."

"Oh. The poor dear. You know everything then?" Her shoulders slumped as if a huge weight had been lifted.

"Not everything, Helena. You are depressed for a reason. Do you want to talk to me about it?"

"Why not? No one else could possibly understand. You know from the passport that my real name was Gretchen. I am the daughter of a Nazi war criminal. My father was the commandant of a concentration camp. He married my mother when she was only fourteen." Helena moved a faded sepia picture toward Ian. It looked like a young girl dressed in a white dress and veil for her first communion. The man beside her looked old enough to be her father. "They don't look like bride and groom, do they?"

"This is a wedding picture of your mother and father?" Ian guessed.

"Yes. Father got special permission to marry Mother. Even in Germany under Hitler, they frowned upon men marrying girls so much younger than them. It was only much later when Mother had found Father and me together in a rather compromising situation that she guessed at his taste for young girls." Pointing to the wedding photo of her parents, Helena said, "You can see that Mother was very tiny for her age and looked more like a twelve-year-old when she got married. As soon as Mother developed, Father got tired of her. I was only eight when he began . . ." Helena couldn't finish, she began sobbing again.

"How did you get out of Germany?"

"I got pregnant, but lost the baby. Mother picked out a young Jewish girl to help in the kitchen in hopes that my father would leave me alone. But Father wouldn't lower himself to have sex with a Jew. So Mother used her jewelry to bribe the guards. They handed me over to a group of people who gave me a false passport and helped me to escape to England. It was just months before the Allies reached the camp. Mother knew that I needed to leave before that happened or I would have no chance for a future."

"And you bought yourself a new identity in England?"

"After I worked as a prostitute just long enough to earn the money needed to get Mother a passport and someone to smuggle her into England."

Ian was at a loss for words. He just stared at Helena.

Finally, she said, "After you have been abused by your father, prostitution is easy. At least you know the men aren't supposed to love you. And they aren't breaking a trust like a parent."

"I'm so sorry."

"So was I. But I was alive, and most of my friends, relatives, schoolmates, and everyone who meant something to me were dead because of that bastard Hitler. I had no choice but to go on. I wanted to die, but I was young and healthy and met a wealthy young man who married me and brought me back to the States."

"But you didn't stay with him?"

"I couldn't bear him any children because of an untreated sexually transmitted disease. So his family bought me off, and I moved to Slatington, where I met Chester, Izzy, and Lester."

"Why Slatington?"

"Why not? Chester fell in love with me and wanted to marry me. But his father was suspicious and hired a detective who traced me back to England. He thought I was a Jew and wouldn't hear of his son marrying one. So we split up."

Helena swung her legs out of bed and said, "Would you hand me my robe?"

Ian picked up a very expensive-looking diaphanous piece of cloth draped over an elegant Louis XIII chair.

"No point in languishing in bed any longer. If Chester can recover from this, so can I." Helena pulled the cord at the head of her bed, and the housekeeper walked in almost immediately.

"Listening at doors again, Mother?" Helena asked the housekeeper.

Ian saw the resemblance between the old woman and Helena.

"I didn't want to embarrass my daughter, so I play the role of housekeeper," admitted the old woman.

"Shall we dine together tonight, Mother?" asked Helena.

"If you wish, Gretchen."

Ian was escorted to the foyer by the old woman, who paused before opening the door for him. "Thank you for giving me back my daughter."

"You are welcome." Ian left the mansion and thanked his lucky stars that his life as a child had been relatively uneventful in a small town in Connecticut.

CHAPTER 66

The Dean Is Awake

WITH LESTER CONWAY and Helena cleared, Ian had only one option . . . to confront the dean and ask him who it was that had stabbed him. He knew that the dean's visitors were limited to family since he was still in the intensive care unit. But Louis had a girlfriend who worked in the unit. Using Louis didn't appeal to him, but Ian wanted to get to this mystery. He was just tired of not knowing and looking at all his friends and colleagues, wondering if they were capable of murder. It didn't make for good working conditions.

"Linda?" The nurse at the station turned and faced Ian.

"Yeah. Louis said to watch for you. Everyone is busy in the backroom. I'm monitoring all the patients on the screens."

Ian watched ten monitors that showed patients connected to tubes, pressure cuffs, respirators, and beeping monitors. He noticed that the dean's eyes were open and the man looked restless. "How is he?"

"Doing really well everything considered. He would have been moved to a regular room by now, but the police figure he's easier to guard in this unit because we limit visitors."

And I am about to go in to see him without permission, thought Ian. He strode quickly to the room and reached up to move the video camera in case one of the nurses left the meeting and happened to glance at the monitors at the nursing station.

"How are you, Dr. Whales?" asked Ian.

"Damn sore! I thought you still had a month left of your ER rotation."

"I do. But I wanted to talk to you. Do you know who stabbed you?"

The dean's cheeks that were deathly pale turned pink. "I already told the detective that I don't remember."

"But you do know, don't you?" Ian could tell by the dean's reaction that he was hiding something.

"Dammit, can't you leave me alone? I am a sick man."

"The person who did this might return and finish what he or she started," warned Ian.

"Not bloody likely. I'd be prepared the next time!"

"So you know!"

"No. Now get out of my room before I yell for security. You could be suspended for harassing a patient!"

Ian had no choice but to leave. As he walked by the nurses' station, Linda looked up from her paperwork. "Leaving already?"

"Yeah. He ordered me out of his room."

"Oh."

"Thanks, Linda. I owe you and Louis."

"No problem, Ian. I would like to see the end of this as much as you. Everyone is on edge and watching everyone else. It's a real strain knowing there's a murderer among us and we don't know who it is."

Ian was running out of people to confront, and he really didn't want to talk to the dean's wife. He was afraid that he might let something slip and she would find out about Brandi.

CHAPTER 67

Interrogating Regina Whales

*A*FTER BEING RUSHED off his feet, the ER was suddenly quiet as if whatever was brewing had come to a head with the stabbing of the dean. With nothing on the board and no one in the waiting room, Ian found himself pacing back and forth. Then he realized it was the perfect opportunity. He decided to phone Paul.

"Hello," grunted the intern.

"Hi, Paul. It's Ian here."

"Goddamn it. Enough is enough! What do you want now?"

"It's really quiet in the ER, and I have someone I need to go see. Can you drop around for a couple of hours?"

"No! But I suppose I don't have a choice. And don't give me your lamebrain answer . . . Yes, you do. I'll come, but this has got to stop. You hear?"

"This is the last time, Paul. I promise."

As Ian passed Paul coming into the ER, he hoped that there wouldn't be too many emergencies because he knew that Paul would not be a good doctor to face that night. "I'll be back in a couple of hours," he yelled to Paul as the slicing doors began to shut behind him. It was so nice to be walking out of the hospital down the street that Ian felt rejuvenated. The only thing dragging him down was the thoughts of talking to Regina.

The dean's wife had agreed to talk to him but seemed puzzled over his request that they meet. He saw her Mercedes parked at the restaurant at the end of the street. Ian still didn't know how he was going to handle her when he walked through the door and settled opposite Regina in a booth at the far corner of the restaurant.

When it was over, Ian had learned nothing except that Regina had an alibi, she was dancing with Dr. Hammersmith when her husband was stabbed. She also said that she had no idea who would want to harm such a wonderful doctor and kind human being as her husband. Ian had to stop himself from choking when he heard her utter those words as if she really believed them.

Much as he hated to return to work, Ian didn't want to push Paul too far. He knew that he might still need him to cover for him later. And Paul might just call his bluff. Ian would never tell anyone that Paul's grandmother hadn't died. But until Paul figured that out, Ian had a ready-made replacement every time he wanted to go somewhere.

CHAPTER 68

Missing Link

HAROLD HAD WORRIED that Reggie would go to the police after they let him go. But Ian knew that Reggie had a lot more to hide than they did. Although what they did was illegal, Ian was positive that Reggie would ever tell the cops that he had been kidnapped in the tunnels of St. Cinnabar and held captive until he finally told two amateurs what he knew about the dean, Helena, and Dr. Conway. He had made enough money off all of them that he was set for life as long as none of them demanded their money back.

What bothered Ian was not what Reggie told them but what he had kept back. He knew that Reggie gave them just enough information so that they were satisfied. But there were still secrets he was keeping just in case he needed to blackmail them again. Of that, Ian was certain. If Harold had not been almost apoplectic over holding Reggie against his will, Ian would have tried to get more information from the blackmailer. But Harold had been terrified that he would lose his job on the police force if Reggie ever complained. That was until Reggie accepted the plane ticket to Haiti that Ian handed him.

Thinking about Harold, Ian realized that he hadn't talked to him since they let Reggie go. Ian was reluctant to call him up for fear that he might tip off the detectives who were still trying to find the strange young man who had showed up halfway through the ball.

Most of the guests had remembered Harold because he was so young that he didn't fit in with the alumni and he had a distinct limp. Only Ian and Marla knew it was Harold the detectives were still trying to locate. With Reggie now out of the country, they didn't have to worry about the detectives coming across him and getting the real story.

Ian walked into the doctors' lounge and saw Paul sound asleep, with the football game blaring on the TV. He nudged him and said, "I'm back. You can go home now."

Paul jumped and said, "Why not sneak up and scare the shit out of a guy?"

"Go home and sleep in your bed, Paul. And thanks!"

"You're not welcome," he growled as he stomped out of the lounge.

Almost as if everyone knew he was back, Ian's pager began vibrating, and he could hear the siren of an ambulance coming into the covered ambulance bay. "Shit! The mayhem had begun again!

CHAPTER 69

One More Suspect

HALFWAY THROUGH HIS shift, the onslaught ceased as abruptly as it began, and Ian slouched down on the couch. Leaning his head against the hard leather cushion, he felt the pager going off. A glance and he saw that it was the same outside line that had rung him earlier. He decided to call it to break the monotony of the night.

"Dr. Ian McLintock here."

"Hi, Doc. You're a hard man to get a hold of," said Harold.

"You're not still mad at me?"

"Heck, no, Doc. It's just that I thought my career was over before it had begun. But I finally talked to Uncle Charlie, and he said not to worry about a lowlife like Reggie Johnson."

"So to what do I owe the honor and privilege of this call then?"

"I forgot to tell you something, Doc."

"You know who stabbed the dean?"

"No. But I know who is stealing the morphine from the medicine room. You were right. Elliot wasn't getting his medication."

"Can you come over here, Harold? I think this is something we shouldn't discuss over the phone."

"Sure, Doc. I'll be there in ten minutes."

"I'll meet you at the entrance to the ER. They've beefed up security so no one gets in or out without an escort."

"See you there, Doc."

Ian was in the process of putting stitches in the arm of a lowlife who had his arm slit open during a street brawl. He was trying to ignore the guy as he quickly sutured the flaps of skin together. When someone tapped him on the shoulder, he almost jumped out of his skin, yanking on the black silk thread.

"Hey, watch it, Doc!" growled the tattooed guy whose arm he was sewing up.

"There's a guy at the entrance who says you want to see him, Doc." The security guard looked like she should still be in grade school, not sashaying around the hospital with a walkie-talkie on her belt.

"That's Harold. Will you bring him here?"

"Sure, Doc."

It was several minutes later when Harold walked into the treatment room. "Hi, Doc."

"What took you so long, Harold?"

"Got a date with the security guard."

"What about Gena?" asked Ian.

"We're not engaged or anythin', Doc."

"Just don't let her find out or you will find yourself with one really angry woman on your hands."

"Don't worry, Doc. I managed to juggle three girlfriends while going through high school."

"Well, it looks like I'm through here." Ian cut the thread and waved for the nurse to come over and bandage the wound.

"Let's go down the street for a coffee, Harold." Ian leaned over at the nurses' station and whispered something in Joshua's ear.

"Okay, Doc. Don't worry!" he answered.

The same scrawny, long-legged, gum-popping girl was working again at the doughnut shop. "Hi, ya Doc!" she greeted him.

"Whatcha want?"

"Two coffees?" Ian looked at Harold.

"That will be just fine, Doc. I've put on a few pounds with sitting around at home and not working."

They retreated to the furthest booth, where Ian could keep a lookout for the waitress.

"So who's the lowlife and how did he get keys to the drug room at the hospital?"

"His name is Carson Stiller, at least that what the rap sheet says. And beats me how he got the keys. You said someone trashed the dean's office a while back?"

"Yeah. But he didn't mention any missing keys. So all we have to go on is the name Carson Stiller."

"This guy's got a juvey record, but it's sealed up tighter than Fort Knox. But he has a rap sheet for drug use and pushing. Nothing major."

"So how did he get started breaking into the hospital?" Ian wondered out loud.

"Beats me, Doc. The only suggestion I have is that I locate the guy and try to tail him. And if he heads toward the hospital, I can call my uncle to get a cop to sit where Gena told me to wait for her. That way he'll see everything if the kid comes in to steal some more drugs. They aren't going to arrest him without proof. And how do we explain that I watched him breaking into the medicine room without getting Gena into trouble?"

"You've got a point, Harold. He'll show up again when he needs his next fix. In the meantime, I've been running into brick walls over the stabbing. Everyone has an alibi so far. You got any suggestions, Harold?"

They discussed the problem of the dean, without getting anywhere. Ian glanced down at his watch and said, "Holy cow, I've been gone for almost an hour. Better get back before someone starts looking for me."

"I'll give you a call if I find this lowlife that's been breaking into the medicine room, Doc, especially if he looks like he's headed toward the hospital."

CHAPTER 70

Tailing the Druggie

*B*EDRAGGLED FILTHY CLOTHES hung on the punk's skinny five feet eight inches frame as he slouched against the graffiti-filled wall. Toting a camera equipped with a high-powered lens around his neck and dressed in a Hawaiian shirt, Harold had kept his distance from the bum and hoped that he looked like a tourist slumming for the day so that he wouldn't spook the lowlife loitering several blocks away. Pleased that he had thought of using the camera for surveillance, Harold could see even the puss-filled pimples on the guy's unwashed face through the telephoto lens.

From the picture on his police file, Harold identified the homeless person as the guy he was looking for—a man in his twenties by the name of Carson Stiller. Only hours earlier, Harold had been arguing with his uncle when his dad's last partner, Paul Randal, sauntered up to them in the station. "What's the problem, Charlie?" Paul asked.

"I think Harold got the sense knocked out of him when he got hit by that car. He wants to find this two-bit drug dealer so he can follow him." Charlie looked at Paul and twiddled his finger around his ear to emphasize that Harold had really lost his marbles.

"And he doesn't want to tell you why?" asked Paul.

"Yeah. How did you know?" demanded Charlie.

"He takes after his old man. I remember one time when Hafferty was on his way home after an early shift. Walked into the bank and saw this guy in line with a bulge in his pocket. Recognized his face from a mug shot. Well, Hafferty left the bank, phoned for back up, then went back in. He got at the back of each line and told the person ahead of him to just walk out of the bank like he'd forgotten something, that there was about to be a bank robbery. Got almost everyone out before he walked up behind the guy and pulled his service revolver and told him, 'Give it up or you're a dead man.' It was all over before anyone arrived to help him."

"Yeah, I remember that," Charlie sighed.

"So who's this guy you want to find?" Paul asked Harold.

Harold showed Paul the guy's picture and rap sheet. After standing and listening to Paul reminisce about his dad and the good old days, Harold finally found an excuse to extricate himself and left him still talking to his uncle as he left the station.

It was only three hours later when Harold got the call from his uncle. Once he knew where Carson was hanging out, Harold had driven down to the part of the city where you could buy any recreational drug imaginable. Harold, now watching Carson from a distance, still couldn't get over how fast the cops had found him.

Harold tried to focus on some of the more colorful buildings that had historical significance so that he wouldn't spook the guy. Even two blocks away, the guy appeared antsy like he needed a fix or had that second sight the hunted developed. Turning his skeletal face covered in a scruffy beard toward Harold, it seemed as if the druggie sensed that someone was looking at him. Suddenly, he turned and took off at a surprisingly fast gait, considering the guy was thin enough for a strong wind to blow over.

Harold kept pace and swore as his leg pained him whenever he tried to hurry. Several times, the guy turned a corner, and Harold lost sight of him only to pick him up after a few minutes. Finally, they hit a crowded section downtown, and the guy stopped as if to catch his breath. Harold took advantage of the break to slip into a phone booth where he dialed Ian's pager number. He really didn't think he would get a hold of the doctor at that time of day. The ringing lasted only a few minutes, and Harold punched in the number at the phone booth. Within seconds, it rang.

"Hi. Ian McLintock here. Who's paging me?"

"Doc! I thought for sure I'd never get you. I've been tailing Carson Stiller, but he looks like he suspects something, and I need someone to trade off with. Don't suppose you could get away or send a buddy over to help me?"

"Just tell me where you are and I'll be there in a few minutes."

"The guy is standing on the corner of Miracle and Center Streets by the Star Bucks Coffee Shop."

"That's right down the street from St. Cinnabar. I'll be there in a jiffy."

Harold watched through the telephoto lens while clicking off the pictures. *This would cost a fortune,* he thought, *if I really had film in the camera.* A couple of times he regretted not having loaded the camera because he could have snapped a really good shot, by which he could have entered into the national photography contest. Once he spotted Ian trotting swiftly from the direction of the coffee shop, Harold breathed a sigh of relief.

Ian turned into Star Bucks and was leaving with a coffee in hand when Carson Stiller began to move again. Ian sauntered nonchalantly behind the guy as he headed straight for the hospital. Ducking back into the phone booth, Harold dialed the precinct number and asked for Paul. He knew his dad's old partner would show up on the seventh floor and ask for Gena without giving Harold the third degree. With any luck, Paul would see the kid break into the drug room and steal morphine himself, relieving Harold of the responsibility of doing a lot of explaining.

After hanging up, Harold tried to catch up to Ian and Carson. It took several minutes before he saw Carson moving toward the alley that ran alongside the hospital. Since Harold already knew where Carson was headed, he entered the hospital by the main door. He had expected Ian to do the same thing and was surprised to see the doctor heading down the alley once the kid was out of sight.

Sure that the doctor would lose Carson, Harold hurried down the corridor to the bank of elevators and took the first one to the seventh floor. He just hoped Paul would get there before Carson made his way to the drug room.

As soon as he stepped off the elevator, he spotted Gena and waved for her to come to meet him.

"What are you doing here, Harold?" The greeting was not exactly warm.

"A detective by the name of Paul is on his way here. I want you to show him to the spot where you asked me to wait for you."

"Why?" Gena looked at Harold as if he had lost his mind.

"There's something I saw while I was waiting for you."

"And you didn't tell me? What was it, Harold?"

"It doesn't matter. I just want this detective to see it so I don't have to explain what I was doing in the hospital."

"You ashamed of me or something? Is that why you asked out that security guard?"

"Shit!" Harold turned beet red and stuttered, "It didn't mean anything, I swear."

"Being with me or with her?"

Harold spotted Paul and seized the opportunity to change the subject. "Right down here, Paul. Just sit here and you can see into the medicine room."

"I take it someone's been stealing drugs."

"Why didn't you tell me, Harold?"

"It would have been my word against theirs. This way Paul can see for himself."

"So what makes you think this guy is gonna show up now?" Gena demanded.

"I've been following him, and he headed right to the hospital. Look, Gena, try and keep everyone away from the nurses' station, and we'll catch him in the act."

CHAPTER 71

Wrong Turn

*I*AN HAD A hunch and decided to follow Carson down the alley. He almost lost him when he entered the hospital through an emergency exit that was locked on the outside. Where the guy had got keys to all the entrances was beyond Ian, and he had to race to get the door before it slammed close and locked him out. Grasping the edge of the door with his fingertips, Ian struggled to stop it from completely closing. It took every ounce of strength in his hands to slowly pry the door back open, and even then the sweat that poured from his hands made the metal slippery, and he almost lost his hold.

Finally, Ian was able to use his shoe to stop the semi-closed door from sliding and got a better grip with his hands. Giving the edge a mighty shove, Ian pushed it open and slipped through. Inside, he could hear the clang of footsteps on the stairs and followed the sound. Ian figured the guy was headed toward the seventh floor but almost ran into him when he stopped at the third floor and was fumbling with keys to unlock the fire exit door.

Suddenly, Ian knew who Carson was and where he was headed, and it wasn't to the seventh-floor drug room. This time Ian knew he had to make it to the door before it closed. Taking the steps two at a time, Ian lunged for the door and barely caught the edge of it before it slid shut. Even so he had to fight to force it back open. By the time he was into the corridor, all he saw was one shoe as the guy turned the corner. Ian had to get to the room before Carson had a chance to finish the business that had brought him back to the hospital.

CHAPTER 72

Who Are You?

*T*HE POLICEMAN STATIONED at the main entrance to the intensive care unit would have stopped Carson if he had tried to enter the unit that way. But the guy was obviously familiar with the hospital and used another stairwell that led to a fire escape door, which was kept locked from the outside. Ian didn't need to follow him. He knew where Carson was headed and entered the unit by the main entrance.

The medical personnel congregated around the nurses' station, and the monitors watched as Ian walked past them into the dean's room. Chester was sound asleep, so Ian stepped into the alcove formed by the garment locker and waited. He hoped he was wrong but wasn't counting on it.

Within a few minutes, the door to the room opened quietly, and the filthy homeless guy slid into the cubicle, reached up, and moved the lens of the camera. It would probably have taken the staff several minutes at best to realize that they could no longer see their patient, and by then it would be too late. Although Carson had not made any noise, the stench of his body odor filled the room, and the dean woke with a start, glanced up, and asked, "What the hell are you doing here, Carson? Haven't you caused enough trouble?"

Ian saw the glint of light on metal as the kid pulled a long-bladed hunting knife and held it to Chester's throat. "I need money, Dad."

"You are as bad as your mother. I refuse to feed your habit. Isn't it appalling enough that I surprised you in my office and you tried to kill me?"

"You screwed around on Mom, and now you won't give her any more alimony, you fat pig. She heard you going at it with your secretary in your office, and she wept for days! She only wanted to ask you for more money to help pay the mortgage. It's not her fault that she can't get any work!"

"That's not why she wanted the money. Anything I gave her ended up feeding your habit. That's why she doesn't have enough money to pay the bills." Ian watched in horror as he saw Carson move the blade into his father's neck enough to draw blood. *Humor the idiot,* he thought. It's not worth your life to tell the kid he's a worthless punk now that he's got a knife at your throat. Ian felt helpless, unable to move from his hiding place for fear that Carson would finish what he started.

"You are not in any position to question where the money goes. I want the number to your banking card. So start talking."

". . . I don't have any money even if you get the number. Someone has been blackmailing me and bled me dry."

". . . Liar! You've got enough to keep a third wife and a secretary on the line."

"Even if you don't believe me, Carson, I beg you, don't kill me!"

"Begging won't help. I need money. And you deserve to die, you useless lump of flab!"

"I'm not begging you because I want to live. It would be easy for me to just let you kill me. I deserve to die. But I know what it's like to live with someone's murder on your conscience."

"Is this one of your patients that you couldn't save, Dad? Doctors can't save everyone, and you can't make me believe that losing someone would ever make you feel that bad. Just give me the damn number now!"

"It was one of the other doctors in our graduating class. We locked him on a slab in the morgue as a joke, but when we went back to let him out, he was dead. That's why I'm being blackmailed. It's not the money I regret having to pay. It's because he was the nicest man you would ever want to meet, and his life was cut short because of my insane jealousy. The other guy who helped to put Izzy in the morgue committed suicide because he couldn't live with the guilt. It's not worth it. I have decided to tell the police that I killed Izzy and take my punishment. But you have the rest of your life. I promise that I won't tell them you were the person who stabbed me."

The overhead intercom startled Carson as a code 99 was called. He pulled the knife away from the dean's throat just long enough for Ian to lunge at the kid. The wrestling match for the knife had them rolling on the floor while Ian, who should have had the advantage because of his height and better physical condition, found that he was fighting for his life as the kid fought back with the strength of the insane.

"Help! Somebody get the hell in here," Ian shouted as he stared at the blade inching closer and closer to his throat.

It seemed like forever before the sound of pounding feet and two heavy men dressed in whites grabbed the kid and forced him to the floor. Ian pulled himself up and turned to look at the dean when the cardiac monitor alarm went off. Startled by the sight of the patient going into cardiac arrest, the orderlies relaxed their hold, and Carson used his feet to propel the one man over his head. Dodging the other, Carson fled the room as a stream of doctors and nurses responding to the code impeded the other orderly form chasing after the kid.

Ian concentrated on dealing with the crisis and hoped the hospital security would catch the dean's son before he got out of the hospital. Despite their efforts, they pronounced Dr. Chesterton Whales dead half an hour later.

CHAPTER 73

All's Well

THE SHUFFLING OF some twelve pairs of feet and the crush of young bodies in short white coats pressed through the narrow corridors of the hospital, stopping abruptly as Ian halted at the nurses' station. After giving the group of new interns their orientation spiel, Ian was about to move on when a stocky, freckle-faced novice raised his hand as if in grade school. "You have a question?" Ian acknowledged the upraised limb.

"Yeah. I've heard that there's a ghost that walks the corridors of the morgue at night and that you saw him. Somebody says that it's an intern searching for the arm he accidentally cut off during an autopsy and that the stump turned septic and killed him."

"You got it all wrong," another intern interrupted. "He was locked in a cold box and died of fright. They also say that the Dean of Medicine was stabbed by a medical student he had failed last year." Curious bright eyes of wannabe doctors stared at Ian, waiting for an answer.

"Not again!" Ian moaned dramatically. "Did you hear what the two of you just told me? Does it sound like any of it could possibly have happened? Every year someone starts a rumor to scare the bejesus out of the new crew, starting their rotation through the various departments. I'm not going to tell you it's a pack of lies. If you want to believe it, that's your business. But from now on the only questions I want to hear from any of you had better deal with medicine. Is that clear?"

Ian turned his back on the group and moved on as he heard a chorus of okays. He patted his pocket and decided to run through the rest of the orientation as fast as possible so he could have extra time to read the mail he had picked up that morning. By lunchtime, he was glad to be rid of the coterie of white-coated interns who thought they knew everything just because they had graduated from some of the most prestigious colleges in the country. One intern had even come from Stanford. Why he chose St. Cinnabar over some of the better-known hospitals was unclear to Ian. But he expected to find out before the month was over.

Turning his nose up at the salads and fresh fruit, he chose a cheeseburger and fries from the cafeteria and headed to a secluded corner. He was still having difficulty realizing that he was the resident now, calling the shots and leading a bunch of green interns through their first day at the hospital.

Sitting with his back to the wall, Ian ripped open a letter from Rebecca Cornwell, who was somewhere on the West Bank. "Dear Ian, Hope you are enjoying your residency. Life in the refugee camp is very hectic with a daily influx of orphans and old people whose children are either prisoners or have been killed in the fighting. Without the money my dear Sam left me, I would be hard-pressed to deal with the overwhelming needs of these people. But I have enough wealthy friends and acquaintances that, what I cannot provide myself, I have been able to raise through them. The camp now has a makeshift hospital and school. The adults still don't trust me because I am a Jew. But the small children have yet to learn to hate. I am teaching them English, and they are teaching me Arabic. It is quite easy to learn from children. They have infinite patience and never make fun of me when I massacre their language. I had a wonderful psychiatrist who made me see that revenge and hate never solved anything. By the way, how is Dr. Mohammed Yeshel? Please tell him that I send my greetings and thank him again for all that he did for me. It is thanks to him that I decided to do something useful with my life instead of hurling myself from the roof of the hospital. He was right. Service to others heals more wounds that I would have believed. Even those Nazi monsters of the concentration camp no longer haunt my dreams . . . ." The letter was over ten pages long, and most of it devoted to the children in Rebecca's classes.

"Ian. You didn't call me for lunch." Marla stood over him with a tray in her hands.

"Sorry, dear." Ian grinned at his wife. "I got sidetracked with the new batch of interns. Here's the letter that came in this morning's mail."

"From Rebecca?"

"Yes." Ian handed them over to his wife.

"By the way, you missed an envelope. Or maybe the postman had it mixed up with one of our neighbor's letters." Marla handed Ian a second letter. The postmark was Slatington.

"You could have opened it, dear."

"It's addressed to you, and if you notice, the bottom left-hand corner says 'confidential.'"

"That's strange. And it has no return address." Ian ripped open the flap and withdrew two handwritten sheets and read them quickly. "Holy shit," he exhaled. Not one to use profanity on a regular basis, Marla was intrigued at what had upset Ian so much.

"May I read it or is it personal?"

"You can read it but may wish you hadn't," Ian said as he handed Marla the letter.

It was in a very spidery handwriting as if the person was elderly or very ill.

It began

"Dear Ian,

"Thank you for your visit. Mother was impressed with you, and it was a great relief for us to be able to unburden our secret. Chester's stabbing was not the only reason I was so upset. The week prior to the reunion, I had undergone tests and had been told that I have cancer with very little time to live. Years of smoking and eating whatever I wanted took its toll. I thought Leon Finegard was a coward to write his confession to Izzy's murder and send it to Rebecca. Now it is my turn.

"You know that Chester and I wanted to marry, but his father discovered something about my past. Everyone believed that Mr. Whales found out that I was a Jew. Could you imagine how upset he would have been if his detectives had dug further and found out my real identity?

"When Chester caved in to his father's demands, it was Izzy who tried to console me. That was so ironic . . . the daughter of a concentration camp commandant being consoled by a Jew. Of course, I couldn't tell Izzy the truth.

"It was my fault that Izzy found the papers. I brought him home and proceeded to get drunk. While we were dancing around, I knocked over the box where I kept my papers. Izzy, like the gentleman he was, started to pick them up and saw my papers with the deutschblutig, certifying that I was 'German-blooded.' Perhaps he could have accepted that, but Izzy recognized my family name. No survivor would ever forget it since my father was responsible for so many deaths. He dropped the sheet as if it were on fire and stared at me in horror. His reaction was like ice water thrown in my face, sobering me up instantly. After that Izzy avoided me like I was a leper. Time stood still as I waited for him to tell everyone the truth.

"After Chester and Leon put Izzy on a slab in the morgue as a joke, they came back to party at my place. It was an opportunity that I couldn't waste, so I made sure they were too drunk to go back and get Izzy out when they planned to. By the time they sobered up and found him, it was too late. All they could do was try and cover up what had happened. So they were not responsible for Izzy's death. I was.

"Strangely enough, I do believe in an afterlife, mostly because I believed that Izzy was the ghost walking the corridors of St. Cinnabar. What I fear the most as I lie here in my final hours is having to face Izzy. I will leave it up to you to tell Rebecca the real truth. Pray for my soul. I live in hell here on earth and have taken up my religion once again in hope that I can be forgiven. The priest assures me that God can forgive anything. I am not sure of that. I find it impossible to forgive myself. It is unfair to burden you with this knowledge, but I need to tell someone . . . besides the priest in confession. By the time you receive this, I will have passed on as I have asked Mother not to deliver it until I have died.

Sincerely,
Helena DuCarthenson"

"Are you going to tell Rebecca?" Marla asked as she folded the letter and handed it back to Ian.

"No. The other letter from Leon almost drove Rebecca to murder Chester and then to kill herself. I will destroy this and say a prayer for Helena. And thank God that my life has been so happy and carefree."

"How can you say that? You deal with suffering and death every day, Ian."

"But it is the normal cycle of life, not the horror and upheaval of war under some madman. We are very lucky, Marla, and this letter from Helena is a reminder."

"You're right." Marla leaned over and gave Ian a long passionate kiss.

"Do you think you could get away from here on your afternoon break, Marla?" Ian ran his fingers up under the bodice of Marla's uniform.

"No. But I will make it home early from work tonight."

"Good. Paul still lives in fear of me telling someone his grandmother didn't die. So if it gets busy, I'll just call him to cover for me."

EPILOGUE

FAINT SUNBEAMS SHONE through the tiny attic window, casting long rays in the dust-filled air. The crib was under several boxes of papers, and Ian grunted in the effort to lift the first one off. The movement sent the whole pile sliding onto the floor with the small ribbon-tied box falling out and breaking open. *It had to have been totally dried out to rip apart so easily,* thought Ian, and he stooped and picked up the letters that scattered on the unfinished beams that formed the floor of the tiny loft. One caught his eye, and he pulled over an old embroidered stool, sat down, and opened it. The memories flooded back as he recognized the beautiful handwriting that resembled calligraphy. "Dear Ian, I want to thank you for all that you have done. I am much happier working with the people in the refugee camps. There is so much that needs to be done. Their leaders still don't trust us but need our help so let the people come for treatment grudgingly. Our hope for the future lies with their children. Enough of our lives. We were overjoyed to hear of Rebecca's safe arrival. And I am flattered that you named your first daughter after me . . ."

Looking at the date, Ian could hardly believe that four years had passed since they had seen Rebecca Cornwell off on a flight to the Middle East. At first, he was sure that the Arabs would never accept an old Jewish woman. But Rebecca's money pulled a lot of strings, and the desperation of the people in the camps overcame their overt suspicion.

The sound of tiny footsteps coming up the long narrow staircase startled Ian out of his daydreaming. Bouncing with self-importance, Rebecca pranced into the attic and announced, "Mommy sent me up."

"That's wonderful, dear! And you look so pretty today, princess, with your new pink dress and barrettes in your hair."

Rebecca immediately spied an old rocking horse and hopped on it.

As a heavier set of footsteps echoed on the narrow stairwell, Ian rose and went to the small door. "Did you want something, dear?"

"Didn't Rebecca tell you, Ian?"

Ian turned and looked at the precocious three-year-old and asked, "Did Mommy sent you up here for a reason, Rebecca?"

"She said to tell you that your son is on the way."

Ian stifled the urge to swear in front of his daughter as he snatched her off the rocking horse and thumped down the stairs. "Why didn't you tell me?" he asked his daughter as he rushed toward the kitchen.

"But I did tell you, Daddy."

She had said that her mother sent her up, but Ian should have asked his daughter why. "How close are the contractions, Marla?" he yelled.

"Calm down, Ian! The suitcase is in the car, and the car is warming up. Harold is driving Gena over in the squad car. We have lots of time. And you have delivered a baby before!"

"Why is Harold coming over?"

"When Gena called him, he insisted that he escort us to the hospital and he won't take no for an answer."

"Just what we need," moaned Ian, "a police escort!"

"Harold said he wanted to make sure that his godson is delivered safe and sound in a hospital. I thought that was so sweet of him."

"Yeah. I suppose so. All the neighbors are going to wonder what a police cruiser is doing outside our house."

"Dear, they already know." Marla motioned toward their daughter who had made the rounds of the neighborhood with her grandmother, telling everyone they met, strangers as well as friends, about the impending happy event.

"He's coming, he's coming!" squealed Rebecca, gleefully clapping her hands.

"I'm going to have a baby brother!"

Edwards Brothers Malloy
Oxnard, CA USA
December 19, 2013